KILLER MIND

NATHAN JOHNSON

NuminouS
PUBLISHING

THIS BOOK IS DEDICATED TO MY PARENTS
WHO TAUGHT ME TO LOVE BOOKS AND STORIES.

KILLER MIND
Copyright © 2014 Nathan Johnson

Numinous Publishing
ISBN-13: 978-0615903262
ISBN-10: 0615903266
BISAC: Fiction / Science Fiction / Adventure

Facebook.com/NuminousPublishing
NathanJohnsonMedia.com/Killermind
Facebook.com/KillerMindBook
Cover Design by M3: Modern Media Magic

THE NEAR FUTURE

CHAPTER 1

The boy heard the footsteps long before he saw the man materialize from the darkness of the dark, subterranean corridor. From the man's unsteady shuffling gait, the boy could discern that he was drunk. The boy's brown eyes—well accustomed to the dim lighting—scrutinized the man. He noticed every detail, from the obtrusive unkempt beard, to the small bulge under a soiled jacket which may have concealed a handgun.

Without showing any outward signs of apprehension, the boy continued walking while slipping his fingers under his tattered coat and around the handgrip of his semiautomatic Heckler & Koch. He stepped to one side as the man shuffled closer. He could not resist a slight grimace of revulsion at the drunken breath and reeking body odor of a person who has not washed in months. The boy locked his face in a ridged scowl and watched the dirty face for any sign of a challenge. Aside from a short, crazed look from his bloodshot eyes, he passed without confrontation.

The boy relaxed his guard only when the plodding footsteps faded away. Relieved, he released his grip on the handgun. If the man had pulled a gun, the boy would have shot him without hesitating. He had done it before. Defense was part of life.

He touched his right eye which was dark and slightly swollen, the markings of a recent fight. A tight, black turtleneck and trousers accentuated his lean muscular body. A body that still ached from the last brawl. He was thankful that he had not been forced to fight the drunk. He was not ready for another bout so soon. But he knew he could never completely relax.

Unless he was ready to die.

The boy might have been sixteen or seventeen. He was handsome—after a fashion—although his face held an air of fierceness which bordered on a perpetual scowl. His knee high boots thudded softly as he walked. His clothes were faded and patched. He seemed claimed by poverty yet he still carried himself with strong presence and pride. He stopped in front of a door.

ON THE other side of the steel-braced door was an office. It felt like a tomb. A single bulb hung in the center of the room yielding a faint light that barely illuminated the person sitting at the desk and left the corners in complete darkness.

It was a young woman. Oasis Trailven. Darting almond-shaped eyes peered from her wary face. A pistol hung at her hip. She closed her eyes and put her hands over her face. Her heart pounded. Her breath escaped in gasps. They were coming for her.

Oasis reached down into a desk drawer and retrieved a small photograph. She leaned forward to see better in the dim light and studied the picture. The smiling faces of a man and a girl about sixteen beamed back at her.

Would he help her? Would he even speak to her after what she had done?

Her lip quivered as she attempted to hold back her tears. She wished she could travel back in time and reverse the horrible thing that had happened. If only she had chosen differently. If only she had known the consequences of her actions.

But the past was the past. She had to make a decision in the present to change the future.

A knock from the door interrupted her thoughts. Oasis jumped like a frightened cat, shoved the picture back into the desk, and put a hand to the gun buckled at her hip. They were coming for her. No! They could not be here already...could they?

The knock sounded again, this time louder and more forceful. With a pulsating heart, she pulled her gun, training it on the door. They would not take her without a fight. Her voice was shaky as she addressed the unknown visitor.

"Who's there?" she asked, half rising from her chair.

THE BOY pressed his cheek against the door so his voice could carry through. "It's me, Creed."

The sound of movement came through the door, then the clink of the bolts being drawn back. A familiar face appeared. She was his only friend in this dark world. "Creed, you surprised me."

She did seem surprised. Her breathing was irregular and her face was flushed. Creed wondered if she had been crying. His intense face broke into a grin. "Were you expecting someone else?"

"Perhaps." She smiled, but Creed knew it was forced and sensed the apprehension behind it. Her furtive glance down the hall confirmed his suspicion. "Come inside."

Creed complied. She threw the bolt, then turned to face him. She was beautiful with a trim athletic figure. Strands of mahogany hair framed her face. Over the past years he had gained a few inches on her. It was strange to be looking down at her, after looking up to her for so long. There was worry in her brown eyes as they swept him with maternal concern.

"What's wrong?" she asked.

"Does something have to be wrong for me to come see you?"

She caressed his swollen eye. "What happened?"

He tried to shrug off the question. "Just the usual, some guy jumped me at the oil refinery. He was probably after this."

He slid a wad of bills from his pocket and placed them in her hand.

"Oh, Creed, you didn't steal this, did you?"

"Have I ever stolen anything?" he said, feigning injured innocence. "Today was payday and they let us off early, so I thought I could walk you home."

"You came all the way out here just to get me?"

"You know I'd walk from here to New York for you, and I'm never comfortable knowing that you're walking these streets alone. Not that this isn't a nice city."

They both smiled at his sarcasm. She drew him into a tight embrace. He relaxed into her soothing, comforting presence. Resting her cheek against his shoulder, she whispered half to him, half to herself, "What would I do without you? Sometimes I wonder why God gave me a better son than I deserve." She pushed aside Creed's locks of dirty brown hair and kissed his forehead. "I just wish..."

He met her eyes. "What do you wish?"

"I wish you could have known Adam. He was a great man. I can see much of him in you."

Adam. His father. She missed him. Creed could see it every time she spoke his name. He knew it was wrong, but sometimes he resented the man for dying and leaving them penniless. It wasn't a subject he liked discussing. "Well, if wishes grew on trees, I'd wish you a silk dress and a rose for your hair."

She smiled. He loved that smile. Something moved in the dark recesses of the room. Probably a rat. Oasis jumped and put her hand to her gun. The grin disappeared from Creed's face. "What's scaring you? You jump at every sound. You reach for your gun whenever somebody looks at you."

The boy looked straight into his mother's eyes trying to read what was behind them. He knew they held a secret. Something she could not—or would not tell. She stroked his hair. "I have a very observant son."

"Why?" he persisted. She sighed and turned away.

Creed could not understand her reluctance. "You weren't always like this. I know you were always cautious, but I've never seen you actually afraid until recently." Creed took her slender hands in his. "Are you in trouble? How can I protect you if you don't tell me what's wrong?"

She was silent for a while, pain clouding her eyes. When she spoke, it was a whisper. "I'll tell you when the time is right."

"Not now?" Creed asked, but he already knew her answer. This was not the first time they had gone over this ground.

"No, my son, not now." Oasis shut down the computer, picked up her purse, and slung it over her shoulder. "Let's go home."

She turned for the door. For a brief moment Creed sensed a deep gulf developing between them. He hated the feeling. Creed caught up with his mother and took her hand. He felt her squeeze his hand with surprising strength that belied her delicate fingers. She did not look at him but kept her gaze straight ahead. He noticed a tear on her cheek.

A rickety elevator took them up to ground level. Outside, the night air was chilly. Oasis pulled Creed closer. Creed felt the cold bite through his shirt. The wind howled as it raced through the wild alleyways of shack houses, slum-buildings, and decrepit apartments. Streetlights were a rarity.

He stepped over the scattered pieces of a broken beer bottle strewn over the ground. Graffiti splattered the surrounding buildings. Aside from the graffiti, everything was black and gray.

Mysterious. Forbidding.

The inner-city had become the under-city. More than fifty percent of the urban dwellings were located underground. It had decayed so much in the past years that the police rarely dared to venture into the dark catacombs.

Creed heard the footsteps before his mother did. They were coming to the end of a long alleyway between two high, steel walls interspersed with brick. He shot a quick glance behind.

In the poor lighting, Creed could determine the vague shapes of men, maybe five. His mother turned and saw them. She froze.

What disturbed Creed most were the blue eyes of one man. They were cold, like two chips of raw ice. Creed had a strange sensation that the eyes were zooming into his face, scrutinizing, probing, reading every minute detail. The feeling unnerved him like nothing he had ever experienced.

The man was now staring at Oasis. He said something to his crew and suddenly they sprinted towards Creed and Oasis.

"Run!" Oasis said in an urgent whisper. Only Creed could have understood the fear in her voice. But her command was unnecessary. Creed was already running before the words left her mouth.

He took the lead as they ran through the labyrinth of alleys. They darted across a narrow side street. A tall, sagging wire fence blocked his path. Gathering a burst of speed, he used a discarded crate as a platform and vaulted the broken fence. Landing on the other side he heard the fence rattle as his mother completed her leap.

A bullet pinged over his head. He threw himself down into a garbage heap. Old clothes, rancid food, and other refuse settled around him. Out of the corner of his eye, he saw his mother dive behind a metal dumpster. The junk pile began shifting under his weight. Then he was tumbling, caught in an avalanche of moving garbage. After regaining his footing, Creed turned to find his mother. She was gone.

Suppressing the urge to scream her name, he scanned the darkness desperately. Nothing. A bullet exploded past his head. Heart thudding, he dropped into a crouch and pulled out his USP, feeling the rubber handgrip against his fingers. Creed ducked beside a tall brick wall. He inched forward.

"Freeze!"

Creed froze.

"Drop the gun," the voice ordered from behind. Creed mentally kicked himself. He shouldn't have let the men circle behind him, but he was careful not to let his thoughts show. His face displayed no sign of surprise, anger, or fear.

Expression was an enemy.

Moving deliberately, not wishing to give the man any excuse to shoot him, he dropped his gun. It bounced once as it clattered on the uneven pavement. Creed was conscious of the short knife at his left hip. The knife was covered by his long black jacket, which flapped around in a cold draft of air.

Broken rubble shifted as the man approached. "Face the wall!"

Creed turned slowly and placed his face against the high brick wall. A gun muzzle was painfully rammed between his shoulder blades. The man did not appreciate Creed's slowness. The red brick cut into Creed's forehead as the man pushed harder, pinning him against the wall.

"Chris, get over here!"

So there were two men behind him. Not good. Creed could feel the man's hot breath on his neck. He was breathing heavily—a welcome sign in any opponent.

"Call Commando and tell him we got the kid."

Commando? Were they working with the military? Not likely. Maybe Commando was some sort of nick name—the blue-eyed man maybe? Was he their leader? Creed heard the tiny beeps of a cell phone. The second man was dialing a number.

Creed weighed his chances. If the first man reacted fast enough, he would put a slug in his heart. But if he didn't . . . there might be chance. A small chance, but a chance nonetheless. And Creed had been in worse places before. If he was going to escape, this was the best time while the other guy was busy with the phone.

Creed accepted the gamble. He rehearsed what he was going to do in his mind. The beeps were coming from his right and not too far away. So when he turned the man would be to his left. The same side as his knife. He took a deep breath, moving his body as little as possible. No need to give the men a warning. He forced himself to relax, letting all the muscles in his body loosen.

Judging from the slight release of pressure from the gun muzzle, the man behind him relaxed also. For a short moment everything was still except for the second man, who was raising the phone to his ear. All that could be heard was the howling wind.

Then Creed disturbed the stillness. With lightning speed and agility, he spun around to his right, using his left arm to deflect the gun. The gun fired with a small explosion, tearing a huge hole in the brick wall, which spewed red powder and chalk, like blood.

In the same movement, Creed reached over his body with his right hand. Yanking out his knife, he flung it with a slight flick. He aimed as he threw, eyes focused on the man holding the phone. The knife blade glinted as it caught the pale light from the street lamps. It twirled easily through the air, once, twice, then buried itself, up to the handle, in the man's chest.

The man fired involuntarily at Creed, but missed by a foot, knocking down a fresh shower of red powder. The man let out a terrible gurgle then dropped the phone and his handgun from dead fingers.

But Creed was not watching. As soon as he had thrown the knife he directed his full attention to the other man who moments before held a gun to his back. He was still holding the man's gun wrist with his left hand. He gave it a sharp twist. The man howled and released the gun, but Creed took a flailing left hook in his right eye.

Fiery pain screeched through every nerve in his body. It felt like the punch had knocked his eyeball out of its socket and into his brain. For a second Creed thought he was going blind. Then his vision cleared—just in time to see the man stooping for the gun. Creed slammed his knee into the man's jaw. The man staggered as he struggled for balance. Creed's fist connected solidly with the man's cheek. One final blow to the chin knocked the man out cold.

Jumping over the prostrate body, Creed seized his gun from the ground. He ran to the second man and pulled his knife free from the body. He wiped it hastily on the man's shirt and sheathed it. He dashed along another badly lit alleyway, recalling the direction his mother had taken when they separated. His eye was still burning and starting to swell. But he hardly noticed. His only thought was for his mother. Was she dead or alive? He prayed to God for the latter.

CHAPTER 2

There was a shortcut across the rooftops. Oasis raced up the fire escape and onto the flat roof. The blue-eyed man was standing there, waiting for her. She was running so fast she almost ran into his arms. She twisted away, but at the last moment he caught her arm with a hard jerk. Oasis turned on him with a right hook followed swiftly by a left upper cut to the jaw. With surprising agility the man dodged aside, avoiding both blows.

"Don't move a muscle or I'll blow you apart!" The voice came from behind her. She lowered her tensed fist. Out of the surrounding darkness, another man emerged. In his hands was an automatic weapon trained on Oasis.

Panting from the long run, she glared at the blue-eyed man standing in front of her, half in shadow. She realized that he was still holding her wrist. She snatched her arm away. The other man raised his gun. "I said, 'Don't move!'" There were only two men. How many had she seen before the chase began? Five? So the other three must be after Creed.

"Well, well, if it isn't Oasis Trailven? As pretty as ever."

She looked up in surprise. How did this man know her? Her lower lip trembled. This last confirmation left no margin for doubt. These were *the men*. The men she had been warned about.

THE BLUE-EYED man was glaring at her. For the first time she recognized that his clothing was much too fine to belong to the under-

10

city. His combat boots, dark pants, and brown leather jacket spoke clearly. He was a professional contract killer.

Something about his face disturbed her. There was nothing apparently wrong with it—it was perfect. But *that* was what made it strange. It was too perfect. There were no bumps, no blemishes, no minute imperfections anywhere. "Oasis." The word came out like sharp wind from an ice cave. "Where is the MCC data?"

"I have no idea what you're talking about."

But she did.

The man lunged, grabbing Oasis by the throat. As if she were a baby, the man hoisted her up into the air and banged her head against the steel wall, pinning her. Oasis gasped, pulling in vain at the choking hand encircling her neck. His fingers seemed to be made of steel. In that one instant, all her fears were realized. She trembled.

The blue eyes watched without sympathy as Oasis writhed in pain and terror. From the look on his face he might have been squashing a bug, instead of a young woman. "If you don't tell me where it is, I will kill your boy. And you know I never lie," he hissed, his mouth scarcely moving as he talked. His breath was strange and deathly cold as it wafted across her face. Oasis tried to answer, "I don't—" She was interrupted.

The sharp report of a gun echoed over the roof top. It was followed closely by a scream. She looked up in time to see his companion lurch backwards with a bullet wound in his chest. He flipped off the edge of the building and plummeted three stories—until his fall was checked by the ground.

The blue-eyed man dropped, pulling Oasis down with him. A spark of joy flashed through her. It was Creed. She knew it in her heart. Her boy was still alive and fighting.

They were now shielded by the short wall which ran around the edges of the building.

When the noise cleared, the man drew his handgun from his thigh and stood up slowly, scanning the area, never relinquishing his hold on her throat. Judging from the direction his comrade had fallen, the bullet had come from one of the tall adjoining buildings.

The murky darkness and fog creeping its way through the air made it difficult to see. Even so, the man's eyes swept over the area with such precision and certainty that Oasis had the impression that his vision was functioning perfectly. She was tempted to try and fight now that his attention was on Creed. But what chance did she have? And he was still gripping her throat. She knew that only a slight increase in pressure would end her life. Her own gun lay just out of reach. If only she could get to it.

The man suddenly whipped his gun up to shoulder height and fired into the darkness. A faint cry came from the rooftop adjoining theirs. Oasis would have recognized that voice anywhere. The man watched the building intently, his gun still raised. Silence reigned again. He turned back to her, satisfied. A lump rose in her throat. The man standing before her had just killed her son.

Something snapped in her mind. A hidden quickness and strength that she did not know she possessed pulsed through her body. She moved so quickly, the man was caught by surprise. Throwing all caution aside, she slammed her fist into the man's wrist. Somehow she twisted out of his death lock. Oasis brought up her forearm in a crushing blow to the man's chin.

It took half a second for the man to react but when he did, he moved with astonishing speed. His knee plowed into her stomach and as her body fell forward, his hand slapped her cheek. Oasis hit the rooftop shingles and all the breath was knocked from her body. The glaring eyes narrowed as he crouched down beside her and yanked her up by the hair. Their faces were almost touching. His tone was horrible and frigid. "Tell me where it is. I hate playing games."

A soft sound caught their ears. They looked up. Creed was standing only a few feet away. Surprise flitted across the man's face. Blood was oozing from a jagged gash on Creed's temple. His left shoulder was also dripping red from a nasty wound. If the bullet had landed only a few inches to the right he would not be breathing now. But he had managed to dodge aside.

A long strand of dirty brown hair half covered his right eye which had swollen completely shut and was tinged with purple. But the other eye focused perfectly. In his right hand he carried his USP, which was trained on the man's chest.

CREED FELT no fear, only an intense hatred for the man who had dared to touch his mother. He squeezed the trigger. Four rounds, fired in rapid secession, thundered into the target. The force of the projectiles lifted the man off his feet. He flipped backwards as he was hurled into a smoking exhaust vent. Before the hot gases swallowed his body, Creed had one last view of the glaring blue eyes, then the man disappeared.

Creed knelt down beside his prostrate mother. Her eyelids flickered open. "I thought he killed you . . ." She reached up and tenderly stroked his face, touching the damp blood on his forehead. "My baby."

Creed shrugged, "I'll be fine. We need to get away from here. Do you think you can walk?"

She winced, "I think so."

He helped her to her feet. They made their way quickly across the rooftop back to the ladder. When they arrived in the ally, Oasis turned to her son, "How many men do you remember seeing?"

There had been five. Creed performed a quick mental calculation, and realized that one killer was still unaccounted for. Instinctively, Creed looked past his mother.

The man was half hidden in the shadows. Death was in his pale green eyes and his lips were peeled in brutal rage, but all Creed saw was the wicked looking submachine gun.

"Mother—" he tried to shout. The loud explosion of gunfire drowned out his futile warning. A bullet whistled past his cheek taking some skin along with it. Another tore out a clump of hair. But they were nothing compared to the heavy barrage of lead which riddled his mother's back.

The world seemed to slow down. Creed let out a ragged yell as his mother slumped down. He could see her face contorted in pain. She made no sound except a slight gurgle, but her eyes cried out a thousand different words. Nothing seemed real.

Oasis had not yet fallen before Creed drew his own gun. He aimed through tear-blurred vision and fired at those pale green eyes.

He did not miss.

Oasis fell into a wide pothole, one of many disfiguring the rough paved street. The hole was filled with muddy water that splashed onto her face and clothes. Creed dropped his gun and cradled her head in his arms, staining his hands with her blood.

"Mother," he whispered, his voice choked with tears. "Don't leave me!" He wiped the mud from her face and stroked her hair with shaking fingers. As he held her close, he could feel her breath expiring in broken gasps.

"Baby," she whispered painfully, "I was such a fool, I should have told you about—" her voice broke and she gurgled. Blood trickled from her mouth.

Creed's hot tears fell onto her face. "Mother, don't say that. It's all right. It's all right . . ." he trailed off, struck by the absurdity of his words. It was not all right. Nothing was right.

With a tremendous effort Oasis spoke again. "Take the data capsule . . . it's . . . it's in my bureau—under the middle drawer. He said it was important . . ."

Creed thought he had lost her and let out a despairing moan. He laid his head on her chest and in doing so caught the feeble words of his mother.

"Take it to Skeddner."

"The neurosurgeon?"

Her delicate fingers traced his face. "Promise . . .me you'll take it to Dr. Isaac Skeddner."

Creed was almost blinded by his tears. "I promise."

She sighed. "And take my ring. He'll remember it."

She held out her forefinger. Creed was barely able to force himself to slip the silver band off her finger. "Don't leave me! I can't live without you."

She smiled softly. "I love you, Creed. Be strong."

He tried to return her smile but failed. "I love you, too," he responded faintly, feeling that something inside him was dying with her. A slight shudder convulsed her body as her spirit ascended, then she fell limp in his arms. Creed desperately wished that he had gone with her. His whole being trembled in agony. He buried his face in her hair and uttered a low, mournful wail from the depths of his soul.

THE BUREAU drawer scraped as Creed dragged it on ancient runners. He had no relatives, no friends, no one to call for help. No one to comfort him when he needed it the most. He could hardly bring himself to believe that she was gone. Again and again he relived her death in his troubled mind. Why had God taken her and left him behind? Gritting his teeth, he forced the thoughts away and turned to the task at hand.

He pulled the drawer, yanking so hard it broke from its wooden frame and fell to the floor. This was his mother's private drawer. He had never been inside. Creed prodded through the scanty contents: a few pictures, miscellaneous scraps of paper, a diary, some letters, and a Bible. Nothing of any pecuniary value. He marveled at her flowery, cursive writing. He frowned as something caught his eye. Brushing aside some papers, he pulled out a small gray object.

A data capsule.

Creed's knowledge of data capsules was limited. He knew they were used to store large amounts of important classified information and usually had special locking codes. Not the kind of thing he would expect his mother to own. What was stored on it? He frowned. How did this fall into her hands? Was this what her killers were after? They certainly were not the normal breed of hoodlums who darkened the streets. They were professional killers. And whoever hired them probably knew where he lived and would send more men to search the house. He had an hour at best.

So, just take the capsule and run?

He would lose his job. His job at the oil refinery had been difficult enough to acquire and maintain. Even if he were absent one day, his boss would rant and rave like the animal he was. There would be no way to explain this. Mercy and grace were foreign concepts to him.

Creed scowled. He would lose the apartment. He and his mother had been living check-to-check as long as he could remember. One sign of an extended absence and the slumlords would snatch the miserable little shack from him.

Creed looked around. What did it matter? His mother was dead. Nothing mattered now. So what if the killers knew where he lived. Let them come. He would kill them all. He would hole up here and pick them off one by one.

Creed stared at the capsule resting in his hand, remembering his mother's final words. There was only one right option. He would honor his mother by carrying out her final wish.

She had told him to take the capsule to Dr. Isaac Skeddner. How did she know him? And why would Dr. Skeddner remember her ring? He was the world famous neurosurgeon who founded Skeddner Pharmaceuticals and discovered the cure for autism. He lived in a colossal penthouse in Bel Aire. Getting in to see him might be difficult.

Reaching into his pocket, he pulled out the ring, noticing a sequence of numbers and letters etched in the interior of the band, like a serial number. Funny, he had never paid much attention to it before. The ring was just another part of his mother, like her hair, her smile or her voice, always whispering words of encouragement and wisdom in his ear. Like a tiny star, the green stone sparkled in the silver band.

He stood. He had to leave before the killers came.

CHAPTER 3

An intricate network of elevated causeways allowed the wealthy to live out their entire lives without touching the earth. Creed pressed his face against the plexiglass canopy which enclosed the causeway.

The beautiful Los Angeles skyline stretched out impressively before him. The rich and vivid colors produced a stunning, majestic picture that was almost unreal. The brilliant orange sun was just beginning to set behind the tops of the shining pinnacles. An endless sea of windows reflected the sun with a soft yellow glow. The buildings seemed to have no bottom and their tops seemed to touch the clouds. Creed had entered a different world.

Elevated buses glided overhead on special tracks suspended between the skyscrapers. Successful men and women in business suits walked through suspended glass tunnels, going to various work-places. The wealthy built estates on the flat roofs, complete with houses, trees, and grass. Wealthy people like Dr. Skeddner.

Creed walked through the swiveling glass doors of the building where the neurosurgeon lived. It had the feel of a grand hotel for the elite. The lobby was elegant and imperial, with gold and brass trimmings. Creed could see his reflection in the polished floor. Behind the visitors' counter, there were several uniformed staff. He held the gaze of two armed security guards as he made his way across the lobby. He knew there were more just out of sight.

Creed adjusted his backpack straps to rest more comfortably on his lean shoulders and stepped up to the counter, trying to act as if he belonged here.

"Can I help you?" a male clerk asked him.

"Yes, I need to see Dr. Skeddner."

The man looked at him with disdain. "Is he expecting you?"

"No, but it is very important that I speak with him."

The man smiled. "Dr. Skeddner is a very busy man. I'm afraid he doesn't have time for beggars without appointments."

Creed pushed aside his pride. It was all he could do to keep some hint of politeness in his voice. "Sir," he said slowly and evenly, "I need to deliver something to Dr. Isaac Skeddner."

"What is it?" the clerk asked, sounding mildly interested. "Every package Dr. Skeddner receives is on his order list, but you don't exactly look like the UPS man."

"I need to give him a data capsule."

"A data capsule!" the man laughed outright. "Tramp, if you expect me to believe that, then you're a fool. You stole it, if you've got one at all."

For a long moment Creed scowled at the man. He had a strong urge to slap the grin off his face. With effort, he shrugged away the thought. Foolish actions would not improve his situation. And would likely land him in jail. He considered leaving the capsule on the counter and dropping the matter. His thoughts strayed back to his mother. She had been so insistent.

"I didn't steal the capsule. My mother gave it to me," Creed muttered through clenched teeth.

The man suddenly lost his mocking tone and grew angry. "Get along, boy, before I call security. I don't have time for this nonsense."

"Before you throw me out, call Dr. Skeddner and tell him I have something from Oasis Trailven."

The man looked at him strangely, then picked up a desk phone. "Yes, there's a boy down here claiming to have something from Oasis Trailven . . . yes . . . okay I'll send him up."

The clerk pressed a buzzer. "It seems that Oasis is your golden ticket. Take the private elevator to your left."

After a long trip—Creed counted fifty levels—the stately brass elevator glided to a stop at the penthouse. When the doors opened, he stepped out. He was outside in a giant courtyard teeming with bushes, potted trees, and arbors covered in hanging vines and brilliant flowers all carefully manicured. A field of grass surrounded the brick courtyard and beyond that a carved ivory fence encircled the edge of the skyscraper. It was hard to believe that all this was created on the top of a fifty story building.

A mansion was built in the center of the courtyard. It was a twentieth century styled house snuggled within the trees. Creed started towards it.

Then he saw the girl.

She was reading *The Lord of the Rings*, resting with her back against a tree. She had a single braid, dyed royal blue, which hung down across her face. The rest of her hair was glossy black and reached her lower back. She had long arched eyebrows and small, slightly pointed ears, giving her a somewhat elfish appearance. She wore designer jeans and a white blouse, and exuded an attractive elegance. A thin silver chain encircled her neck and two small diamond earrings dangled from her ears. She was lost in the book and didn't notice him.

The wind caught up her hair and blew it gently around her innocent face. Casually, she glanced up and met his eyes. Creed got lost in the two pools of blue and long black lashes. Something about her seemed almost familiar. He wondered if he had seen her before, maybe on a magazine cover.

How it happened Creed could never figure out, but in the blink of an eye she had thrown down the book and launched herself through the air. Her first punch took him in the cheek. For a moment Creed's mind slipped into a mental freeze. A full thirty seconds elapsed as the girl pummeled him before it even occurred to him to fight back. He was not afraid, just floundering in dumbfounded shock. He had never seen a girl move like that before.

But she was still a girl. Not even a contest. Grabbing her wrists firmly, he pinned her up against the tree, taking care not to hurt her. He didn't know who she was but he had a feeling that injuring her could land him in more trouble than he desired. She struggled like a cornered cat, flailing her arms and scratching him with her nails. When she found her wrestling useless, she stopped. Closing her eyes, she turned her head away and braced herself like a person expecting to be decapitated. Her blue braid dangled over her face. Just that quickly she had slipped back into a meek child. She cowered before him.

When a long moment passed and nothing happened, she opened her eyes. "Are you going to kill me?" she asked eyeing the gun buckled to his hip. She spoke with a slight British accent that was foreign and strange to Creed.

"No."

"Are you going to kidnap me?"

Kidnap her? Creed almost laughed to himself. What an absurd idea. "No."

This answer seemed to confuse the girl. Her eyebrows puckered into a perplexed frown. "Then what are you going to do to me?"

"Nothing."

Creed let her go. He did not think she would fight him again.

He was wrong.

The instant he released her hands, she drove her knee into his groin. Creed crumbled. She managed to snatch his gun right off his belt as he fell. Creed found himself staring up at the gun muzzle aimed right for his heart. She was breathing heavily and he noted a trace of a smile which she tried to hide. She was obviously proud of herself for flooring him. He could have died of embarrassment. She had taken full advantage of his gentleness. Creed scowled.

He found himself admiring the girl's grit. This was not the way he expected to deliver the data capsule to Dr. Skeddner. Creed could tell by the way she held the gun, that this was not the first one she'd handled. He studied her face. She did not seem capable of killing him.

Yet, she had surprised him twice already in the space of a minute. Anything was possible. His mother's gun was still at his waist and his knife at his hip. The data capsule pressed against his thigh pocket.

"Wait!" he shouted. "Before you shoot. Can you give this capsule to Dr. Skeddner?"

He put his hand to his pocket, but was deterred by an aggressive movement from the girl with his *own* gun. For an instant he had an opening. The gun was close enough to knock away. He deliberated. Odd, for some reason he actually didn't care if she pulled the trigger or not. He only wanted her to take the capsule.

"Do you take me for an idiot?" she asked, wisely taking a step back and eliminating any possibility of Creed disarming her. "I'm not going to take anything from you. It could be a bomb."

"It's not."

"Then what is it?"

He felt scarlet creeping up his neck. "I don't know, but it's very important."

The girl rolled her lustrous eyes. "Whatever. I'm calling the police to have you arrested for trespassing." She took a step away from him, "Stand up slowly, and put your hands on your head."

Creed obeyed. "I didn't trespass. I have Dr. Skeddner's permission."

Her eyes flickered over him and she gave him a sly smile, "I'm sure you do."

Creed pictured what he must look like to the girl—the ragged scar under his eye which had marred his face for eight years, ever since a guy had tried to gouge out his eye with a knife; his faded, patched and bullet-torn jacket; and of course the gun. The image was completed with his customary scowl—which had darkened considerably in the last minute. He licked a few drops of blood from his cracked lip, an adornment inflicted by the girl's knuckles.

"Please," Creed said, employing a word he rarely used. He tried to hide the exasperation seeping into his voice. "Please, take this capsule to Dr. Skeddner."

"For all I know you might be an assassin dispatched to kill my father. Now start walking."

Father? Dr. Skeddner was the girl's father. He let out a mental sigh of relief. It was fortunate that he had not injured her. "What are you planning on doing with me?"

"I will direct you to my father. He will decide what to do with you."

It was a short, tense walk to the house. At the girl's bidding, he rang the bell. After a few seconds, the door was cracked open by a man whom Creed assumed to be the butler. When he caught sight of Creed his eyebrows shot up in surprise. "Why Alexis," he said. "I must say I'm a bit concerned about your choice of friends."

Like the girl, he spoke with a trace of British accent. The girl's eyes were dancing with mischief.

"I just caught him sneaking up on me in the garden," she responded coolly.

The butler's face clouded in distrust. "Did the waif harm you in any way?"

"I'm fine, but I would like to tell father about him. Do you think you could keep an eye on him for me?"

"Why certainly, Alexis, but shouldn't the boy be kept outside until you have informed your father?"

"Oh, he'll be fine in the house," she said nonchalantly, giving Creed a wink. "He's not much of a fighter."

Under different circumstances, Creed might have laughed. The butler remained unconvinced. "But I'll have to search you. We can't have you carrying weapons into the house. Dr. Skeddner is a powerful man, and there are many people who would like to benefit at his expense."

Creed recoiled. He hated the idea of parting with his weapons, but he could see no alternative. Reluctantly, he unbuckled his utility belt and holster, and handed over his knife, stealing a look at Alexis.

The butler admitted them inside. Creed found himself in a stylish foyer. The soft breath of the air-conditioner was cool and fresh. Alexis disappeared up a long Cinderella staircase.

They entered an enormous living room. The floor was made of intricately cut marble, decorated with large rugs. Suits of armor from centuries long past stood on pedestals. Everything in the house was massive, from the huge glass windows and beautifully arched doorways to the overstuffed arm chairs and expansive wall hangings. Decorative swords and antique guns adorned the walls. It was like a private museum.

The butler directed him to a sofa. "Dr. Skeddner *might* be able to see you shortly," he said stiffly and retreated from the room. Creed sat rigidly, refusing to lean back in the soft chair. He would wait just long enough for the doctor to come, give him the capsule and go home. Home? No, his mother was dead. There was no home to go back to. He gripped the arm of the sofa. He wanted to scream. Yell. Break something. Destroy something.

He looked up as the butler returned. "Dr. Skeddner will see you now."

Creed stood and followed the man down a hall. The girl appeared and flashed him a disarming smile, but he could not determine whether she was encouraging or mocking him. The butler pushed open a set of doors then shut them as soon as Creed stepped inside.

The office was elegant and refined. The desk and chairs were built of polished oak. On the far wall a framed painting of a horse covered almost half the wall. Creed felt out of place in his old faded clothes amidst the rich finery around him.

Dr. Skeddner sat in a brown leather chair positioned behind the desk. He was dressed casually in slacks and a blazer. His black hair was streaked with gray. His age was difficult to discern, but something in his manner caused Creed to think of him as older—wiser. He was certain the doctor was measuring him up but was uncertain as to what conclusions he drew.

A young African-American woman dressed in a dark business suit sat across from him reading from a sheath of papers. She stopped as Creed entered.

"Have a seat." Dr. Skeddner's voice was deep and firm, the sound of a man who never second guessed himself.

Creed obeyed. He sank down in the soft velvety cushion of the large oaken chair. Even though the chair was deep and comfortable, Creed sat as rigidly as a stone carving.

"I understand you have something for me."

Gravely and silently, Creed reached into his shirt pocket, drew out his mother's gold ring and the data capsule, and deposited them on the desk. The doctor seemed to ignore the capsule and picked up the ring. The ring's green crystal caught in the sunlight from the window. It sparkled and sent faint green lights dancing across the wall.

The ring had a strange effect on Dr. Skeddner. It seemed as though a thousand memories flashed across his face, not all of them pleasant. The man was wandering deep into his past. He brought the ring up to his lips and kissed it.

Creed frowned.

He had anticipated some form of recognition, his mother had told him that much, but the man's reaction to her ring took him by surprise. Jealousy crept up his spine at Skeddner's apparent affection for his mother. He almost snatched the ring back. A sudden suspicion leaped into his heart. Was this man his father? No, no that couldn't be true. His mother had told him that his father was dead. She had never lied before.

But that was before.

"Where did you find this?" Dr. Skeddner said, clutching the ring in his hand. "If you harmed her . . ." he looked up quickly and stared at Creed with new eyes. "It can't be . . . " then he added incredulously, "Are you her son?"

"Yes."

"Creed?"

He was taken aback at the man's knowledge of his name but nodded again. A significant look skipped between the woman and Dr. Skeddner.

"Yes, you have her eyes. . .Where is your mother?" he said rising to his feet. "Did she come with you?" Creed stiffened and gritted his teeth. The man's gray eyes widened as he read the misgiving in Creed's body language. Furrows of apprehension creased Skeddner's forehead. "Boy! Where is your mother?"

Creed focused his eyes on the papers spread across the table, taking deep measured breaths to calm himself. He refused to cry in front of this man. "She's dead."

Skeddner paled and dropped into his chair. "Are . . . you sure about this?"

"Of course I'm sure!" The words vaulted out more forcefully than he had intended.

For a moment the doctor closed his eyes and sat with his head bowed. "This is terrible. Forgive my asking, but how did she die?"

Creed steeled himself, clenching his jaw. "She was murdered."

"Murdered." He fingered the ring in his hand. "How did it happen?"

"Some hired guns shot her down in the street."

After a moment, the man stood up and paced to the window, his hands clasped behind his back. "She was such a sweet angel. I wish . . . I wish it could have turned out differently," he murmured, clearly not speaking to Creed. Skeddner slipped the ring into his breast pocket. The action did not escape Creed's notice. Was the man stealing his mother's ring in front of his eyes? What did the man take him for?

"May I have my mother's ring back, Sir?" He spoke with stiff politeness, yet something in his voice suggested that he was not requesting but demanding.

Skeddner turned back to face Creed. He seemed surprised and dismayed at Creed's question. "My boy, I'm sorry." He handed the ring back to him. Dr. Skeddner massaged his forehead. "I am not entirely myself. This is difficult and shocking news. I suppose she never mentioned me, did she?"

"Only once, just before she died, when she told me to bring the capsule to you."

The man nodded sadly as if he had expected the answer. Creed shifted in his seat. He decided to ask the question that had nagged at his heart for the past five minutes.

"Are you my father?"

The blunt question pricked Skeddner. A lingering beat passed before he answered quietly. "No . . . no, I'm not your father, but I should have been."

What was that supposed to mean? Creed searched the man's face, but his gray eyes were difficult to read. He looked ready to say something else, then changed his mind with a shake of his head. "Tomorrow, I'd be grateful if you would tell me your story in full. There are many important matters which need to be addressed. But not now."

The black woman, who had not uttered a word during the entire discourse, now spoke. "Young man, did your mother say anything else?"

"No."

Dr. Skeddner walked back to the desk. "Creed, I'm sorry, let me introduce my attorney, Jennifer Jones."

Jennifer smiled warmly. "It's a pleasure to meet you."

Creed gave a curt but polite nod. The attorney's eyes kept straying toward the data capsule. Dr. Skeddner, seeming to recognize this, swept it off the desk and into a filing cabinet behind his chair. "Do you have a place to stay the night, Creed?"

"Well, I . . . " Creed faltered. What was the point in lying? "No."

"You are welcome in my home as long as you wish to stay."

The offer struck Creed broadside. He was unused to even the remotest forms of generosity and his first thought was one of suspicion. "I'm not here to impose," he said, rising from the chair.

"Please stay," Dr. Skeddner pressed. "I understand what it is to lose a loved one. It's the least I can do for you."

Creed nodded slowly, placing aside his pride. The man seemed genuine. "I suppose I could. Thank you."

"I'll have someone escort you to your room." Skeddner pushed an intercom on his desk. A manservant entered. "You called, Sir?"

"Yes, take this young gentleman to one of the guest rooms in the east wing. Make sure he is comfortable."

It wasn't until Creed was outside in the hall, that he realized Dr. Skeddner had not even questioned him about the data capsule.

The girl, Dr. Skeddner's daughter, was lounging in a chair twirling her single blue braid around her finger. She dropped it as Creed was led in by the servant. She eyed him as if he were a dangerous but intriguing animal.

"So, were you able to deliver your precious capsule?"

Creed nodded. From the sarcastic tone in her voice Creed assumed she still didn't believe him—not that he cared.

"I hope he wasn't too hard on you?" she asked.

He shook his head. Her face held a mixture of amusement and curiosity.

"I'm sorry about your lip. I didn't mean to hit you that hard."

Creed wasn't sure if she was teasing him or sincere. He studied her face as she studied his. "I'm glad you came. This has been so exciting." She cocked her head. "You weren't actually fighting me in the garden were you?"

Creed shook his head.

"So you had no intention of hurting me. Correct?"

He nodded.

She smiled coyly, a smile that would have melted the toughest boy. But it had no effect on Creed, who countered the look with disinterested eyes. She offered him her hand. Creed stared at it, noticing her blue nail polish. Shaking hands was not something he did often—in fact he could not recall the last time he'd had the occasion to perform the action. Awkwardly, he stuck out his hand. He was conscious, as he touched her hand, that his rough fingers were streaked with dirt. Quite a contrast to the girl's carefully manicured fingers and painted nails. "I'm Alexis Christine Skeddner."

"Creed," he returned tersely.

CHAPTER 4

Father still hates me, Adam . . . I don't know what to do. He comes out of nowhere and sets himself up as a dictator over my life. He's demanding and cruel and I . . . hate him. I can't stand it much longer. I'm afraid I'll do something desperate.

Creed held his mother's letter closer to the table lamp. He had read most of the letters searching for any mention of the data capsule, but so far there was nothing. He settled himself better on the feather bed, a welcome change from the thin rubber pad he was accustomed to sleeping on. The shower had been a taste of heaven. He had never felt so clean in his life.

A fifty-inch plasma screen occupied the corner. He had flicked through the list of movies, a few old ones looked interesting, *Terminator* and *I, Robot*. He might watch them if he had the time.

As he lay there, he pondered the day's events. Where did his mom get the capsule? His mother had said that Dr. Skeddner was a good friend of hers. So why had she never spoken of him before? He turned on the pillow. And Alexis did have a nice smile he decided. With that last thought he drifted off to sleep.

Creed saw himself in his mind's eye. It was almost ten years ago, and once again he was six years old. Something had awakened him. He sat up in bed and shivered. It was cold. It was always cold. Heat cost more than they could afford. Creed's watch was lying on the small table next to his bed. His mother had just taught him how to tell time. 4:21AM. It was early. What had disturbed him?

Then he heard it again. A quiet whimpering.

Pulling the blanket around himself like a cloak, he crawled off the bed. The door emitted a rusty squeak as he pushed it open and looked out from his room into the dark hall. The house was small, only two closet-sized bedrooms, a sparse livingroom, a bathroom, and a tiny kitchen which was not more than a microwave and a refrigerator.

His small feet barely made a sound as he crossed the hall to the adjoining bedroom, the blanket trailing behind him like a king's royal robe. His mother's door was ajar. The woeful sounds floating out drifted through the house. Silently he peeked into the half-open door.

Oasis lay curled in a small ball on the bed. His mother was crying. Her eyes were closed but the tears found a way out. Creed could not understand what he was seeing. He only cried when he was hurt or unhappy and she was always there to wipe away his tears. Now she was crying.

The scene disconcerted him. He slipped through the door and stood beside her bed. The small boy reached out and tenderly wiped the tears from her face. At his touch, her eyelids flickered open. "Adam?" she asked in a dreamy voice.

"No mother, it's me," he said quickly. Surely his mother had not forgotten who he was? Why had she called him by his father's name? Creed studied his mother's face as he pushed aside a loose strand of her mahogany hair with his small fingers. Gradually her eyes seemed to focus and come back to reality.

"Oh, Creed," she smiled sadly, "for a moment I thought you were Adam. You look so much like him. I wish he could have seen you . . . " her words broke off and she started crying again. Creed threw his arms around her neck. "Why, are you crying, mother? Are you hurting?"

Creed woke up suddenly. The darkness was threatening. He felt the strange shock of his mind tumbling back from dream to reality. He was not home. He was in a room in the Skeddner mansion. His mother was not with him. He was alone. His mother was gone. Dead. His pillow was moist. Tears? The dream had felt so real.

DR. ISAAC SKEDDNER stared down at the small titanium data capsule. His fingers trembled. If this was what he thought it was . . .

Alexis slipped to her father's side, wrapping her arm around his shoulder. She started when she saw the capsule in Skeddner's hand. Then she frowned. "I thought he was lying, father."

He nodded still gazing at the small titanium capsule. "I know, sweetheart. So did I."

She leaned her chin against his shoulder. "What's on it? Why did he bring it?"

Skeddner's response was low and diffident. "I'm not entirely certain."

She smiled, her eyebrows arching. "But you must have an assumption?"

"Maybe . . . or maybe not. Normally, they are used to store military intelligence or other highly sensitive information. They are supposedly indestructible. But I doubt it has any relevance to us," he said, brushing aside her question. He pulled open his desk drawer and placed the capsule inside.

It was obvious from the way the girl pursed her lips that this answer was unsatisfactory, but she did not press the subject. Skeddner knew the explanation was absurd. Granted, he did not want to lie to her, but she could not be involved with this.

"What did you think of the boy, Alexis?"

The girl brushed aside her dark hair. "He is fierce, but I think there's something sweet behind his hard exterior. I can see it in his eyes. It's an attribute only a mother can instill."

In a second Dr. Skeddner seemed to melt from his large imposing form to a whimpering child. Sighing, he sat down in his chair and buried his face in his hands. His body shuddered as he began to sob. Concern was etched across the girl's gentle features. She slid off the desk and slipped her arms around his neck. The doctor held her close. For a long moment they held each other, neither saying a word. Finally, Alexis kissed his check. "Don't cry, Father."

He smiled at her through his tears. "Ah, my darling, what would I do without you?"

She was watching him intently. "Tell me what is troubling you."

Skeddner stroked her hair. "It's nothing you need to worry your pretty head about," he said, averting his face. She took his chin in her hand and pulled his face up so they were looking directly into each other's eyes—her royal blue eyes and his dark gray ones. "It's Mother, isn't it? Oh, I'm so sorry. I shouldn't have mentioned Mother. I know how much you miss her. I didn't mean to unearth your sorrow."

The man smiled through his tears. "I know, darling. I know."

CREED WOKE to the smell of bacon, eggs, hashbrowns, and the heavenly aroma of freshly baked bread. The hot breakfast lay on the small coffee table. His clothes, which had been clean and ironed sometime during the night, lay folded on the upholstered bench at the foot of the bed. He dressed quickly then tackled the food. It was a royal feast compared to the tasteless mush he normally ate.

As he ate, he pondered what he should do. He rehearsed what he could tell Dr. Skeddner about his mother . . . or he could just leave. He was not ready to discuss his mother with anyone.

He got up and stepped out into the hall. It was still and quiet. He saw no one. As he passed doors, he peeked into the different rooms. There was a billiard room, an old-fashioned dance hall, and a stylish dining room. The enormity of the house amazed him. The Skeddners were extremely wealthy. But he could not quell the feeling that the house was missing something. A missing component. Odd.

He stopped inside a well-stocked library, fascinated by the rows of books. Never had he seen such a wealth of knowledge. He stiffened. Someone was watching him. He wheeled around. Alexis was standing in the doorway.

She smiled. Creed wondered how long she had been standing there. He should have heard. Was she spying on him? She was dressed in jeans and a sky blue top. A beret covered her black hair which seemed even silkier than last night. She was barefoot and, like her fingernails, her toenails were carefully manicured in blue nail polish. This girl was obsessed with blue.

"Did you sleep well?" she asked stepping into the library and closing the door behind her.

The bed had been wonderful. Creed nodded, maintaining his stoical, distrustful attitude. "Yes, thank you."

"How did you come to speak so well?"

The question caught him off guard. What an odd question. He knew that he spoke a bit differently; his mother had always pressed him to use proper English. Down in the slums, slang words, missing articles, and curse words were so pervasive that it was practically a different language.

Creed stared at her blankly, a skill he had developed in the streets. If he appeared a bit dull, most people left him alone; but sometimes it had the opposite effect.

"You know, how did you learn to speak?" she repeated.

"My mother."

His answer seemed to puzzle her. "Well, who taught your mother to speak?"

"I don't know."

"Does your father speak well?"

"I've never met my father."

"Oh, I'm sorry."

There was an uneasy silence. Creed hated interacting with strangers, especially girls. He wished she would stop staring with those beautiful eyes and go away. She was beginning to make him nervous, which was not an easy thing to do.

A SHINY black Chrysler pulled out of traffic and turned down a street leading to the Skeddner penthouse.

Behind the tinted windows were five men. All were seasoned killers.

On cue, all four security cameras mounted around the entrance to the underground parking structure clicked off. The alarm system had already been disabled. As the sedan neared the gates, they swung open of their own accord. It always helped to have a man working on the inside.

CHAPTER 5

The rattle of a sub-machine gun exploded the silence. The sound echoed around the house like a thousand fireworks, rendering its location impossible to determine. Creed and Alexis both jumped. Instinctively, he knocked her to the ground.

The noise ceased just as suddenly as it had begun. From his position on the floor, Creed scanned the room. They were alone. He stood up slowly. "Where did it come from?" he asked, helping Alexis to her feet.

"I don't know, but I hope it wasn't my father," she ran towards the door.

"You shouldn't—" Creed began, but Alexis was already at the door. She tried to push it open, but the double doors did not budge. She pushed it again, yet it still did not open. She slammed it with her fist.

"It's locked from the outside. What's going on?"

"Stand back," Creed ordered. He took a running start and kicked the doors. The lock gave way with a crunch and the doors flew open. Alexis dashed past him.

"Wait, girl!" Creed cried. But she refused to listen. That stupid girl was going to get herself killed. He caught her at the end of the hall. Grabbing her arm, he dragged her back. "Don't be a fool!" he whispered in her ear. "Are you trying to get shot? You don't know who's down there."

She halted and bit her lip. "Don't be obtuse. Of course I don't want to be shot. But I wasn't thinking about that. My thoughts were on my father. Let go of my arm."

Creed released her. "This might be a good time to think about it.

35

It's usually too late after you're dead." He did not even try to hide the sarcasm.

"Someone might need help and I didn't see you offering to take the lead," she answered coldly.

"I will. But what did you have my in mind to do after you rushed headlong into the middle of a firefight? You don't even have a weapon."

"I would have thought of something."

"Sure. Where are my guns?"

Alexis hesitated only a moment. "Follow me."

In the back of a closet, she pushed aside some clothes revealing a safe. She spun the lock and opened it. The two pistols and his knife sat there. Creed reached in and clipped his gun belt to his waist. He felt a greater sense of security with it close to hand.

Despite all her bravado, Alexis stayed half a step behind him as they tiptoed down the halls expecting at any moment to come across someone who was not supposed to be there. As they neared Dr. Skeddner's study, Alexis slowed down, almost stopping completely.

"Father?" she called in a halting whisper.

The unnatural stillness was threatening. Her face betrayed the sickening feeling in her heart. Rounding the office door, they witnessed a grisly scene. The butler's body was slumped across the desk at an unnatural angle; half a dozen bullet wounds marred his body. Blood dripped down the desk, forming a small red pool on the oriental rug. His eyes were bulging out of his head and his mouth hung slack. Alexis paled and gasped in revulsion. Unconsciously, she grabbed Creed's arm to steady herself.

For a moment, Creed thought she was about to faint or puke. "Are you all right?"

"Yes . . . yes. I think I'm fine."

Creed looked back at the room and swallowed. The sight was not a novel one to him. He had experienced death from an early age, in some of its most violent forms. Still, after seventeen years, he had never been able to shake off the deep feeling of horror that accompanied it.

"What . . . happened?" Alexis asked in a choked voice. Neither felt any inclination to step inside the room. Creed stared. He was assaulted by the memory of his mother's murder.

The bullet holes were in the walls and furniture around the desk. Clearly the fight had been one sided. The room had been ransacked as well. Drawers were pulled out. Papers and computer disks were strewn over the floor. Dr. Skeddner was nowhere to be seen.

"Father!" Alexis cried, near to panic. "Where are you?" The silence seemed to be mocking her. She ran down the curved hallway but froze, and flew back. "Creed, please come help me find my father. They might still be hiding in the house."

He joined Alexis in her search, glad to escape the office, but he knew it would prove fruitless. The perpetrators would be long gone. If they had intended to kill him and Alexis, they would have already made the attempt—not that they would have succeeded.

They scoured the mansion and found the bodies of three other servants who had been brutally slain. They retreated to the living room.

Alexis was twisting her braid around her finger. She bit her lip, ignoring the taste of lipstick on her tongue. She sank into an arm chair and covered her face with her hands.

Alexis told Creed that most of the servants were away. This was an ideal time for a kidnaping. How they had managed to infiltrate the house without activating the alarm system was still a mystery to him. The place was loaded with security. Whoever had done the job had executed it perfectly. He and Alexis were the only living people in the house. She had already contacted the police and they would be arriving shortly. There was nothing left to do, but wait.

Creed stood by awkwardly. He watched a tear escape through the girl's fingers. He knew she was hurting, but he had no idea how to comfort her. Sniffling, she wiped her eyes and tucked a few loose strands of hair behind her ear. "Creed," she whispered, attempting to recover her emotions, "I know that my father offered lodgings to you, but under the circumstances I don't believe you can stay."

Creed nodded his agreement. At least she did not suspect him for her father's disappearance—or did she? "Who locked us in the room? Somebody didn't want us out here."

She looked up, then frowned. "What do you mean? You think my father...?" Creed shifted uncomfortably. He could see the anger building up behind her eyes. Her voice was low and level. "How dare you even suggest such a thing! You know nothing about my father."

Creed lifted his hands in a gesture of surrender. "Look, all I'm saying is something happened. I'm just trying to stay open to the possibilities."

"He was kidnaped. End of story."

Creed groped for the right words. "Are you going to be all right alone?"

"I don't intend to stay here. I'm going to call my cousin in New York. She and her husband will let me stay with them until my father is . . . is . . . found." Her sentence broke with her composure. "Oh, God," she cried imploringly, "Why?"

The unanswered question floated through the empty mansion. Her eyes held such a faraway look that Creed believed she was indeed crying out to God.

"He never hurt anyone."

This last statement was directed toward Creed. Not sure how to respond, he said nothing. Alexis looked up with a start. "His phone!"

She pulled her cell phone from her pocket and punched a speed dial on the keypad. It rang. But it was not answered. She sank back into the chair.

Creed ran back upstairs and retrieved his backpack. Coming down again he made up his mind to leave. He had no obligation to stay. He had delivered the capsule as his mother had requested. His part in this mess was finished.

Alexis had not moved from the chair. Her head was bowed as if in prayer. Her thin shoulders were shaking with silent sobs. She did not look up as Creed sneaked past her, down the hall and out of the house. If she heard him, she paid him no heed.

After the death of his mother, Creed had decided to fulfil her wish and then find a place to die. There was nothing left for him. But now he did not feel the same. He did not feel ready to die. What had happened to him? He almost felt disloyal to her. Before, his body, mind, and soul were ready to shut down to join her, but now...

Creed pondered this question for a full five minutes before he discovered the answer. He was uncomfortable leaving Alexis alone.

Was he delirious? No. Of course not. Then why on earth would he care about this girl? His guilt increased by the second until he felt completely rotten inside.

Creed scowled.

He continued walking through the courtyard. But the nagging feeling refused to leave. He was just about to turn around when he became aware of a slight rustling in the bushes. Someone sprang out. Whipping out his gun, Creed found himself aiming at an FBI agent. Not an ideal situation.

The officer also had his Glock trained at Creed's chest. Creed, having no wish to get entangled with the law, immediately dropped his gun. "On the ground!" the man barked.

"Sir, I think there's a mistake. I didn't do anything," Creed said while following the agent's commands. The agent snickered. "Of course you didn't do anything."

Two police officers appeared beside Creed. The first officer called into his radio, "We've apprehended a suspect, leaving the house carrying a handgun."

"I told you I didn't do anything!"

But he knew how ridiculous his words sounded.

CHAPTER 6

Alexis Skeddner wiped her eyes on her sleeve as she opened the massive double doors. A team of FBI agents crowded her doorstep. She was expecting the police, but she was not expecting to see Creed in handcuffs. Both guns and his knife were in the possession of the officer.

"Miss Skeddner," one agent said, nodding a greeting. He introduced himself as Carl Wayne. "Are you all right?"

"Yes, I'm fine."

He shoved Creed forward. "We caught him leaving the premises."

The look in her eyes immediately caused Creed to regret his decision to leave. "Thanks for coming back," she said, then looked away.

How could he answer that? The officer frowned, still gripping Creed's shoulder. "Was he the trouble?"

"No, sir, the boy's innocent. I don't believe he had anything to do with it."

The officer seemed disappointed. "Are sure he wasn't bothering you?"

"Yes, I'm positive. He's just an acquaintance of the family. Please release him."

Reluctantly, they uncuffed him, and Alexis led them to her father's office. As the FBI team began to snap pictures, collect bullet casings, and dust for prints, another agent, Jerry Anders, questioned Alexis on a wide range of subjects. Creed remained aloof. He picked a chair in the livingroom and waited. Most of the officers gave Creed a wary, suspicious eye. He was out of place here, like a skunk in a bed of roses.

Alexis suddenly bolted up.

"Wait, I just remembered. My father keeps hidden security cameras in his office. We can play them back downstairs."

A few minutes later, they sat around a television screen. The image flickered then revealed Dr. Skeddner typing at his computer. After a few seconds, the door was knocked in. A man in a brown jacket gripping a Sig Sauer pistol stood framed in the doorway.

Creed had to grip his chair to resist leaping from his seat. His eyes were riveted to the screen. A cold fear clenched his chest as two unnerving blue eyes stared back at him.

It was the man who had killed his mother. The man he had killed.

Commando.

No. It could not be true. He had killed him, killed them all. Was it some kind of trick? He could vividly remember Commando falling. Even if he had somehow survived the impact, he would be in traction for months if not forever. There was no way he could have healed so fast. But there he was alive and breathing.

He was obviously the leader. Four other men came up behind him dressed similarly, black leather and knee-length combat boots. All carried pistols. But these were not the men who had chased him and his mother through the alleys.

One of them, a young man no older than twenty-five with long sideburns and short, spiky, red hair, trained his handgun on Skeddner. "Put 'em up!" he shouted in a high tenor. "And get away from that desk!"

The doctor rose angrily, but still composed. "What can I do for you?"

"I want the capsule with the MCC data," Commando said.

"What are you talking about?"

The leader turned to his followers. "Search the room, boys. Crultt, Trex, disarm our friend."

Crultt grabbed Skeddner by the shoulder. He was an imposing African with well-developed biceps and coarse black hair dangling in dread locks. The red headed man darted forward, a cocky grin flickering across his face. He seized a taser that was hidden under Skeddner's jacket. Skeddner shoved Trex away.

"Hyndrix, take a crack at the computer." A thin weasel-looking man with squinting eyes—eyes which appeared never to have left a computer screen, began going through the open computer files. Behind him lumbered a man weighted down with more firearms and weapons than all the rest combined. His lower lip was twisted into a continual grimace. The men methodically searched the room, opening cabinets and going through the desk.

Skeddner looked straight up into the camera. "Whatever you're looking for, it's not here."

Commando smirked. "I might be inclined to believe you except that your loyal attorney told me otherwise when I gave her the proper coaxing. It was a good try, though."

A few tense moments elapsed before Trex shouted,"I've got it!"

He waved a data capsule aloft.

"Well done, Trex. Give it to me," Commando ordered, snatching it. "You old liar," he said, turning toward the doctor as he stroked the capsule solemnly in his hands. "Rolls was a coward. He was afraid to use it and afraid to destroy it. But I must say, I'm glad he didn't."

"I don't know who you are, but what you're holding is incredibly dangerous."

"Don't try to preach to me, Skeddner. I know exactly what I'm holding. Don't worry. I'll take good care of this baby."

He motioned to Crultt and Lynch, who clamped hands on Skeddner and dragged him out of the doorway. The doctor struggled. "You have the capsule. What else do you want? Money? Give me a pen and I'll write you out a check."

Slipping the titanium capsule into his pocket, Commando holstered his pistol. "I don't want a thing from you. I just want you."

"Why?"

"If I had my way, I'd skin you alive. So you had better leave it at that before I forget my orders and kill you by accident."

The men trooped from the room with Trex herding Dr. Skeddner. Off camera, they heard the fearful voice of the butler. "What are you doing!"

The same awful explosion they had heard only a few hours ago shook the speakers. The butler's body came flying back, landing in a bloody heap on the desk.

They continued to stare even after the screen had gone black.

Creed raked his fingers through his hair. So, *that* was what Commando had wanted from his mother, that stupid data capsule. What was on it? Why didn't she just give it to him? His mother was not an idiot. She must have had an extremely good reason for resisting. But what was it?

Baffled, Creed bent his attention to the other faces in the room. A tinge of pity touched him as he watched. Alexis buried her face in her hands. Recalling her words when she caught him on the grounds sent a shudder through him. *It could be a bomb*, she had said.

The capsule was a bomb. A bomb which had just detonated, shattering her world. Agent Wayne handed Alexis a small box of tissue and stood up. "There seems to be conclusive evidence on that tape. I'll make a copy and take it to the station. You wouldn't happen to know—what did he call it? MCC data? Do you know what that is?"

Alexis shook her head. "I'm sorry, sir. All I know is that Creed brought it."

After a grueling cross examination, Creed told the interrogator everything he knew about the capsule and Commando. Nothing.

But Wayne was having difficulty believing him. "You must realize that suspicion falls heavily on you as both you and Miss Skeddner freely attest that you brought that data capsule."

"If I was in league with them, do you think I would've stuck around?"

The man smiled. "You have a point there. But I think it would be best if you stayed here until we clear this business up."

"What if I don't want to?"

"Then I will have to get a warrant for your arrest. It's your choice."

AN ARMY of police and forensic investigators streamed in and out of the Skeddner premises for hours. The kidnaping of Isaac Skeddner was headline news.

In the den, Alexis Skeddner flicked on the screen. Inserting the recorded footage from her father's office, she watched closely. There must be something they had overlooked, some hint, some clue that would give them a lead on her father's kidnaping. She felt like she was watching a scary crime drama, except that this was real. Much too real.

The images of her father and the kidnapers flashed across the screen. Her father was talking. She noticed that he was tapping his foot. At first she dismissed it as a nerves, but it was out of character for him. His feet were out of the kidnapers' view, yet in perfect view of the camera. He kept tapping, then pausing. Tap. Pause. Tap. Pause. The realization was startling. He was speaking to her. Morse code.

"SEE? HE'S using his foot to tap out a name in morse code: David Mason. He is a friend of my father. He can help us."

Alexis and agent Wayne were watching the kidnaping play out on screen again. Her rush of words was greeted with a rather blank stare.

The agent crossed his arms. "Look, Miss, I'm very busy. I don't have time for all this."

"I'm certain Mr. Mason has some information—"

"Or Father wouldn't have tapped his foot. Yeah, I know."

She caught his arm. "Please, believe me, sir! You must believe me! I know my father."

"I understand that this has been a stressful day, Miss Skeddner. But you're running on speculations and assumptions."

"What else do I have?"

"I don't know, but I do know that I need to get back to work."

"Fine, I'll go by myself."

"Miss, I'm afraid that's not possible. You're not allowed out of the house. It's for your own security."

ALEXIS HESITATED in the hall, uncertain how to proceed. Through the open doors, she could see Creed slouching, stoic and motionless, on a brown leather couch. Anger filled his fierce brown eyes. She could not understand why she trusted him. He was just some boy off the streets. No, he was more than that; exactly what, she was still unsure.

Creed's backpack lay at his feet. He was loath to let his possessions out of sight, as if someone might want to steal his miserable things. Hesitantly, she approached the sofa until she was a few feet away. He didn't look up or show the slightest acknowledgment of her presence, but kept his gaze on the far wall. How was she going to do this?

Taking a deep measured breath, she accosted the boy. "I think my father left me a clue on that recording."

No response.

She had the notion that her words had collided against a brick wall, not that she had expected much more. She tried again. "If you watch the tape, you'll notice that before the blue-eyed kidnapper—,"

"His name is Commando," Creed said without moving.

Alexis caught her breath and stared at him. "How do you know that? Nobody mentioned his name on the video. You're not . . . you're not in cahoots with him, are you?"

Creed lifted his almond eyes. His brown locks hung across his face. Folding his arms across his chest he related his story in the sparsest words possible. "Two days ago, he and some other men chased me through the streets. One of them called him Commando."

"Why didn't you give his name to the police? It could help them find my father."

"Trust me, it won't help them. It's not his real name."

"You don't know that."

"Look, I've already tangled with these men. They know exactly what they're doing. Those clowns in the other room are out of their league."

Alexis frowned. What else did this boy know that he wasn't telling? "So you knew the kidnapers were coming after the capsule before you brought it to us?"

"Of course not," Creed snapped back. "If I had known they would come here after the capsule, I would have told you."

"What was on that wretched capsule? Why do these men want it?"

He sighed. "If I knew, I would've told you, I would've told the FBI. Did you come here just to pester me with stupid questions?"

She ignored his comment. "It didn't dawn on me until I watched the security recording again, that my father was tapping his feet in morse code. He spelled out Mason. I met Mr. Mason once when he visited our church. I need to talk with him."

"And you're telling me this because . . . ?"

"The police don't believe me."

"What makes you think I'll believe you?"

"I'm praying that you will."

"Just call the guy. They'll let you do that, won't they?"

"Yes, but I cannot locate his number."

"Look in a phone book."

"I already have. It's not listed. But I remember where he lives."

Creed dropped his voice. "So, what you're really trying to say is, 'Help me bust out of my police protection?'"

The girl blushed, but nodded, matching his voice level. "I don't think I can do it alone."

Creed's tone held genuine pity as well as genuine defeat. "Sorry, but I can't help you there. I'm in enough trouble as it is."

Alexis's face darkened and her eyes blazed. "I don't believe this! You brought that horrible, horrible capsule, and my poor father gets kidnaped because of it. Now my life is falling apart around my ears. And you're simply sitting there like a filthy coward."

Creed clenched his fists, but kept his tone level. "Look, girl, it was my mother's dying wish that I bring the data capsule to your father. And as for your father, I'm not throwing my life away for him. His kidnapers are professionals. You mix yourself up in this and they'll kill you just as easily as they killed your butler."

"I'm already mixed up in this. I just told you the police don't believe me. If I wait for them to act, it might be too late." Her lip trembled. "You don't care. That's your problem. You just don't care. You don't care what happens to me, or my father, or anyone else on this planet. All you think about is yourself."

Creed was on his feet in a second, advancing on her. Backing away, she could feel the danger lurking behind his calm but, deadly expression. She had cut a nerve. A hint of fear brushed her as she found her progress barred by a wall. Would he attack her? He was still coming, cornering her. He stopped with his nose nearly touching hers. She could see the muscles tightening his face as he spoke.

"If I didn't think about myself, I'd be dead today."

Alexis shivered.

"I couldn't..." he faltered. "Those men killed my mother."

Even as the words left his mouth, the protective fierceness melted away. His eyes carried a faraway look of sorrow and fear. For a moment she caught a glimpse of the boy without his mask. She was startled by how easily she could see through him.

"You weren't there," he said again reliving the moment. "Those bullets tearing away her flesh. I saw her die."

His lip trembled and he gritted his teeth at the remembrance."Her blood mixed with the mud of the street and my tears. She lay there, dying in my arms. I had to watch helplessly as her life ebbed away . . ."

His voice started fading as he struggled to control his emotions. He turned away. "I'm not the one to help you. My life is nothing. It's over. I don't care what happens anymore."

FOR AWHILE Alexis stayed quiet. Creed knew she was processing everything he had said. His words had come out unbidden. He hadn't meant to tell her so much.

"That's awful," she said at length. "I'm sorry, I had no idea." She paused. "I lost my mother too, only six months ago in a car accident. I understand the trauma you're going through."

It *was* awful. Somehow he felt better for her sympathy. He nodded, somewhat embarrassed at her witnessing his breakdown. With difficulty he returned his face to its normal, emotionless expression. He stared past her. "My mother is dead. If there was anyway humanly possible to bring her back, I'd do it in a heartbeat. But there isn't."

"Creed, this isn't over. Your life isn't over until God says it is. Everything happens for a reason and everyone has a purpose. I think you still have a part to play."

"Chasing after those men will do nothing to solve my problems."

Alexis leaned closer to him. "What about my problems?"

"They're yours now, not mine."

She stood up. "I'm disappointed in you, Creed. When I first saw you in the garden, I assumed you were just what you looked like—some street thug. But then I saw something in your eyes that was different," she wavered, "I don't know how to explain it. My heart told me that I had come across a rare jewel. Unfortunately, I was mistaken. You're nothing but a worthless, miserable, street urchin and I hate you!"

With those final words she spun on her heel and marched off, head held high. Creed watched her go. Her feet pounded the stairs as she began to run. His conscience pricked him like a razor blade. He tried to smash it down and ignore it. But it resurfaced in the form of his mother's disappointed face. She was disappointed in him.

Then the image of his mother's murderers flashed across his mind, those eyes that seemed to be made of ice, that tight, violent face. He shuddered. But could he run from it? Creed found himself climbing the stairs.

As he stepped up to the open double doors of her bedroom, he was stunned by what he saw. It was a room that would make an Asian princess jealous. Everything was beautiful and costly. From the artistically carved fireplace and intricately woven tapestries that adorned the walls, to the black and orange tiger skin on the floor and the enormous canopy bed. The luxurious bedroom was bigger than Creed's entire apartment. It was a miniature palace.

Alexis was crying on a feather bed surrounded by silk pillows. He could imagine Alexis and her father gathering these things from their travels to the four corners of the globe. But all of her treasures would be empty without her father.

Her father—the man whom she might never see again.

He rapped on the door frame. "Alexis?"

"Why are you still here? Get out!" she ordered without looking up.

He walked up to the bed. "Look, Alexis—"

"Are you deaf? I said, 'Get out.'"

"Alexis, you were right about me. I am afraid of those men and I was acting like a coward."

It was difficult to force his mouth to construct his next words. "I'm sorry."

He said it quickly to get it out of the way. He had never apologized to anyone in his life with the exception of his mother.

Alexis lifted her head. "All I want is my father back." She reached out and touched his arm. "Please, won't you take a risk for him?"

Creed glared at her so fiercely that she drew her hand back in alarm. His face was harder than bronze. "No."

Ignoring the imploring look in her eyes, he turned away. He would not lift a finger for that man. Her final plea stopped him short. "Will you do it for me?"

He couldn't face her.

Her voice rang in his ears. "Don't you want to know why they killed your mother?"

Her question was like a revelation. "Yes."

Brushing aside her braid, Alexis sat up, bestowing him with full confidence. "How do we get out?"

CHAPTER 7

In all, there were ten policemen stationed in the Skeddner house. They had set up extra security cameras around the property and reset the security system to sound if any door or window was touched, but it was clear that they didn't expect any trouble. This was merely protocol. They lounged in the foyer, eating and talking in hushed tones. They were hulking men each decked out with flak vests, guns, and radios. Every fifteen minutes or so, one made a round of the house. But they were guarding against people entering, not escaping.

Creed crouched at the juncture where the hallway branched into the living room. The only option was to slip past them, because he was not ready to add police assault to his record. He needed his pistols; there was no way he was leaving without them. To his surprise, he saw them lying on the side table. Somehow they had been overlooked in all the excitement. Well, that certainly made his life easier.

He slid out on his stomach. Holding his breath, he retrieved his twin pistols and holstered them. Creeping forward on his toes, he retraced his steps back up the stairs to Alexis's room. He still wasn't sure how to get out. Alexis met him at the door, a glimmer of hope in her eyes. "Did you find a way past them?"

He started to say no, but stopped. The escape route was absurdly obvious. "Maybe."

He crossed the room to the wide ornamental fireplace and slid open the grating. "Do you have a car?"

Alexis trailed after him. "Yes, my Corvette is in the garage."

Creed had to resist rolling his eyes. "That'll work."

He dropped to his knees and peered up the chimney, wrinkling his nose at the sharp, burnt odor. "Is there a cap?"

"Well, I suppose so. Wait, you're not thinking about climbing it, are you?"

"You said you wanted to get out."

She crouched beside him, looking up doubtfully at the rugged, brick shaft. "What if I fall?"

"I'll be right behind you to catch you."

She was still hesitant.

Creed shrugged. "If you don't want to go, it's all the same to me."

He started to turn away, but she grabbed his arm. "No . . . I'll do it."

"Then help me tear these sheets."

Together, they ripped up the fancy sheets from her bed and knotted them until they had improvised a rope to Creed's liking. He looped it around his shoulder like a mountain climber and motioned to the chimney with a mock flourish. "Ladies first."

Alexis braced herself against the brick walls and began her ascent. Creed tied his backpack to the sheet rope so it would hang beneath him, and followed her up. It was a tight fit. Creed doubted Alexis would fall; she probably couldn't fall even if she tried.

The next few minutes were torture. Hands scraped on rough surfaces. Feet searched for footholds. The climb was arduous and awkward. At one point they could hear the police officers laughing and joking with each other through the wall. Creed had expected Alexis to meet some difficulty, but she surprised him. She was much more athletic than he had given had supposed.

Halfway up, the sunlight from the room disappeared entirely and they were climbing blind. He could hear her rhythmic breathing above him. "I'm claustrophobic you know."

Creed groaned. That was great. The last thing he needed was for her to freeze up and refuse to go up or down. "We're almost there," he encouraged. They shuffled upwards alternating between pushing with their hands, legs, and backs.

To his relief, Alexis continued, knocking soot and dirt on him. Then she stopped. "Okay, I've reached the top. Now what?"

"Try and push the cover off."

The steel cap, which kept rain and birds out of the chimney, squeaked angrily as it was pushed aside. Sunlight poured down through the swirling dust. Alexis dragged herself out of the hole and up onto the curved, sloping roof tiles. Creed followed suit, blinking in the light.

He put on his backpack and unwrapped the makeshift rope from his waist. He looped one end around the chimney, secured it with a quick knot, and threw it across the roof. Now came the hard part. He led the way as they inched down the roof. Arriving at the edge, Creed leaned over.

The cameras were positioned at the corners of the house facing outwards. He slid over until he found a spot that was out of their line of vision. Creed took hold of the rope and slid down. After he landed, he held the rope steady for Alexis as she descended.

They crossed the floral courtyard, and took the elevator down to the garage. A brand new Chevrolet Corvette sat in a reserved space—blue, of course. Alexis slid into the driver's side, and Creed strapped himself in the passenger seat. The engine purred to life.

A HELICOPTER droned over the tranquil waters of the Pacific rapidly approaching its destination. Commando cracked his knuckles. This mission had been easier than he had hoped. He was feeling good about himself. They were one step closer to the goal. Very soon, all the pieces of the puzzle would fall into place. The cell phone clipped to his waist vibrated. He read the caller ID. Taylor Whitefield.

He swiped the phone open. "Everything is going smoothly. We're right on schedule."

Whitefield ignored Commando's reassuring remark. "My dear Commando," he began in a voice infused with sarcasm, "have you, by any chance, had the opportunity to watch any of the major news stations?"

It was an odd question. And it was everything Commando could do to keep his cool. He would never get used to Whitefield's curious, roundabout way of asking a question. Commando's irritation colored his words. "I've been a little busy as of late."

"Well, maybe if you had seen the news, you might recognize an interesting video clip of the man who was filmed in the act of kidnaping Dr. Isaac Skeddner and catapulted to international fame."

Commando almost crushed the phone to block out the mocking tone of Whitefield's voice. He groaned inwardly. He had been so careful! He glared loathsomely at Dr. Skeddner who was slumped in his seat, his hands still manacled to the chair. "How?"

"A hidden camera, of which I assume your associate spy was unaware, conveniently located in Dr. Skeddner's office."

Commando growled. "Well, I got him didn't I? Nobody followed us. And I can change my face."

"Don't you mean that *I* can change your face?"

Every word the man spoke seemed intent on mocking the life from him. Commando's patience, never in great supply, shredded away to its last strands. "I could change your face, too. Nobody would know you had a face when I'm finished with it."

Whitefield shrugged the threat away with little concern. "You need to be a hundred times more careful. If you're caught, it could place this entire operation in jeopardy."

Commando winced hard at the absurd understatement, thankful that Whitefield could not view his reaction. "Then we should make sure that doesn't happen. I'll watch my end and you worry about yours. Remember, if anything unfavorable happens, little Rachel will be the first to die, slowly—by my own hand."

A pause ensued. This threat extinguished Whitefield's mockery and reprimanding. When he did answer his voice had dropped to a hoarse whisper and lost its placid tone. "If you so much as touch her, I'll kill...myself, then where will you be? All your crooked schemes will be for naught."

"I will be arriving shortly," Commando said, reveling in victory. "You can explain the situation to Skeddner."

CREED STOOD next to Alexis at the door of Mason's condominium expecting trouble. He scorned her impulsiveness, yet at the same time, admired her courage. Alexis knocked but there was no response. She tried the knob. It was unlocked and turned under her fingers.

Creed and Alexis found themselves in a living room of moderate size. Black leather couches, a glass coffee table, and a giant wide screen TV made up most of the room.

Alexis stepped around a potted plant. "Hello? Mr. Mason? Is anybody home?"

Creed glanced around the empty room. Something was wrong. "Are you sure this is where he lives?"

Alexis nodded. A voice came from behind them. "When I heard that you'd run off, I had a hunch I might find you here. Mason is dead."

Creed spun around, whipping out his gun. Blocking the doorway, was Dr. Skeddner's lawyer Jennifer Jones.

She blinked with surprise and fear. "Put the gun down. I only want to help you."

Alexis frowned at him. "Creed, this is our family attorney. Please put the gun away. This is not the streets."

Still unable to dismiss his initial suspicion, Creed slid the gun back into its holster. Jennifer turned her attention to Alexis while keeping a cautious eye on Creed. "Alexis, I just found out about your father. I can't begin to explain how sorry I am."

"Please help me. I'm completely at a loss."

Alexis stepped forward as if to hug her. But Creed caught Alexis by the arm, preventing her. Alexis looked at him in disbelief and shook him off. "What is wrong with you?"

"Something's not right . . ." Creed muttered.

Jennifer looked uncomfortable. "There's still a chance to save your father, but you need to tell me where he hid the data capsule. We'll use it as a bargaining chip."

Alexis frowned, "But I don't have it. Commando took it when he kidnaped my father."

"I think there's been a mistake. Commando took the wrong one."

Creed stiffened. "How do you know which one he wanted?"

The woman paused a fraction too long. "Only one is valuable."

Creed's question burned in his mind. "*Why* is it valuable?"

"It contains plans for some type of secret weapon. That's all I know."

Creed didn't like the way Jennifer was staring at him. There was something fearful in her expression.

"He's coming back for it," she said darkly. "He'll hunt you down."

A warning. In an instant, Creed yanked out his gun.

Everything happened at once.

Alexis jumped in his way yelling, "Creed, no!"

An arm suddenly looped itself around Creed's neck cutting off his wind pipe and almost pulling him over backwards. Jennifer leaped into him snatching at his gun. Creed gasped for air. Somebody was clinging to his back and attempting to tighten the choke hold. Jennifer and Alexis crashed into him. In the chaos, the gun was peeled from his fingers.

CHAPTER 8

Alexis saw Creed's gun sliding across the floor. She knew if she didn't get it, someone might end up dead. She and Jennifer both lunged after the gun. Diving head first, Alexis swatted the weapon away. Jennifer's face clouded. "I'm sorry, Alexis."

Before the girl had a chance to comprehend the words, the lawyer's knuckles transferred waves of pain tingling across her jaw. But the betrayal stung more than the blow. Confusion filtered through her mind. This was their lawyer, her father's friend. Why did she strike her? Jennifer was going after the gun again. What would happen when she got it? With a final effort Alexis reached out and grabbed her ankle.

SKEDDNER HAD always known it could happen. It happened all the time in movies. It had even happened to one of his closest friends. He had just never expected it to happen to him. Nobody woke up expecting to be kidnaped.

Kidnaped. The word possessed such a belittling, and at the same time chilling, sound. His friend had returned in a body bag.

He shook the thought from his head. This was no way to be thinking. He rubbed the back of his neck. Every muscle was tight. His armpits were damp. The helicopter had become stifling.

How was Alexis handling this? If only he could warn her, tell her to throw that capsule into the sea.

The floor shifted under Skeddner's feet as the craft landed. Commando climbed out of the cabin. Trex loosened the blindfold that had rendered Skeddner oblivious to their location.

"Out, Skeddner," Commando ordered, encouraging him with a rough shove. Skeddner flinched. He guessed they were in some type of laboratory. Commando handed the capsule to a man coming to meet them. "Dr. North, take this up to the lab and let me know as soon the files have been opened."

The man hurried back the way he had come. Skeddner was hustled into a small room. Commando handcuffed Skeddner to a chair, then sat down opposite. "We have great plans for you, Skeddner."

"I'm sure you do."

He watched Commando. The man was as cold-blooded as they came. Dr. North reappeared. "I'm sorry, but this data capsule is blank."

Commando jumped up knocking down his chair. "What!"

In one amazing bound he leaped across the room and jerked the man up by his shirt collar. The man cowered, mesmerized by Commando's chilling eyes.

"What did you say?" Commando's voice had risen to a savage, grinding screech. Sweat poured from the doctor's face like wax from a burning candle. He swallowed. His Adam's apple bobbed up and down as he tried to repeat his message. "There was no information stored in the capsule," he stammered. "We scanned the whole thing, but there was nothing. It was empty."

"Impossible! Was the information erased?"

"Not necessarily. I don't believe there was ever any data on it."

Casting a murderous expression at Skeddner, Commando liberated the quaking technician who slumped to the ground. Commando dashed from the room as Dr. North touched his neck tenderly, checking for damage.

A wild thought entered Skeddner's head. The man probably had a phone. True, Skeddner was in handcuffs, but Dr. North was kneeling with his back toward him. This might be his only chance.

There was a brief, hard scuffle which ended when Skeddner's elbow hit the doctor's throat. Dr. North groaned and flopped over. Pain sizzled up Skeddner's leg where he landed hard on his knee. But he barely noticed. In his hand he held a cell phone. Commando certainly was not working alone; Skeddner could only pray that his cohorts had not located Alexis already.

He hammered out a well-known number.

TURNING TO one side, Creed jammed his elbow into his adversary's ribs. The choke hold loosened and Creed took the opportunity to wriggle away. He spun around, fists flying, but stopped his punch midway when he caught his first glimpse of his opponent.

It was boy. He could not have been any older than himself. He was a black boy with chestnut colored skin, small ears, and a sharp jaw line. He bore a striking resemblance to Skeddner's lawyer Jennifer Jones. There was fear in his brown eyes. Creed's rapid evaluation was cut short as the boy threw a punch.

Dodging to his left, Creed avoided the weak swing. Creed doubted if the boy had ever fought before. Not wanting to hurt him, Creed placed a measured blow to the boy's stomach and knocked him down.

Spinning on his heel, he scanned the room for the gun. It was still lying near the armchair, safe for the moment. But there was a more pressing concern. Jennifer was kicking ruthlessly at Alexis, trying to break the girl's dogged hold on her ankle.

Creed covered the distance in two steps. Launching himself into a low flying kick, he aimed for the chin. A resounding crunch announced the completion of his kick as the heel of his boot contacted solidly with the woman's jaw. The force of the blow sent her sliding across the floor. Creed bent over Alexis hoping she was alright.

Jennifer got to her knees and crawled after the gun. Creed was not about to let her get there. But before he could attack, pain smashed into the back of his head. Bits of broken pottery fell around him.

It was a vase. That boy had thrown a vase at him.

He turned in time to see a heavy picture frame slicing through the air. He dropped to the ground, saving his head. Alexis had an odd expression on her face. "Troy! Stop fighting him. He's my friend."

The black boy looked at her in surprise and confusion. It was apparent that they knew each other. More importantly, Troy was distracted. Now for the gun.

Too late. The distraction had been long enough for Jennifer to reach the gun. "Ok, everybody freeze!"

Jennifer menaced them with the weapon, but her hands were shaking. Creed examined the way the woman held the gun. She had never touched one before—which made the situation even more dangerous. Whatever composure the woman had possessed previously was completely lost. She gestured violently with the gun as she screamed at the boy. "Troy! Come away from them. I thought I told you to stay in the car!"

"I guess it's a good thing I came. What are you doing?"

Alexis rose to her knees. Disbelief rather than fright washed over her face. "Miss Jones, you're the one who locked us in the library aren't you? But why? Why are you doing this to us?"

"Alexis, don't you understand? He will kill me!" the woman shouted almost hysterically.

"What are you talking about?"

Creed never lost sight of the gun from his peripheral vision as Troy turned questioningly to the gun-wielding lawyer.

"What's going on? You told the police you didn't know anything about Dr. Skeddner's kidnaping."

Jennifer inhaled sharply. "I'll explain later. We're in a precarious situation. If we don't tread carefully, we could all end up dead. Right now, I want you all to get in the car."

"This is ridiculous! What are you doing?" Troy turned to Alexis, "There's been a mistake. You—."

Jennifer cut him off. "Troy! Shut up and get in the car."

She swivelled, training the handgun on Troy's heart. The boy gulped. "Aunt Jennifer? You're not gonna shoot me, are you?"

There was shock in his voice.

Then Creed made his move. He darted forward, making a swift grab at the gun. For a few nerve wrenching seconds, they both fought for possession. Between their struggling fingers the gun discharged. Jennifer let out a ragged yell. She broke away from Creed, clutching a bloodied hand.

There were tears in her eyes. "I'm sorry. Commando threatened me. I didn't have a choice. I'm sorry."

Alexis looked ready to cry herself. "Where's my father?"

"I don't know." Jennifer's words came out fast and wild. "But I have to call Commando and tell him where you are."

She pulled out a cell-phone, but Creed slapped the phone away. Jennifer back pedaled. "Okay! I'll never speak to him again. I'm leaving the country. Troy, come with me. We'll run together. Commando won't find us. He only wants Alexis and the capsule, not us."

"We can't just leave—,"

Jennifer had worked herself into a frenzy. "Yes we can!"

She grabbed Troy's arm, but he jerked away. "No."

"I promised my brother that I'd take care of you!"

"Like this? I don't think this is what dad meant."

"Fine!" she shouted and bolted from the apartment. They heard the squeal of tires as her car spun out of the lot.

"Wow, my day just got interesting," Troy muttered sarcastically and dropped into one of the chairs. "I was always wishing she would go away and leave me alone, and now she has." He snapped his fingers. "Gone. Just like that. I just can't believe she would do that to me."

Alexis, wide-eyed, buried her face in her hands. "Oh, God, can I trust anyone?"

Everyone jumped when her phone started spouting classical music. Alexis lifted the phone to her ear. "Hello?"

"Alexis?"

She lit up. "Father! I was so worried about you. I—"

"Thank God, you're safe. Now, sweetheart, listen carefully. The data capsule Creed brought is in the library. I want you to—" he gasped as if someone had just slugged him in the stomach and knocked the wind from him.

Creed saw the complete story in her eyes. For a brief moment Alexis had dreamed that her troubles were over. Her father would come home, and everything would be normal again. But she heard another voice on the phone and her high expectations were dashed into a thousand little fragments. It was the unmistakable voice of Commando. "Don't come after us, or I'll kill him!"

Static crackled, and the connection died—right along with her hopes.

SKEDDNER GROANED as he leaned back in his chair. His head was still ringing where Commando had clubbed him. He braced himself for the next blow. With an effort Commando lowered his gloved fist. Skeddner knew Commando would not kill him—at least not yet.

Skeddner licked his bleeding lip. He had needed thirty more seconds, just thirty precious seconds to warn Alexis.

His kidnaper hissed in his ear. "It doesn't matter who you called. Nobody is going to find you here. So you might as well tell me where the real capsule is. I'm sick and tired of your little games." He waved the blank data capsule in Skeddner's face. "Where is the capsule, Skeddner, the real one?"

"I was wondering how long it would take you to figure that out," Skeddner said grimly.

"You lied! You knew it was blank the whole time!"

"I didn't lie. You assumed it was the data capsule you were searching for. You never bothered asking me."

Commando roared and slapped the doctor across the face. Snatching Skeddner by his glossy black hair, he crouched down until they were both on eye level. With his free hand, he picked up the phone from the floor and scrolled down the list of outgoing calls. "Who's number is this? Is it Alexis's? Were you telling her where you hid it?"

As much as Skeddner tried to stay impassive, Commando was quick to observe his subtle repulsion of fear.

"Ah, so it was Alexis," Commando's face twisted into a sickening smile. "A friend of mine installed a bug in her phone. Don't worry, I'll find that girl and the capsule. And she'll be praying for death before I'm finished with her."

"You're too late. I've already called the police and they'll have it before you can get there," Skeddner returned quickly—too quickly.

"Don't play the fool with me Skeddner, you know just as well as I do, that you would never dream of handing that capsule over to the police."

CHAPTER 9

Alexis bit her lip, closed her phone, and slid it into her pocket. Conflicting thoughts circled through her mind. She did not know whether to be happy or sad, relieved or anxious. Her father was alive that much was certain, but how long he would stay that way was a separate question. Why hadn't the men asked for a ransom? What did they want with him?

She twisted her braid around her finger.

"Well, what did he say?" Creed encouraged finally.

"He said *your* data capsule," she began, giving Creed a spiteful look, "Is still in the library, but Commando interrupted him before he could finish. So what Miss Jones said about the fake capsule is true."

"Don't call it my capsule," Creed said defensively, folding his arms across his chest. "But you ought to be thankful. At least Dr. Skeddner is still alive."

Alexis sighed. "I'm going back to my house to retrieve that miserable capsule."

She had almost forgotten about Troy, who was staring at her. She had met him a few months ago at her church youth group. When his father died, his aunt had taken him in.

"I had no idea what was going on," Troy said, and looked at the floor. "I'm really sorry about what she did to you. What can I do to help?"

Creed shook his head. "Believe me, you don't want to be involved in this. If I were you, I'd get as far away from us as possible."

Alexis nodded. "I appreciate your offer, Troy, but I think he's right."

Troy gave Creed a dirty look and tugged on Alexis's hand. "Can I talk to you a minute?" He pulled her out of earshot of Creed and whispered. "How long have you known this guy? I probably don't have to tell you this, but he's from the lower levels, the under-city. They're all druggies and gangbangers down there. You're not safe with him."

"I'm not safe around your aunt."

Troy looked down. She knew it was a low blow. "That wasn't fair. You obviously didn't know what she was doing. I know you're not involved with this. We should keep it that way."

"But are you actually ready to trust this guy? Are you ready to trust him with your life?"

Creed was peering through the mini blinds overlooking the street below. "Are you guys done? Alexis, we need to go. It's not safe here."

Troy touched her shoulder. "At least let me go with you."

She was moved by his concern. She looked into his eyes. "Are you sure?"

THE FANCY sports car coasted down the elevated freeway en route to the Skeddner mansion. Evening traffic in L.A. was as bad as ever. Troy had the backseat to himself. "I had a friend, who knew a guy whose father was kidnaped. They found him three days later on the side of the road. The only way they could identify him was by his wallet."

Alexis bit her lip. "Troy, please!"

He winced. "I'm sorry. I didn't mean for it to sound like that. My point is, maybe it would help us find Dr. Skeddner if we laid out all the information we have. Starting at the top. Who's this Commando guy?"

"The scoundrel who kidnaped my father."

"And you're sure it was him on the phone?"

"Positive. Once you've heard that icy, inhuman voice, you never forget it."

"So he's after a data capsule?"

Alexis nodded and frowned, her arched eyebrows furrowing, then she vented on Creed. "Why didn't you destroy that rotten capsule instead of dropping it off at my house like some time bomb?"

"Alexis, I told you, my mother told me to bring it. I didn't know those killers were after it, and I still don't know what's on it. I don't even think she knew."

"Whoa! Time out! Your *mother* had it?" Troy asked. "Where'd she get it from?"

Creed scowled wishing he had kept his mouth shut. "Look, Troy, if it were up to me you wouldn't be here. Apparently, I'm stuck with you, but it doesn't mean I have to like you, and you're not exactly growing on me. You're one more person I need to watch out for. So you had better tread with care around me."

"Sheesh. I'm just trying to get some answers."

"He doesn't know where his mother got the capsule," Alexis began. "Yesterday, he and his mother were attacked by a gang." She paused, giving Creed a chance to expound, but when he didn't offer a word, she continued. "They killed his mother. Before she died, she told Creed to bring this data capsule to my father. So Creed brought it to my father, and then today Commando kidnaped my father and stole the vile thing. Creed thinks that Commando is one of the mercenaries that killed his mother."

"I don't *think* he was one of the killers; I know he was one. I shot him—shot him through the chest."

"He didn't look shot on the video," Alexis said dubiously. "He actually looked quite healthy."

"You sure it was a genuine data capsule?" Troy asked.

"Yes, I saw it myself and my father confirmed its authenticity. When I get my hands on the wretched thing, I'm going to destroy it."

Troy threw up his hands. "You can't do that. Data capsules are almost impossible to destroy. Plus the info programed into the capsule has got to be extremely important, or else these guys wouldn't be chasing after it."

"Obviously," Alexis said, rolling her eyes. "It is valuable to the most evil slime on the face of the earth."

"But how can you say that?" Troy countered. "You don't even know what's on it."

"I don't need to know. Your aunt said it was a weapon. The capsule is cursed. Evil and death follow it like a dark cloud."

The poetry was starting to annoy Creed. "You'll need it to bargain with," he said. "If you don't have it, your father is as good as dead."

Holding the wheel steady with one hand, Alexis pulled out her phone and dialed the number the FBI agent Thomas Wayne had given her.

"Agent Wayne?"

"Yes? Who is this?"

"It's Alexis Skeddner."

"Miss Skeddner! Where are you?"

"I'm leaving Mr. Mason's condo. I apologize for breaking out, but I could see no alternative. Your men wouldn't listen to me."

"That was very foolish. What happened?"

"Mr. Mason wasn't there. I think someone killed him. My father's lawyer tried to kidnap me...then she ran away. Then, my father called and told me to obtain the capsule which, presumably, is still at my house.

"Didn't the video show the kidnapers taking it?"

"I thought so too, but my father seemed adamant that the capsule is still at the house."

"All right, Miss Skeddner, I'll go along with this for now, but try to be more careful in the future, okay? This is not a game. Those men who kidnaped your father are very dangerous. Men you don't want to be involved with. When will you be at the house?"

"About two hours depending on traffic."

"I'll meet you at the house in two hours. I'll want a full report when you arrive."

Alexis closed her phone.

"Why did you tell him two hours?" Troy asked. "We can't be more than twenty minutes away."

"We need time to find the capsule."

CHAPTER 10

Alexis leaned back in the black leather seat. The car skimmed over the road. Shining white headlights from a thousand vehicles illuminated the elevated freeway. She eased the vehicle onto the main superhighway, kicking it into high gear. Her phone rang to life. The caller ID was unknown.

She held it to her ear. "Father?"

"No, but if you want to breathe another day and just maybe see him again, you'll pull off the freeway right now," a voice hissed threateningly in her ear. A voice which was the breath of frost itself.

She would have driven through the protective railings if Creed had not grabbed the wheel, narrowly averting disaster. Sweat broke out on her forehead. She knew that voice. It was Commando. She could taste the panic accumulating in her throat. How did they find her? With shaking hands she pressed the phone closer to her ear.

"Where are you holding him?" Alexis asked, in the most fearless voice she could muster. Creed was instantly alert.

"Who is it?" he demanded, leaning toward her and straining to hear the conversation. Covering the mouthpiece, Alexis whispered to him. "It's Commando!"

Troy moaned, slouching down in his seat and covering his head with his arms as if he expected bullets to come flying through the rear window at any moment. "I knew I should've gone back home," he muttered.

Alexis trembled visibly. "What should I do? He says to exit the freeway, or he'll kill me."

"Don't you mean kill *all* of us?" Troy corrected.

"Ask him what he wants," Creed advised. But she already knew. They all knew. Alexis relayed Creed's message into the phone.

"Sweety, all I want is that little data capsule. Give me that and nobody gets hurt."

Alexis bit her lip. "I don't have it and to my knowledge the last place I saw it was in your hand when you kidnaped my father."

"What did you do with it, girl?"

Alexis had the impression that Commando would savor the idea of throttling her through the phone if it were physically possible. She scrambled for an answer. "I don't know . . ."

"Pull off the highway."

"And if I don't?"

"We'll kill your father and leave your pretty carcass to rot on this freeway."

"How do I know you have my father?" For an answer, a cold hiss sounded in her ear. "Just take my word for, girl. You've got exactly thirty seconds."

The phone connection died.

Defeated, Alexis leaned back in her chair, clutching the wheel with bloodless fingers. "How did he find us?"

"It's the phone!" Troy exclaimed as if he had just discovered the Second Law of Thermodynamics.

"Of course!" Alexis rolled down her window and tossed the phone out onto the freeway.

THE BLACK SUV roared down the crowded highway challenging the speed limit with Marvin Crultt at the wheel. Next to him in the passenger seat, Commando studied the map on his phone, tracking the location of Alexis's phone.

"Slow down, Crultt. I don't want her to see us yet. We need to wait until they get to a more secluded area before we move in."

Trex, Lynch, and Hendrix shared the commodious backseat. All had stashed their weapons beneath the seats except Lynch who always preferred to have his guns in hand.

Commando was the first to spot the car they were pursuing. "There they are."

They followed his finger until they caught sight of the Corvette.

Trex whistled through his teeth. "Now that's what I call a sharp car, right there."

Even though the vehicle was more than a hundred yards away, Commando's eyes focused like a satellite camera. The girl driving was Skeddner's daughter. He knew that much. There were two boys, one was Jennifer's nephew, but the other was unfamiliar. Then the boy turned around in his seat. Instantly, Commando recognized the brown haired boy, from the jagged cut across his face to his solemn, penetrating brown eyes.

Anger erupted in Commando's veins. He half drew his gun, his normally expressionless face twisted into a horrible glower. With his opposite hand, he reached under his jacket and touched the spot on his chest where Creed's bullets had collided with his body. Grudgingly, Commando lowered his weapon. He would bide his time. He had assumed that the death of his mother would discourage the boy from nosing where he did not belong. He had been wrong.

Retribution was about to descend on the boy's head in the form of lead bullets and when it did, nothing short of God would save him.

But why was the boy here with Skeddner's daughter? The question stumped Commando. And more importantly, which one had the capsule? Or did any of them have it? Occupied with these thoughts, he failed to notice Tony Lynch rolling down his window. Then Lynch leaned out of the open window. Pulling his modified sniper rifle to eye-level, he sighted. His right forefinger squeezed back on the trigger.

ALEXIS SCREAMED. A resounding crack exploded in Creed's ears. The car swerved as two bullets ripped through the rear window, tearing up the headrest and whistling a hairs-breath from Alexis's silver earrings. They continued, uninterrupted, through the windshield leaving a huge spidery crack in their wake. A few shards showered over Troy and the backseat, but most of the glass stayed in place due to the protective plastic film. "Oh, man! Oh, man! Somebody's shooting at us. We're gonna die!"

Creed scanned the sea of vehicles rolling behind them. Whoever was firing at them was shrouded in darkness. "Get a grip, Troy!" Creed ordered, calmly sliding the USP from under his jacket.

His fingers drifted over the familiar rubber handgrip. Images of the last time he had fired the gun flashed through his brain. With a practiced hand, he knocked out the magazine, checked it, then reloaded. He laid the weapon across his lap. A low whistle of surprise sounded from Troy.

"Whoa, Man! Is that a real gun?" he inquired, leaning over Creed's shoulder.

"It's real enough for my purposes," Creed said, adjusting his headband which restrained his long hair from dangling in his eyes and obscuring his vision.

Troy was still gaping at the gun. "Are you gonna . . . well . . . use it?"

Creed looked back over his shoulder, brown eyes focused. "I'm not wearing it for decoration."

THE CRACKING report of the gun echoed powerfully in the small confines of the SUV. As soon as it went off, Commando knew who had fired the gun. Only one person would take liberties without orders.

"Stow the gun, Lynch!" Commando ordered. Turning in his seat with frightening speed, he caught the barrel of the gun in his hand. The blue eyes glared coldly.

Lynch was afraid of Commando, but was doing his best to disguise it.

"Why wait?" he demanded, his twisted lip adding a growl to his voice. "You said you would kill her, and it's not like I can't hit them from here," he responded, sulkily pulling the sniper rifle back inside the car.

"Yeah, Lynch, I know you could hit the moon if you wanted to—that's why I hired you. I can't risk the capsule or the girl being damaged, understood?"

Lynch nodded. Commando released his grip on the gun.

Trex leaned forward. "Are you sure the girl still has the capsule? It's been almost an hour since Skeddner made contact with his daughter. If he's got any brains, he told her to get rid of it."

"She still has it, and even if she doesn't I can't afford to kill her—yet. How is she going to tell us what she did with it if she's dead? Answer that one."

The red tracking dot on the computer monitor blinked and disappeared. Somewhere on the freeway, the phone had just been flattened into a razor thin strip of metal. Commando muttered under his breath and hit the dashboard with vengeance.

"Change of plan. I just lost the signal," he growled. "Step on the gas, Crultt, we can't let them out of our sight."

ALEXIS BRUSHED slivers of glass from her lap onto the black carpeted floor. It was taking considerable will power to keep from screaming—let alone drive a car. This could not be happening. When she woke up this morning, the world was perfect, then her father was kidnaped and her day plunged into a tragic spiral which showed no signs of relenting.

Well, at least the shooting had ceased.

For the moment.

Alexis glanced in the side view mirror. An ominous black SUV was baring down on her. The shiny grill looked like a row of grinning teeth. The car was pulling up behind them weaving its way through the traffic. At first she tried to ignore it, hoping—praying—it would go away. But every time she glanced in the mirror, it was there.

It was not long before Creed noticed her apprehension. "What's wrong?"

"Do you think that car is following us?"

The boy scowled at the image reflected in the review mirror. "You mean the SUV? Yes. I've been watching it for the past five minutes."

The certainty in his tone unnerved her. Sometimes she wished he was not so blunt.

"Is that him?" Troy swallowed, "The Commando guy?"

"I'm unsure. Perhaps. But I can find out," Alexis said, spinning the wheel. She sliced through three lanes and merged onto a different freeway. The SUV executed a brilliant maneuver around a large truck, staying right behind them.

Troy voiced his deduction. "If they're not following us, then they sure aren't trying to stay away from us. This is really, really bad, guys."

Alexis took charge. "Troy, call the police."

Troy fumbled for his phone. "Uh, sure. What's the number?"

"Troy! 911."

"Oh, yeah." He attempted a nervous laugh, "I don't know what I was thinking."

They entered a residential area. The intersection light burned yellow. Instead of slowing, Alexis floored the gas pedal.

A little girl darted across the street, right into the path of the car.

"Watch out!" Creed shouted. Alexis gasped and wrenched the wheel narrowly avoiding the child. The car swerved up onto the sidewalk and crashed through the floor-to-ceiling window of a Japanese restaurant.

A little Japanese man dove out of the car's path. Chairs and tables were snapped like matchsticks. Small packets of soy sauce and chopsticks flipped through the air. The car cut a furrow of havoc through the building before passing out the opposite window in another explosion of glass.

Bouncing over gravel, they rumbled down a cramped ally. The SUV was still on their taillights. This needed to end. Creed lowered the window, leaned out and fired at the SUV. The front right tire exploded and the car spun out of control. It stopped only after it had slammed into a lamppost.

Troy let out his breath. "That was completely, utterly, and totally crazy."

CHAPTER 11

Skeddner tugged at the cuffs chaining his hands together as his sour-faced guard ushered him inside a well lit room. The guard removed the handcuffs and left abruptly, closing the door behind him. From the opposite end of the room, a man strode forward offering Skeddner ample time to assess him. He was small and refined with prominent Greek features. His green eyes seemed to hide desperation and pain. Although Skeddner had a fleeting moment of recognition, it dissolved into the uncomfortable knowledge that he should know this man.

"Ah, the great Dr. Skeddner. What a pleasure to see you again! It has been far too long. I apologize that I was unable to see you earlier, but I was conducting some important business in Europe and have just returned. There is much that needs to be discussed. Why don't we sit down?"

The man pointed to a well-furnished desk at the end of the room, situated near a window.

"I'll stand," Skeddner muttered.

"Suit yourself." The man sat behind the desk in a large armchair. He produced a bottle and two glasses from behind the desk. "Wine?"

"Do you honestly think I'm in the mood for wine? Don't try to soften me up. Just tell me what you want!"

"Oh, my dear, this is a poor response from you. I was certain that you would have guessed already, seeing as we've accomplished so much together in the past. I thought you would be overjoyed to see me again. Or at least," his eyebrows shot up expressively, "Remember my name."

"Stop the riddles."

"My dear doctor, I'm surprised at you! Do you pretend to have a memory disorder or has your mind actually failed you in your old age?"

Skeddner shouted, "Tell me who you are!"

"I'm Dr. Taylor Whitefield." His voice was calm, maybe even humorous. He was enjoying his little game. "But maybe you know me better as Kevin Faulkner."

Skeddner started in surprise. That name he knew all too well. "What! Kevin! I thought you had—I mean you look so . . ." he stumbled over his words.

Whitefield did not share his problem. "Plastic surgery can do wonders and newspapers can sometimes be deceiving, can they not? But I'm sure you know that. After all, you didn't believe everything they published about dear Oasis Trailven, did you?"

With an ashen face Skeddner leaned forward, muscles tensed. He was ready to leap over the desk. "You brute," he whispered fiercely. "You killed her, didn't you?"

Calmly, Whitefield drew a handgun from under his white coat. "Please Dr. Skeddner, this is not the time for rash and violent actions. I would hate for there to be more bloodshed. Even if you managed to subdue me, you'd never slip past the guards."

Skeddner dropped into the chair. "But why? What possessed you? She was innocent in this ordeal."

Skeddner was astonished to see anguish on Whitefield's face.

Whitefield shook his head and stared off into space. "First, I had nothing to do with her death. It was her own choice. Even so, it was a dark and unpleasant business. You know it was Adam's fault. His pride was the downfall of his career and their happy lives. Even so, the poor girl might still be alive if she had only heeded my advice. I knew what he wanted, and I told her that if she relinquished it, nothing would happen to her or her son. There would have been no violence. I warned her, but she was stubborn and defiant—like you. Maybe she should have left you sooner."

Skeddner felt the blood rush to his head. He sucked a deep breath trying to quell the anger. He needed to think, and he could not think when he was angry. He looked away.

Whitefield leaned closer. "Oasis wouldn't give him the data capsule containing the plans for the MCC, but you already know this don't you?"

He smiled at Skeddner's sullen silence. "Commando is still searching for it, and I've never heard of anything escaping from his clutches. He always finds what he is searching for, no matter how many men, women . . . or children he has to kill to obtain his prize."

This last sentence was a knife to Skeddner's heart.

"Now look here, Whitefield," Skeddner said, forced politeness in his tone. "We can talk this through. No one has to get hurt."

He thought he could detect a hint of relief in Whitefield's answer. "My thoughts exactly, dear doctor. I congratulate you on using your intellect to resolve this situation. We wouldn't want anything . . . unpleasant to happen to young Alexis now, would we?"

"Leave her out of this."

"Then let us hope it doesn't come to that, shall we?"

The air was still.

"You've changed," Skeddner said. "You're a disgusting excuse for a man. I never imagined that you would stoop this low."

"My dear Skeddner, I need you for your scientific mind, the little that's left of it."

Skeddner didn't take the bait, instead he crossed his arms and found an interesting spot on the wall. Whitefield leaned back in his chair. "The reason I invited you here—,"

"You mean kidnaped."

Whitefield glared at the interruption.

"Just had to make sure that was straight. Continue."

"Help me create the MCC. If you do, you will go down in history as the most brilliant scientific mind of our time. And the world will thank you a thousand times over."

"You're out of your mind."

Whitefield smiled. "Maybe I am."

CHAPTER 12

"But your dad never said *where* in the library," Troy reminded them for the third time. He, Alexis and Creed stood in the middle of Skeddner's giant library. All four walls were adorned—from floor to ceiling—with books.

"You don't actually read all these things do you?" Troy asked. "I never open a book if I can possibly avoid it. Haven't you guys heard of the Internet?"

Each wall had its own wheeled ladder, which was connected to a track allowing it to glide over the shelves. A daunting task awaited them.

Stepping forward to a shelf, Alexis trailed her fingers over the leather bindings. "Maybe my father hid the capsule inside a fake book."

Troy nearly exploded. "A fake book? Oh great, that's a ton of help. There's a million books in here. I'll be an old man with a cane before we find it. It could be anywhere!"

Alexis shot him a meaningful look, "Thank you, Troy, for that very informative statement. Try to show a bit of optimism, if you can."

Creed started hauling out books, checking for secret compartments. "Troy's right. Commando could be here any second. We'll split up. Alexis take that wall, Troy you've got the far wall, and I'll take this one."

His words spurred them into action. Thirty minutes later, they had gutted the library. Mountains of books lay scattered on the floor. Creed tapped walls listening for hollow spaces. He didn't find anything. Discouragement was sinking in, when his gaze fell upon a thick encyclopedia. He pulled open the leather bound covers. The capsule stared up at him.

"I found it."

The other two hovered over his shoulder as he scooped the object from the book. Creed didn't know whether to be pleased or disappointed. He scowled at the capsule, the heart of all his troubles. What dreadful secret did it hold? Why did Commando want it so badly?

Alexis bit her lip as though the very same ideas were occurring in her mind. "Can I see it?" Handling the capsule like it might explode, she examined it as if expecting to discover its mystery.

All three jumped as the sound of shattering glass came from downstairs. The capsule dropped with a clatter from Alexis's white fingers. Alarming thoughts rushed like wildfire through three different minds. Cold eyes. Perfect skin. Sub-machine guns.

Creed snatched up the capsule. Troy dropped into a nearby chair, looking ready to bolt and hide under a bed.

"I guess we stayed a little too long, huh?" But his attempted joke, didn't hide his despair. "Oh, boy, we're gonna die."

Creed ignored his quickening heart rate and reached for his USP. He pulled the weapon from his thigh holster while addressing Troy.

"That's the third time you've said that today, and it had better be the last time. I never want to hear those words come out of your mouth again. Got it?"

The boy nodded numbly, taken aback at the rebuke. Creed flicked the safety off his Heckler & Koch.

"I've been in tight corners before. There's always a way out if you look hard enough."

Troy swallowed. "But aren't you afraid?"

"I don't allow my fear to control me."

His words seemed to strike a chord in Troy. Creed could tell he was making a conscious effort to emulate him. Troy sucked in a breath and tried to calm himself. "Well . . . all they want is the capsule, right? So we give it up, they let us go, and everybody's happy. Right?"

Creed scowled, recalling his experiences with Commando. "I'm not about to gamble my life on it. I think they'll try and kill us either way."

"Plus, the capsule is the only leverage we have," Alexis added.

Unless Commando had recruited more henchmen, he still had four with him. Five trained killers. If it came to fighting, Creed knew he couldn't expect much help from Alexis or Troy. The only reasonable option would be to sneak past Commando and get to the car.

The house was dark with only a few lights on. The kidnapers could be hiding anywhere. Creed needed to determine where the men had broken into the house. After the initial shattering of glass, there were no other sounds to indicate where the men might be. The house was a labyrinth, allowing half a dozen paths leading from the library to the garage, where the Corvette was waiting.

"We need to get down to the garage," he murmured half-aloud.

"Yeah, but without getting killed," Troy added, as if to remind Creed that arriving at the garage alive was an important aspect to consider in his calculations.

"Why don't we jump out a window and then run around to the garage?" Troy suggested. Creed ran over to the window, wondering why he hadn't thought of that already. The window offered a perfect view of the moonlit courtyard—and the wraith-like man standing next to the elevator, cradling an assault rifle. The man flipped his weapon up and fired. Creed threw himself aside as the window exploded, flinging bits of glass over the room.

There was no way they were going out the window. Checking to see that Alexis and Troy were unharmed, Creed made for the library door. "Follow me. We're going to the garage."

Troy grabbed his shirt, "Hey wait, man, have you lost your mind? We can't just waltz down there. They've got guns! Guns with bullets!"

Creed's face remained undeterred as he tore the boy's clutching hands from his shirt. "You don't need to tell me what a gun is. Look, I don't think we're going to get out of this house without a fight, but I'm open to any suggestions."

Troy licked dry lips, but was unable to come up with a reasonable, cohesive idea. Creed made his way to the double doors. "That's what I thought. Now stay close."

He put a finger to his lips, signaling the others to silence. He opened the door and stuck his head out, his USP at the ready. The hallway was clear. He stepped outside the room and waved the other two ahead. "Hurry!"

COMMANDO WAS a very cautious man, but he was beginning to feel the pangs of desperation. The capsule had eluded his grasp for a full four days. Four days too long. Now that boy had it.

Commando slid his Sig P226 from under his jacket, unlocked the safety, and rechecked the 12 round magazine. That boy would die today. He jumped through the broken window. His combat boots crunched on fragments of crushed glass as he landed inside the formal dining room. The table still had the remains of a hurried meal.

"Commando, are we going in or what?"

Commando glowered back at the redheaded Trex who shifted his machine gun from where it hung on his shoulder to a more accessible position. Commando did not bother to answer the ridiculous question. Trex was young and naive. Commando was well aware of this fact and didn't let it annoy him—too much.

Hendrix, who was posted outside guarding the elevator, had just radioed that he had caught sight of the kids on the third floor. The birds were trapped in the nest. Tony Lynch climbed over the broken window frame, followed by Marvin Crultt, whose body and features might have been hewn out of a slab of granite.

Commando turned and addressed his men. "I want the girl alive. I don't care about the other two. Be especially wary of the white boy. He's far more dangerous than he looks. Crultt, take the front stairs.

Lynch, check out the kitchen and cover the back stairs. Go systematically and search every room throughly. But don't take all day. I don't intend to be here when the cops show up. Trex, come with me."

THE HOUSE felt like a wild, dark, death maze where any nook could conceal a gunman. Creed took the lead. He darted down the curving staircase, past the exotic furniture and decorations.

"The ballroom is the next door on the left," Alexis panted. "We can cut through there and take the back stairs down to the kitchen. It's faster."

As Creed sprang into the kitchen, the first thing he noticed was a man on the opposite side of the room. Combat boots, black leather, a submachine-gun, and a twisted lip.

Tony Lynch.

Rising up like an animal, the man let loose the gun, spitting slugs into the doorway. Alexis hurled herself to the tiled floor, flattening to produce the smallest possible target. Screaming, Troy went down as well. Creed threw himself sideways avoiding the bullets and focused on the middle of Lynch's chest. He squeezed the USP's trigger.

The storm of bullets stopped abruptly.

Fury and shock registered on Lynch's face as he clutched at the two holes draining out his blood. Alexis looked up in time to see Lynch tumble over dead.

She screamed. Creed thought she had been shot. He dropped to her side. "Are you all right?" he demanded.

"I'm fine," she gasped.

"Then don't scare me like that," he returned brusquely.

"But you . . . you killed him," she said, staring with unconcealed horror at the body lying at her feet.

"Well, he didn't kiss him, that's for sure." Troy said eyeing the man's face with disgust. He got up from the floor. Creed looked him up and down. "Where did you get hit?"

Troy shrugged sheepishly, not a scratch on his body. "I'm good. Bullets just make me a little nervous."

"They'll have heard the gun go off," Creed muttered more to himself than to his companions. As if to punctuate his thoughts, the pounding of boots thundered behind them.

He grabbed Alexis's hand and ran for the doors. Shoving Troy out first, Creed slammed the door shut. Even before he turned back around, he smelled the danger. He spun, gun at the ready.

He took in the whole scene in one swift glance. Though there were no lights, the moon offered enough luminance for him to see that they had run into a large den. Two sofas faced each other in the center of the room. Tapestries covered the walls. Three men were facing him in a wide semicircle. Creed recognized them all from the recording of Dr. Skeddner's kidnaping. There was the African, Crultt, holding an ugly looking machine gun, and Trex who was packing two semi-automatics.

And Commando.

They were trapped. Creed scowled, tasting defeat on his tongue. So much for sneaking by them. Commando held his gun in an outstretched hand. Up to this point, Creed had successfully pushed aside his numbing fear, but now with the killer so close, he could not escape the mind stopping dread. This man was supposed to be dead. The man locked eyes with Creed, his tight skin stretching to capacity over his bony frame.

"Where's your mother, boy?"

The taunt struck Creed like a bullet. He tried to restrain the wince but failed. All his thoughts of hatred came storming back. He saw his mother with Commando's fingers clenched around her neck. For a moment his vision was frozen in red fury. Then he snapped back into reality. Commando was standing before him, a smirk riding across his face. Creed raised his gun to shoulder height. His finger itched against the trigger. He would kill him.

The giant black man with dread locks growled. "Don't try it, boy. I'll riddle your girlfriend full of holes."

Creed checked himself. What was he thinking? Even if he pulled off one shot, Alexis and Troy would almost certainly be killed. Commando nodded, seeming to know that Creed would not resist.

His picture perfect face revealed nothing. "Have a seat and I think it might be a good idea for you to lay those guns on the coffee table."

Without removing his eyes from Commando, Creed eased himself onto the other end of the sofa. Like a man losing his last good cards, he placed his guns on the table.

Pale-faced, Alexis complied with Commando's suggestion and seated herself. The all-too-real weapons provided sufficient motivation. But her calmness surprised Creed. Without a moment's hesitation, Troy dropped down beside them. He played with a loose thread hanging from his windbreaker.

The atmosphere was surreal. Commando sat across from them as though he was about to make a simple business transaction. The man's knee-length jacket fell open exposing two pistols secured to his hips and another strapped across his muscular chest. He pulled out a lighter and ignited the two ornamental candles on the coffee table. Eerie shadows flickered across his face.

Behind Commando and off to one side, Crultt rested gun in the crook of one arm keeping the muzzle trained on the sofa's three young occupants. Grinning, Trex cocked his gun. Together they formed a tight semicircle blocking every avenue of escape.

From his peripheral vision, Creed glanced down at the table. His twin pistols were lying just within reach, between the pair of glowing candles. He calculated how quickly he could snatch up the weapons, fire them, then dodge the machine gun.

"By the laws of nature, you should be dead, boy," Commando began. "You were lucky I missed. You won't be so lucky again."

Creed did not acknowledge the remark, instead he dropped his eyes and stared stonily at his boot laces. He slouched forward feigning a sense of defeat and added a convincing sigh, not exaggerated but audible. He was rewarded by Crultt lowering the submachine gun slightly and releasing his grip on the trigger. Officer Wayne should be pulling up any moment. If he could somehow stall Commando—

Commando's eyes narrowed as he turned his laser-like gaze upon Alexis. "And where's my capsule, little girl?"

Do not tell him, Creed pleaded silently. That was their only leverage. He was acutely aware of the capsule's presence in his pocket, like a living entity. He had to force his eyes not to look at it. If Commando had any intuition that the capsule was only inches away . . .

It did not take much for Creed to imagine what Alexis was feeling. Before today, he doubted she had ever been threatened with a gun. Her experience with them had probably not extended beyond movies. Guns were a thousand times more terrifying in real life. The muzzle of Crultt' gun seemed enormous. He knew that if Crultt applied the slightest amount of pressure on the trigger thirty slugs would tear through the three of them in the space of a second.

Alexis straightened her shoulders. "Where did you take my father?"

Commando's face twitched in what appeared to be amusement. "That's actually irrelevant at the moment. Let me explain how this works, kid. I ask the questions, and you answer them, or we start blowing parts off—starting with your toes and working our way up."

Fear radiated off Alexis, but she didn't crack. "The police will be here any second."

Creed was impressed with her composure. She was trying to buy some time. Smart girl.

For the first time, Creed spoke to his mother's killer. "Why is the capsule so important to you?"

"You don't know?" Commando sounded amazed at his ignorance but then shrugged. "Well, then that's all the better for you. I won't be forced to kill you after you tell me where it is."

Commando inclined his head.

A click sounded behind them. The sound was not loud, but from the searing terror which raced down Alexis's face, it might have been a bomb. Creed watched as the cold gun barrel was shoved against her head. The savage face of Hendrix stood only inches from her own. A face ready and capable of blowing her head off. Leaning across the back of the sofa, the man caught her hair, holding her still. Alexis gasped involuntarily, a solitary tear squeezing from her eye. Troy was swallowing uncontrollably, waiting for the inevitable.

Commando's expression remained impassive. "Hendrix hasn't killed a girl in almost a year now, and he's getting a little restless. I'm only going to ask this question once more, so you had better answer. Where is the capsule?"

With a barely discernable movement, Creed slid the toes of his boots into the underside of the coffee table. The table was rustic but not too heavy. Good. He would only get one shot at this. No second chances. There was no restart button. If he made a mistake they were dead, but what was the alternative? They would be dead either way. He whispered a silent prayer and took a deep, measured breath, reviewing his plan.

Then he acted.

A sudden burst of energy erupted from Creed. He spun, caught Hendrix's gun wrist and jerked forward, prying away the weapon. Carrying his momentum through, he leaped up flipping the table over at Commando and heaved the shocked Hendrix over the back of the sofa. The two candles pitched through the air landing on Commando's clothes. His jacket and undershirt burst into flames.

The move was so daring, so unexpected, so impossible that nobody even breathed for a full three seconds.

Nobody except Creed.

Howling, Commando leaped up, tearing at his blazing jacket. Hendrix crashed to floor, unconsciously discharging his gun and firing bullets past Creed. Troy threw all his weight backwards against the sofa.

It flipped. Head over heels, Creed found himself flying backwards through space. The sofa formed a type of shield as Crultt wrenched back on the gun's trigger unleashing a hundred bullets exploding and ricocheting through the room.

CHAPTER 13

Whitefield knew his attempts at persuasion were having little effect on the stony Isaac Skeddner. Another method was necessary. He leaned forward in the high-backed chair. "I would like to show you something."

Skeddner refused to look at him. "I have no wish to indulge you."

"I'm sorry to persist, but you don't actually have a choice. Follow me." Whitefield snapped his fingers. Two burly security guards came over, hoisted Skeddner up by his armpits, and escorted him behind Whitefield. He led them outside the room and pressed his left hand against the black panel next to a thick sliding door. He waited as an orange laser scanned the ridges and swirls of his hand print. "I find it amazing that every hand has a unique print, a virtually impossible task for evolution."

As the elevator doors separated, Whitefield turned to the security guards.

"Wait here for us." Laying his hand on the pistol he wore under his coat, Whtefield cautioned Skeddner, "And please don't test me."

Once inside the elevator, Whitefield slid a keycard through the detector on the control panel. Then he typed a complicated password into the keyboard. Skeddner experienced the falling sensation as the tiled elevator floor dropped out from under him.

Whitefield grasped the side rails. "We are going to a place that only three people in this world know about. The men who designed and constructed it experienced unexpected deaths soon after its completion."

The light ran down the numbers above the doorframe. After the elevator hit the last level, it continued plummeting downwards.

"We are below sea level now," Whitefield explained. The doors slid open with a swish. The new corridor was long and dark, lacking the neon lighting Skeddner had become accustomed to in this place. He still didn't know where he was. A deep musty smell penetrated his nostrils. The walls were bare. Bronze pipes and electrical wiring which would normally be covered by wall paneling were exposed.

Whitefield stopped in front of a door and tapped out another password. "Come witness my life's most important accomplishment."

With a low grinding sound the steel door slid off to one side. Skeddner could only stare in dumfounded amazement.

EVEN AS Creed dove on his stomach for cover, he was calculating. The door was to his right. He slid behind the bookcase. A score of wild bullets clipped overhead tearing up walls, furniture, and decorative bookcases. The gunfire was a deafening roar, blocking everything else. Wood chips and bits of drywall burst around him. He winced as a piece of splintered wood bit into his shoulder.

Commando had finally disentangled himself from his fiery jacket. Flinging the burning remains away, he flung himself at Crultt. "Fool!" he shouted. "Stop shooting!"

Heedless of the heat, he grabbed the glowing muzzle and twisted downwards sending a seam of bullets puncturing the oak floor. His jacket had not been completely extinguished when he dropped it on the carpet. In seconds the floor was ablaze.

Creed saw Alexis roll into the adjoining kitchen. She would be spotted in a second. Hot sparks popped and fizzled, jumping about the room. Creed was still holding Hendrix's gun. He popped up and spewed half a round, giving Commando and Trex something to think about.

Both men dove aside. Trex ducked behind the corner of a wall unit. Alexis crawled across the tiles keeping the kitchen island between herself and Commando. The glass cabinets exploded as Trex fired over her head. Plates and glasses toppled to the floor. "Get the girl," Commando ordered. "I'll take care of him."

Troy followed Alexis and they made their way to the service door which led to the garage. Creed needed to give them more time. He could see Trex sliding on his stomach trying to cut Alexis off from the service door. Creed and Commando broke their cover simultaneously. There was no time to aim. No time to think, just pull the trigger. Two guns fired. Commando's bullet clipped Creed's ear. Creed's bullet ripped off half of Commando's face.

But strangely, there was no blood—only a cybernetic, chrome-plated skull.

There was a stunned calm.

They stared at each other, Commando in mortal anger, Creed in numbed shock.

Half of Commando's face was constructed of chrome alloy plates and casing. His left eye was completely mechanical, built with micro motors, optic camera lenses, and wires. It roved madly in its socket, glowing an unholy blue. His face was beyond eerie. It was unearthly. Demonic. Creed could see his reflection in the polished surface.

Then the entire room was on fire. The flames leaped up, engulfing everything in their path. Creed was never sure how he got out of the room—but he did.

He crashed out the door, and across the courtyard to the elevator. Trex and Hendrix let off a few parting shots but did not give chase. Arriving in the subterranean parking garage, Creed darted through the rows of expensive cars. A car horn blared. He spun around. The Corvette screeched to a stop beside him. He caught a glimpse of Alexis and Troy's frightened faces as he jumped inside.

The Corvette roared out of the garage. They drove in silence, each nursing their own thoughts of fear and bewilderment. The only sound was the gentle hum of the Corvette's engine.

Troy shut his eyes. "What have I gotten myself into?"

The silence was depressing.

"He was not a robot," Alexis said finally. "I know I must be dreaming."

Creed wished he could believe her, but his ear still stung from Commando's slug. The police had no idea what might be waiting for them.

Troy shifted uncomfortably in his seat. "Technically, I think he's a cyborg not a robot."

"Cyborg, robot, who cares?" Alexis sounded indignant.

"A robot is just a machine. A cyborg is a fusion of human and machine. That thing was breathing. A true machine wouldn't breathe. I ought to know. My uncle worked at the Whitefield Institute of Cybernetics Engineering and Organisms Development for two years, I know a bit about robots and cyborgs."

Alexis looked at Troy in the review mirror. "Are you referring to the robotics museum on Shell Island?"

Troy nodded. "Bull's eye. It's owned by a scientist named Taylor Whitefield, one of the most renowned robotics engineers of the century."

Creed pondered the name. "Wasn't he the guy who designed those Mars robots and new satellite probes for NASA?"

"Yep."

"You think he has anything to do with that . . . that monster?"

"I dunno, maybe. That cybernetic bill was passed a few years ago making most of the genetic cyborg research illegal. People were afraid of creating Terminators. If the thing that kidnaped your dad actually is a cyborg, this will be the biggest thing since splitting the atom."

Alexis eased the car into the Friday freeway traffic. "Troy, may I use your phone?"

HIS CLOTHES still smoking, Commando inhaled deeply through his lungs, one warm and alive, the other cold and artificial. The flames leapt around the room like living beings. He stood fuming in the middle of the den. Steel plates and bolts protruded from his head like silver bone where the artificial skin had been blown away by Creed's bullet. This mission was no longer just about the capsule. It had become personal.

His men stood around awkwardly. They were trying hard not to stare but were finding it impossible not to. They all knew that Commando had been in some type of horrendous accident, and parts of his body were reinforced with robotic equivalents but never had they imagined anything like this.

He seemed normal from the neck down, dressed in combat trousers and a brown leather jacket, but his robotic face appeared to have stepped out of some science fiction horror movie. The combination was unnerving. It left them wondering how much of his body was robotic. Was he a man or was he a machine?

Commando's short black hair stuck out sharply from his chrome skull. They heard the hum of the tiny micro motors controlling the cold blue eye which glared at them. Without flesh surrounding it, the mechanical eye was something from a hellish dream. The normally solid Crultt, who had gunned people down without batting an eye, swallowed visibly. Hendrix's face had dropped to a deathly pallor. Each man wished to ask Commando a dozen questions, but Commando's stare froze the words on their lips.

Trex, who considered himself closest to Commando, cautiously approached his leader. "Uh, Boss, we probably shouldn't hang around here. The cops will be here any minute."

"Get rid of the bodies," Commando spat. The spittle was incongruent with the mechanical mouth that ejected it. "I don't want a single scrap of evidence left behind."

AS SOON as agent Wayne caught sight of the smoke he flipped on his siren, but his instincts whispered that he was too late. Not a soul remained on the Skeddner property. Smoke billowed from the windows accompanied by wisps of bright red flame in vivid contrast to the blackness of the moonless night.

CHAPTER 14

Skeddner finally summoned the presence of mind to shut his gaping mouth. Standing not three feet from his face on the platform was his waking nightmare.

Whitefield smiled with satisfaction.

"It is the FX-6. The next generation of machines."

Like a grinning human skeleton, the blue and silver plated robot stared back at Skeddner with dead eyes. Chrome alloy plates covered thousands of wires, servos, and motors. Whitefield pushed a button on a remote he was carrying and the eyes lit up like two blue lasers—much like . . .

Skeddner spun around to face Whitefield. "Commando?"

Whitefield smiled again. "Yes. Commando is a cyborg, or at least half of him is. The other half used to be a young man named Sklade Browning. He is one of my first successful cyborgs. Surely, you must remember the prototypes I showed the company shortly before my . . . my departure. Rather impressive is it not?"

Skeddner put his hand against the rough walls to support himself. It was too much. He wasn't sure he could grasp the magnitude. "Sklade Browning? Not Sklade . . . "

"Yes, Skeddner, your old friend Sklade. He would have killed you yesterday instead of kidnaping you, but I convinced him that you are more valuable to us alive than dead."

The news only added to the smothering blanket of dread settling over Skeddner. "He killed Rolls?"

"Murdered him in cold blood. And I assume you know why he did it?"

"The MCC plans."

"Yes, but he never acquired them. Rolls had supposedly destroyed them before he got there. It wasn't until later that Browning found out that Rolls had somehow managed to smuggle the information away. After years of searching, Sklade Browning, or Commando as he prefers to be called, traced it to a young woman named Oasis Trailven."

Whitefield inclined his head. The tough Skeddner was beginning to break down. "So he just killed her?"

Whitefield nodded. "But again it seems that Commando was a step too late. She had already sent the plans off to you."

"And now he's hunting down Alexis," Skeddner breathed hollowly.

Whitefield shrugged. "Yes, I'm afraid so. She—like Oasis—stubbornly refused to relinquish the capsule."

"This cannot be happening," Skeddner murmured. "We agreed to destroy it in order to prevent this nightmare."

"Unfortunately, the nightmare is already in motion and cannot be stopped. People have already begun to die."

"But you can stop it. Stop Sklade. Call him off. I'll make the MCC. I'll do whatever you want but don't hurt her. I can't lose Alexis, too."

"There, Skeddner I was confident that you would eventually arrive at my point of view. I have a lab already set up for you."

"You know I can't do anything without that capsule, assuming Rolls did copy all the MCC information onto it."

"Never fear. Commando will bring it here shortly."

Skeddner jammed his finger in Whitefield's face. "If he so much as touches my daughter, you will regret it forever."

"AGENT WAYNE?"

"Miss Skeddner! Where are you?"

"We got to the house before you did and we found the capsule but Commando came and—Oh, it was absolutely horrible! He's a robot!"

The agent chuckled. "A what?"

"It's not funny," Alexis snapped. "You would not be laughing if you saw what I saw."

"Okay, I'm listening. But first, are both of you all right?"

"Yes, we're fine. "

"Now, take a deep, calm breath and tell me what happened."

"He's a robot, an android, oh, I don't know what you'd call it . . .a . . .a . . cyborg."

"Who was?"

"My father's kidnaper is a cyborg!"

"Now Miss Skeddner—,"

"Don't 'Miss Skeddner' me! You must believe what I am saying. I know it sounds insane—and it is—but it's the honest truth. The man is a real live robot. Like something out of a film. Half his face is a robot skull."

"You're not feeling well, Miss Skeddner. Your father's kidnaping is affecting you. Why don't you come over to the station, and we'll talk this through."

Alexis hung up the phone. "He didn't believe me," she said at last to Creed.

"I told you he wouldn't believe you."

Troy chuckled nervously from the backseat. "Can't really blame the guy. I don't believe it either. We're gonna have to turn around you know. Police station is back that way."

Her lips pursed in a thin line and she made no move to alter the car's direction.

Troy shrugged. "So, I take it we're not going to the station. Where are we going?"

"The cybernetics museum," Creed answered.

Alexis stared at him. "How did you know?"

"That's the logical choice. Besides, that's where I'm going whether you go or not."

Troy bolted upright in his seat. "Wait a minute. Maybe I missed something. Don't we want to get *away* from that cyborg? It was trying to kill us!"

"That's the only lead I have. I need to find my father and if the police won't do it, then I will."

"You are insane!"

"No, the situation is insane, and calls for . . . well, unusual actions. My father owns a private jet. It's at the airport. That's where we're going."

"You guys sure you want to do that?" Troy asked, "I mean, there's gotta be another way. You're going in way over your head."

Alexis smiled grimly. "Then I'll just take a deep breath."

THE AIRPORT terminal was a huge building made entirely of glass panes. Creed and Troy followed Alexis through the crowds of people milling about looking for relatives and friends, checking luggage, and purchasing tickets. Monotone voices played out over the public address system. Alexis had already informed her father's pilot that they were coming—a pilot whom she insisted would take them anywhere without questions.

Creed tapped Troy on the shoulder. "I need to talk to you."

"What did I do now?" Troy returned.

"Nothing, just saved my neck back at the house. If you hadn't knocked the sofa over . . . "

Troy's countenance brightened at the compliment. It dawned on Creed how much Troy looked up to him.

Troy shrugged, "Thanks, but you did all the fighting. You were amazing. I was just . . . just trying to follow your lead."

"Commando might have killed me if you hadn't acted as quickly as you did. I won't forget it." He reached out and clasped Troy's shoulder. "I don't make friends easily."

Troy grinned and returned the clasp.

"Let's go," Creed said. "We have to keep that crazy girl safe."

"Excuse me?" Alexis asked, looking back and giving Creed a look of playful shock. "I hope you weren't referring to me?"

"No, I was talking about that girl over by the luggage rack. No relation to you."

She smiled outwardly. Creed smiled inwardly.

"You know," Troy said, "somehow, I think this is getting beyond Dr. Skeddner. I think we're just scratching the surface of what is actually happening. I mean whoever this Commando-guy is working for is really serious. Creed, be straight with me. Do you think the cyborg died in the fire?"

"No."

Creed answered without hesitation. It would take more than a little fire to destroy that thing.

"You think it's following us?"

"Probably."

"And you're still not scared?"

"Possibly."

Troy shook his head. "Well, this is the most excitement I've had since, well, since forever. I need a soda. You guys want one?"

They shook their heads. He walked off searching for a soda machine.

Creed glanced sidelong at Alexis. She had sobered considerably since he had first seen her reading her book in the courtyard. She sighed. "Personally, my appetite for excitement is satisfied. I've had enough to last me a lifetime."

"Let's hope it doesn't get more exciting."

Suddenly, he grabbed her arm and pulled her behind a set of metal seats. As an explanation for his action he said only two words. "They're here."

Creed felt like hitting his head against the back of the chair. Alexis seemed to wilt. She bit her lip and shut her eyes. "How do they keep finding us!"

Creed poked his head over the seats as far as he dared. He spotted Trex immediately. The man stood out with his red hair, and there was a definite purpose in his step. Hendrix and Crultt were right behind him, shoving their way through the people. Although Creed didn't see Commando, he could not be far away.

An exasperated sigh escaped from Creed as he dropped back. A creepy sensation was climbing up his spine. They were being stalked by a cyborg monster.

"What are we going to do?" Alexis said in a panicked whisper. She was on her hands and knees. He could practically hear her heart thumping in her chest.

"Just give me a second," Creed snapped back.

The lethal consequences of the situation imparted an additional sharpness to his answer. A thousand wild thoughts bolted through his brain cells, which he quickly discarded. Frustrated, he ran his fingers through his brown locks trying to clear his mind.

Alexis leaned closer to him. "Creed, I'm afraid."

Her simple statement was unnecessary. Creed could see she was terrified. But he was not about to voice his own fear, especially to a girl. Creed would never allow fear to conquer and subdue him. Her vulnerability stirred something in him. She was his responsibility. He needed to be her protector. "Alexis, listen to me. I won't let anybody hurt you. Okay?"

She nodded.

Creed could see Troy at the soda machine. "Alexis, we're going to get Troy and then run for the escalator. Okay?"

She nodded like a puppet on a string. Creed reached for her hand. They would have to move quickly. He could feel her blood pounding down her veins. They crawled behind the chairs. When they found Troy, Creed grabbed his arm. "We've got to go."

"But I didn't get my soda . . . " One look changed Troy's mind. They ran doubled over, using people, chairs, anything, for cover. They arrived at the hangar through a side entrance.

The hangar housed three Learjets. Alexis raced for the largest one. The sleek, 12 million dollar aircraft commanded attention. It boasted a 43 foot wingspan and two turbine engines. A small wiry man, who looked like a strong wind would lift him into orbit, jumped down from the hatchway. He wiped his hands on the rag and waved. Alexis did not return his wave.

"Mr. Coleman, start the engine! We need to go right now!"

"Whoa, hold on, Alexis. What's the rush? Are you running from the cops or something?" He winked. Creed assumed Alexis had informed him about the situation with Commando. She gripped the man's arm and all but threw him into the open jet hatch.

"Mr. Coleman, *please*, I don't have time for this. He's after us."

"Okay, okay! You don't have to get pushy. Let's go."

They boarded. Creed had never flown before and wasn't sure he would like it. Troy nudged him. "Hey, you all right, man? You're looking a little green."

"I'm fine," Creed muttered.

Strapping himself in, he felt the engine power to life. The plane taxied from the hangar and onto the airstrip. As the plane entered its takeoff run, Creed caught a glimpse of Commando running out of the hangar. A swath of bandages covered his face, but they didn't cover his blazing blue eyes.

THE POWERFUL engines of the Learjet defied gravity as it thundered into the sky, exhaust rippling through the air leaving heat waves in its wake. This was impossible. An outrage. Standing on the open runway, Commando watched his quarry vanish into the sky. He clenched his fists, his chrome fingers hidden beneath black leather gloves.

Trex stood beside him, still skittish and uneasy after witnessing Commando's true identity. He had been unable to muster enough nerve to question his boss—and wasn't sure he even wanted to. The young redhead jumped as he was accosted by the cold, steely voice of Commando. "Who is the pilot?"

"Rick Coleman."

"Where are they heading?"

"Shell Island. Do you want me to book a flight?"

"Shell Island?" Commando echoed in surprise. Both his eyes, authentic and artificial, narrowed pensively. "Why would they go there unless . . . Yeah, go ahead and call up William. Tell him we need a lift, right away."

CHAPTER 15

The setting sun was just kissing the tranquil sea. The water was like crystal glass, not a single ripple disturbed its surface. A shining white form streamed from the sun. A woman came toward him, her bare feet gliding over the water, her flowing white gown blowing gently in the breeze. It was his mother. She smiled and held her arms out to him. He rushed forward but she melted in his arms.

Creed awoke cold and shivering. He was curled in a plush chair flying across the Pacific. Troy was dozing in the window seat next to him. His earphones were still plugged in and he was clutching a half-empty soda. Beyond the window, the dark sky rushed by. Creed pulled off his black headband allowing his brown locks to fall around his face. Raking his fingers through his hair, he wondered if there was any hope. He pulled out his mother's ring, running his fingers over the serial number impressed on the band. Stroking the green stone, he whispered, "I can't do this any more, Mother."

"Was that her ring?"

Startled, Creed found Alexis sitting across the aisle. She was leaning on the armrest, balancing her chin in her hands. His initial reaction was to shove the ring into his pocket. It was like a secret he had kept with his mother. But for some reason he stopped. "I thought you were asleep. Yeah, it was hers."

"It's exquisite."

Creed started. Those were the exact words his mother had used to describe the ring. Embarrassed, he nodded his agreement. "She thought so, too."

"May I see it?"

Creed recoiled. Alexis blushed, sensing his reluctance, "I'm sorry. I didn't mean to—."

"No, it's all right. Here."

He placed the ring in her palm. Alexis ran her fingers over the thin silver band as she studied the green jewel. "My father gave me a ring like this." Her eyes misted. "He was always so protective of me. He hired private tutors for me. He never let me go on dates. He's hardly let me out of his sight for sixteen years. I suppose it was recompense for my sister."

"Your sister?"

"My father hates talking about her, but she was the daughter of my father's first wife. His wife died only a few years after their marriage. It was a dark time for my father. He quarreled often with my stepsister, and eventually she ran away. After my father remarried, he got rid of all the family photos with her in them. But my mother saved one for me. She said I should have a picture of my sister."

Alexis pulled out a photo from a small wallet in her pocket and held it out to him. "There's my sister in the middle with her fiancee."

Creed gave the picture a quick half-interested glance. Four faces smiled back at him. There were two men, one was obviously Dr. Skeddner, and a woman who was, presumably, his wife. But it was the pretty brunette who made Creed catch his breath. Forgetting his customary caution, he snatched the photograph from Alexis and held it as still as his shaking fingers would allow.

At first he thought his eyes were deceiving him. She was much younger, probably no more than seventeen, but there was no mistaking the mahogany hair, hazel eyes, and athletic figure.

He was staring at his mother. A wild turmoil raged in Creed's head as every clue, every gesture, fell into place in his mind. He laid his finger on the man holding his mother's hand. "Who is this?"

"That was her fiancee, Adam."

Adam. His father.

He felt Alexis gently rub his shoulder. "Is something wrong?"

Creed didn't want to tell her. He didn't even want to look at her. But she deserved to know the truth. Even though he knew what he had to say, it was difficult to find the words. When Creed willed his mouth to speak, only a broken, strangled sentence came out.

"She . . . she's my mother," he said in a barely audible whisper, jaw clinched and rigid. Alexis looked as if he'd just twisted out her heart. Taking Creed's face in both her hands, she pulled him to face her. She was almost breathless. "Look me in the eyes and tell me what you just said."

With painful slowness, Creed raised his eyes until they met hers. "She's my mother."

He couldn't stop the tears from forcing their way out of his eyes. He felt her fingers trembling on his cheeks. "Oasis?" she asked, sounding half afraid of the answer she would receive.

Creed didn't have to respond. His brown eyes revealed all. He stood rigidly, every muscle in his body tensed. "What did he do to my beautiful, beautiful mother?"

The pain in Alexis's eyes was unmistakable. "Creed, I'm sorry. I had no idea."

For a moment he thought she was about to hug him, but she stopped midway and dropped her hands, probably afraid he would take offence.

"It's a little weird. I guess that means you're my nephew," she said instead.

Creed barely heard her. "I guess," he responded absently, staring off into space. Suddenly, he caught her by the shoulders. "Alexis Skeddner," his voice was low and strained. "Tell me the truth. What happened between my mother and . . . Dr. Skeddner."

He gripped her shoulder harder. Alexis blushed uncomfortably, but kept her eyes on his. "I don't know, Creed, honestly. I wouldn't lie to you. She left before I was born."

Her face reflected pure innocence, and deep inside he knew she was telling the truth.

"Well, what do you think happened? Why were we left to grind our way through life, while that man lives like a king?"

Alexis's shoulder was pulsating. "Creed . . . you're hurting me."

He snatched his hands away. "I'm sorry," he whispered. Dropping his head in his hands, he sank back into the chair.

Impulsively, she slid her arms around him. Creed flinched, not returning her hug. Then, slowly, he squeezed her back. After a moment, Alexis pulled away so she could see his face.

"Father and mother never talked about it. Truly, I don't know anything. I know I could never fill her place in your heart, but I'll be your ever devoted sister."

"Thanks, Alexis, but I need to be alone right now and think. Why don't you try and get some rest?"

She nodded, retreating to her seat. "I wish I could. My thoughts keep mulling over my father, and my brain won't calm down." She dropped her voice, "Actually, I'm afraid to sleep. I know I'm going to have nightmares of that horrible Commando."

INSIDE THE cockpit, Rick Coleman took his hand away from the yoke to switch on his headset. "Commando? Yes, this is Rick Coleman. I have the kids in the back. I would have contacted you earlier but it took longer than I expected for them to fall asleep. What do you want me to do with them?"

"Just bring them to the museum. I'll meet you there."

"And my money?"

"You'll have your money when I have those kids."

"I'm on my way. I'll touch down in about fifteen minutes. Over."

He shut off the phone, looking pleased with his success at handling the assignment, and glanced back to check on his captive passengers.

He was staring into Creed's scowling brown eyes.

Creed had learned to sleep with his ears open, and this was not the first time that skill had proven useful. Shock delayed Coleman's reactions.

Creed couldn't resist teasing. "It's a small world isn't it? I didn't know you were a friend of Commando," he said, before slugging him. Alexis and Troy were asleep, ignorant of the fight unfolding in the cockpit.

The pilot recovered himself with surprising quickness. He went for his pocket, probably after a gun or a knife, but Creed was already in too close and caught his wrist. Despite his size Coleman fought fiercely, twisting around and forcing Creed's head between the dashboard and his knees. Creed kicked Coleman hard in the chest. They rolled to the cabin floor pummeling all the way.

Coleman broke away and scrambled to gain his feet. His gun was halfway out, when Creed hit him. The gun discharged.

The noise shocked the sleepers into wakefulness. Troy bolted upright, spilled his soda on his pants and yelled. The bullet missed Creed, but blew a hole in the instrument panel behind him.

The plane rocked, and Coleman flung out his arms to keep his balance. It was a fatal error. He clutched at the emergency latch on the door. The door sprang open and he was sucked out. His scream was long and haunting.

Gripping the handrails, Creed crawled to the hatch and slammed it shut.

The plane shuddered as if in pain. Creed returned to the cockpit where Alexis and Troy stared hopelessly at the instrument panel. Sparks skipped across dozens of switches and dials. Warning lights blared. Buzzers whined as a paralyzing fear seized everyone in the cabin.

Troy swallowed. "Anybody know how to fly a plane?"

His question broke them from their stupefied daze. Alexis took command of the situation. "Creed, there's a fire extinguisher in the locker. Hurry!"

The plane lurched again. Creed almost heaved. With difficulty he reoriented himself, found the lockers, and grabbed the red canister. Another tremor attacked the plane. This time Alexis lost her balance and hit her head against the back of the seat. She moaned. Creed rushed to her side. "Alexis! Are you all right?"

"Yes. I'm fine."

He helped her up. A line of blood trailed from her forehead. She dropped into the pilot seat. Flames leaped angrily over the instrument panel. Fire-extinguisher in hand, Creed sprayed down the dashboard hoping he was not doing more harm to the instruments.

"We're going down!" Troy warned.

"It would be wise for you both to strap your seatbelts," Alexis said, buckling her own. Hesitantly, she flipped some buttons on the control panel. "This might be ugly."

Troy followed her example. "You sure you can fly this thing?"

"I flew the plane once, for a few minutes, but not alone, not at night, and not damaged."

Creed felt like the chair was melting and becoming a part of him. The air pressure was squeezing him tightly making it difficult for his lungs to draw in a breath. The color evaporated from Troy's face.

"Um, Alexis, don't you think we'd better slow down a bit?"

"I know, Troy," Alexis said, watching the dials carefully. "I think she can hold."

Creed could tell she was nervous but calm. It struck him how closely she resembled his mother. Then he chided himself for entertaining such a thought, especially at a time like this.

Troy clutched his stomach. "But I don't know if I can hold."

Cloud and sky were going by at an alarming rate. All that could be seen were flashes of white and grey clouds. The fog was extremely heavy. Creed felt like they were cutting a path through mashed potatoes—with a chain saw. The ground was invisible.

Troy was gripping the seat with his fingernails. "We're going too fast."

Alexis spoke without turning around. "I know, Troy. It's not responding properly."

Desperately, she flipped switches and pulled the throttle toward herself. The plane slowed somewhat, but not enough for Creed. "Alexis! Pull up the nose so we don't flip when we hit the water!"

She grabbed the yoke and pulled. There was nothing else Creed could do. He could only look on in horror as the plane plummeted. It was not right to die like this after all they had been through. All at once the ocean appeared before them.

The sea stretched beyond sight, blending seamlessly with the sky. The plane was dwarfed by the great expanse of water, as it crashed in a cascade of white. There was a great whooshing and splashing sound as the sleek plane sliced the water. Through the cockpit shield, Creed saw a wild kaleidoscope of water, foam and bubbles rushing past him at a terrific speed.

But they were not dead. Not yet.

Whipping off his belt, Creed stumbled to his feet. "We need to get out before we're submerged!"

Water was spilling from some cracks and splashing onto the cabin floor. Alexis pulled open an emergency hatch in the ceiling. A short ladder unfolded from the hatch door. She grasped the rungs and hauled herself up. Troy clambered up behind her. Creed sloshed back to his seat and rescued his backpack and pistols before following them out of the hatch.

Outside, Creed had to squat to balance himself on the sloping plane. Fog hung thick in the air. The wrecked aircraft floated haphazardly, rocking and bobbing like an abandoned cork. Flicking aside her drenched hair, Alexis climbed farther up the plane, which was slowly descending nose first, giving the illusion that it was shrinking.

"We're sinking," Troy observed sadly. The chilly sea air nipped at Creed's face. He was sitting on top of a sinking plane somewhere in the middle of the Pacific ocean. Soon the water would close over his head.

It would drag him down to its dark depths. It would fill his mouth and flood his lungs. It would choke out his life. Creed trembled.

"Creed?"Alexis was looking at him with concern. "What's wrong? Are you hurt?"

He could not answer. Then Alexis's eyes went wide as she saw something behind him. "Hold on! There's a wave coming!"

A turquoise wall of sea rose up, poising over them like a cobra preparing to strike. Creed gripped the slippery sides as best he could, knowing all to well that if he was ripped off, he would die. He snatched a deep breath. A second later the horrific water smashed into them, smothering everything in its path. Creed fought to keep his hold. Salt water stung his eyes. Then it was over.

He prayed that Troy and Alexis had secured themselves. They had. Troy was shivering, his teeth clacking like castanets but he was still there. Alexis was clinging with desperate determination. She looked like a wet rag. Creed's fingers were freezing. Much more of this and he would not have to worry about holding on, his fingers would be melded to the plane.

Alexis gasped. "That's the silver tower."

Creed was flooded with relief. At that moment a shining ray of light broke the fog. Gleaming like a polished jewel, a tower rose imposingly out of the sea.

The early morning sun sent white rays playing over the glistening surface. Hundreds of tinted picture windows adorned the walls. White foam rippled and rolled where the water line met the tower. It seemed as though it had been built before the sea even existed. It was an architectural marvel of the modern world.

In the distance, through the drifting mist, Creed could make out what seemed to be a small island surfacing through the mists. The drifting wreckage, which had once been an airplane, ground to a stop as its belly scraped against rocks and seaweed on the shoreline. Creed slid off the edge and began wading quickly up the beach. He wanted to put as much distance between himself and the water as possible. Alexis followed ringing out her hair.

Troy pointed through the trees. "There's a little town on the other side. Probably a ten minute walk. We can get some food."

The three of them splashed through the shallows. Creed looked back at the plane only to see it disappearing beneath the waves to take one final trip—to the bottom of the Pacific.

CHAPTER 16

At the motel door, Creed swiped the plastic card. A green light blinked as the computer read the magnetic strip and unlocked the door. The room was standard: green carpet, two full beds, and floral wallpaper. A King James translation of the Bible rested on the night stand.

Troy was sipping a soda and tapping away at the laptop balanced on his knees. He was nodding his head in time with music from his earphones. "Hey, man, glad you're back. I was just wondering if I should go after you. What were you doing out there anyway?"

"Checking the layout."

"The layout?"

"The layout of the building. Stairs. Elevators. Exits."

Troy still looked befuddled. "Like in case of a fire?"

"No, like in case of a robot."

Troy nodded slowly as the significance hit him. "Oh, I get it now. Pretty smart. I wouldn't have thought of it."

"If you had grown up in the under city, it would have been your first lesson. Always know the exits."

"What's it like down there?"

"Dark. Dirty. Dangerous."

Creed dropped his backpack on the floor and dropped himself on the unoccupied bed. Wearily, he stretched out. Maybe he could sleep without having those painful dreams about his mother. "What were you doing on the computer?"

"It's just a journal. If we live to get out of this mess, I want to

111

remember it.”

Creed frowned. “We were chased by killers, had a shootout with a psycho robot, and crashed an airplane into the Pacific. How in the world could you possibly forget?”

Troy grinned. “Well, you know, sometimes things slip your mind.”

“I wouldn’t underestimate the power of your mind. It’s been said that one mind is more powerful than a thousand supercomputers.”

“Who told you that proverb, your dad?”

“No. He never told me anything.”

“Yeah, I know what you mean. My dad was kinda like that too. Tough and silent type. ”

“My father died before I was born.”

“Whoa. That’s rough. But I feel you. My dad died in the war. Do you ever wish you could have met him?”

Creed looked away. “Everyday.”

Troy had a pained expression in his eyes. “I remember when he died like it was yesterday. When I opened that letter, I cried for weeks. He went missing in action . . .” He swallowed. “But I’m proud of my dad. He was a great man and a great soldier.” Troy dropped his head. “I’m nothing like him.”

“Well, you’re definitely not the silent type, but I think you may be tougher than you realize.”

“DID YOU two get settled in all right?” Alexis asked, stepping inside the boys’ room. It was the next afternoon, almost fifteen hours since she had stumbled into bed the night before and cried herself to sleep.

Troy gestured at Creed, who stretched on the bed, oblivious to the world. “Well, Creed settled in. I think he went into a coma. Never knew a guy could sleep so much.”

Alexis watched Creed, surprised at how calm and tranquil the boy appeared when sleeping. His brows were relaxed and unfurrowed—so different from his normally fierce countenance. Without his scowl he looked handsome. Almost dashing. This was her sister's son. Her nephew. It was all so strange. "If he wants to sleep, we should let him. He certainly deserves it. If it weren't for him . . . "

"We would've eaten a bucket load of bullets for dinner last night," Troy finished.

Alexis shuddered. "Or worse."

She sat down at the edge of the bed. A lone tear trickled down Creed's face. Hesitantly, she reached out and wiped it away. Drawing her finger across his face she brushed the long jagged scar lining his cheek. Fresh scabbing suggested a recent wound, only a few days old. What type of life did this boy lead?

The brown eyes suddenly flicked open. He caught her wrist almost wrenching off her arm. He flipped her to the floor, pinning her in a single motion. His clenched fist was raised over her.

Alexis cringed. "Creed?"

His eyes widened in recognition and he sprang off her. "Alexis, I'm sorry. It was a bad dream. Did I hurt you?"

He held out his hand.

"I'm fine," she answered, tentatively taking his hand and pulling herself up. "I came to see if you were ready to go the museum."

"Give me five minutes." Four minutes later, Creed clipped his gun belt to his waist, and slipped into his long windbreaker. "Ready."

Troy tossed Alexis a brochure advertising the museum. "Hey, I found this down in the lobby."

Spreading the brochure open, her eyes fell on the museum emblem. A computer-generated image of a figure, half man and half robot. Alexis paled.

Troy shook his head. "This whole thing is a mad venture."

He had voiced the very thought that was plaguing her. Was it pure foolishness? But she had to try something. Troy was not done. "What are we going to do? Just waltz in and demand to see Dr. Skeddner? He might not even be there and even if he is, what then?"

Alexis crossed her arms. "I need to try."

Creed traced the handgrip on his pistol, "We need some sort of battle plan."

Alexis gave him a grateful look. If there was one person on earth she could count on, it was Creed.

"Okay," Troy said, relenting. "I like the plan part, but let's try to keep the battle part to a minimum."

"DADDY, I'M afraid."

Whitefield glanced down at the attractive girl sitting on the table. She looked young for her sixteen years. The innocent smile that usually parted her lips was gone. Her green eyes were even wider than normal. She looked forlorn and vulnerable, gripping the table edge with white knuckles.

"What is bothering you?"

"I need to ask you something."

He set down the syringe he was filling and wrapped his arm around the green-eyed girl. "Go ahead, Rachel. I'm listening."

Rachel toyed nervously with his lapels. "Why can't we run?"

Whitefield slumped. "They would apprehend us before we even left this room."

"I'm surrounded by cold halls and cold stares. I hate this place."

The sigh rose from the bottom of Whitefield's soul. "As do I."

"Commando scares me," Rachel said, "I hate that awful man—if there still is a man underneath all those nuts and bolts. Why did you ever agree to work for him?"

He felt a sudden twist in his heart. How did she know? He had been very careful to hide his . . . agreement with Commando from her. But he always knew he had to tell her someday.

Rachel stroked his hand. "Why, Daddy?"

"When you were four years old, you had some medical complications. Commando offered me the money I needed to help you.

In return, I promised to finish building the robots."

"I'm afraid for you, Daddy. Commando hates you, just like he hates me."

Whitefield pulled his daughter closer. "I don't much care what Commando does to me as long as I can bring you safely through this ordeal."

The door banged open and the cyborg himself trooped in. "I hope I'm not interrupting anything."

Rachel looked at the floor and clutched her father's hand. Whitefield frowned, wondering if he had overheard their conversation. "Actually, you are, but that would not trouble you much, would it?"

"No, it wouldn't. Has Coleman landed yet?"

"Not to my knowledge," Whitefield answered stiffly.

"Well, I'll just wait here for him. He's not answering his phone."

Whitefield looked down at his daughter, "Okay, Rachel, we're all done. You can go up to your room."

"Be careful Daddy," she whispered as she left.

Commando removed the bandages from his face. The lights reflected across the chrome half of his skull melded to his flesh. "She's a smart kid. Daddy should be careful."

Whitefield pulled out a rack of synthetic face masks from a locked drawer. He selected one and handed it to Commando. "You're the one who needs to be careful. The cyborgs are of no use to you or your employer, unless they can be controlled."

"Don't remind me," Commando hissed, sliding the mask over the naked machinery which constituted his head.

"I hope you realize they will be powerful—too powerful for us to harness if they decide to defy our orders. My dear Commando, my point is, put simply, you must recover that data capsule or all is lost."

The cyborg frowned. "We would have a nightmare on our hands."

A sudden change flashed over Dr. Taylor Whitefield. His voice dropped an octave and lost its smooth classy style. His face quivered with emotion. "This has been nothing but one endless nightmare since you murdered my wife and hurt my poor daughter."

Commando grinned wickedly. "Oh, I'm sorry to hear that. If I were you, I'd be very careful, Whitefield."

The cybernetics engineer turned away. He would never let Commando see his tears.

CHAPTER 17

The boat chugged away from Shell Island, which was probably named after the numerous shells dotting its beaches. Creed and Alexis leaned against the ferry rail along with the rest of the museum visitors. Looming over them, the museum tower blocked out the sun, leaving the boat in shadow.

A giant pair of cargo doors opened up in the side of the tower, and the boat passed into an indoor docking area. The air was cold. Steal support beams crisscrossed the walls. Creed felt like he had slid into the belly of a submarine. Shimmering light particles reflected off the water and played over their heads on the domed ceiling. The boat pulled up to a curved platform which served as a dock.

Steps led up to the museum entrance doors. Emblazoned above them were the words: "The Whitefield Institute of Cybernetics Engineering and Organism Development." Beside the words was the Institute's logo, a figure who was half man and half robot.

Creed swallowed. Looking at a picture of a cyborg was one thing, seeing one in real life was a completely different experience.

"Well," Troy said, "if you guys are hoping to meet more cyborgs, I think this is our best bet."

As they stepped off the boat, the two electronic glass doors slid open and they filed inside the main building. The interior design was an unusual mixture of Greek architecture and modern technology. It was beautiful, but cold. Giant slabs of intricately cut marble made up the floor. The walls were fashioned from gray panels. Wide windows allowed a stunning view of the island and the surrounding ocean.

The information desk was at the far wall. Troy jabbed Creed with his elbow. "You check out those security guards?"

Creed nodded. The guards wore a standard brown uniform with a US flag and eagle emblem. But their uncommon aspect was their faces. They were the roughest, fiercest-looking law enforcers Creed had ever seen in his life. None looked hesitant to pull weapons and use them.

"Looks like they pulled those guys out of a terrorist training camp," Troy muttered. As they found a place in the ticket line, he pulled out the pamphlet. "The museum is divided into two sections. The lower section is where the exhibits are, and the top is where they research and develop the robots."

"It's ELEVEN o'clock," Troy remarked, glancing down at the glowing LCD face of his watch. The trio were squeezed inside a broom closet. "The museum closed at eight. I haven't heard a sound since nine. You guys think we can get out now? Not that the last three hours haven't brought us closer together, and I enjoyed the life stories, but I got cramps in my leg, in my arm—."

Creed leaned over Alexis to poke Troy in the ribs. "If you don't pipe down, you'll have something worse than cramps when I'm done with you."

Alexis smiled despite her efforts to suppress it. "You shouldn't be complaining, Troy. After all, as I recall, this was your idea."

Troy sighed. "Yeah, I know, I know. But it worked, didn't it? We're inside."

"I'm not the one who's complaining. In fact, I thank you for it. You're brilliant."

Troy shrugged nonchalantly but basked in her praise. "Aw, it was nothing."

As Creed watched Alexis, he was struck again by how much she reminded him of his mother, the way she tossed her hair, her smile, her composure.

He slid outside. "It's clear."

After they traversed the hall, there was another set of doors which opened out into a circular corridor. The far wall was a plexiglass window. Underneath them was a laboratory.

Scattered about the room were more than a hundred technicians and engineers in lab coats, busily working in their own cubicles. Mechanical devices cluttered the room. Some of the technicians were constructing complex motors, and others were tinkering with wires, processing chips, and data cards. A few were welding metal plates. Some of the modules were no more than small articulating fingers which were controlled by masses of optic fibers as thin as a strand of hair. What they were building was obvious.

Robots.

The sound of boots echoed down the hall. Creed's mind screamed out one solitary command. Hide!

A few yards ahead the hall opened into a wider corridor. Creed pushed Troy to one side and pulled Alexis into the alcove on the other side of the wall. Flattening themselves against the wall, they were hidden from the view of anyone coming down the corridor.

Creed pressed himself closer to the wall, wishing that he could somehow pass through it. He could see Troy huddled in the corner trying to make himself as small as possible. Alexis closed her eyes. Creed could hear her breath escaping in stifled gasps. He gave her hand a comforting squeeze. He wasn't sure, but he thought her breathing quieted somewhat. He knew the best way to calm his own fears and his pounding heart was to take deep measured breaths. He had learned that years ago in the alleys.

They were trespassing after hours and Creed suspected that the guards might shoot first and ask questions afterwards. The boots grew louder in Creed's ears until it sounded like a massive army clopping down the hall. To his relief, all the guards passed without looking to the sides. One man was pushed past in handcuffs. He was hunched over and shuffled his feet in defeat. Even though he didn't see the man's face, he recognized Dr. Isaac Skeddner.

Alexis saw him too. The word "Father" had almost escaped her lips when a hand clamped over her mouth, smothering the sound.

Creed, who had guessed her reaction, held on tightly. It was a relief to find the doctor and yet at the same time frustrating. There was Dr. Skeddner not five feet from where they crouched and there was no way to get his attention. Creed waited until the footsteps died away and his heart rate returned to normal. He took his hand from Alexis's mouth.

Troy got to his feet. "Do we follow them?"

Lights flipped on with a burst of brightness. Creed found himself blinded by powerful flashlight beams. He was disarmed and handcuffed before he even saw the half dozen security guards glowering down at them. Since when did security guards carry handcuffs?

"Walk!" one of them growled. They marched them to an elevator.

"What are you going to do with us?" Creed asked his captor. The man only grunted and shoved them through a code locked door marked *Security Only.*

Creed suspected, from the way the security guards acted, that they weren't guards at all, but mercenaries. This museum was certainly hiding something.

Their prison looked like an unused office. He performed a quick check of the room, hunting for anything that might serve as a weapon or a tool to pick the lock. Troy dug in his pocket and produced his phone. "What would we do without phones?"

He threw it down a moment later. "No reception. Should've known. Guess there aren't too many cell towers in the middle of the ocean."

Creed dropped to his knees and ran his fingers around the doorframe. Alexis was looking at the window. "Creed, what about the window? I know it's a long way down, but I think we can do it."

Creed winced. He had hoped that the idea would not occur to them. Pretending not to hear, he continued, half-heartedly running his fingers along the doorframe. Alexis grabbed Creed by the shoulder and shook him. "Creed!"

"I don't want to go that way," he muttered.

"Why not?"

"I can't swim."

She looked confused. "What?"

Creed turned on her in an unexpected outburst. "I can't swim! Okay?" His voice vibrated around the small room.

Troy shrugged."Maybe we should try and find another way. This could be dangerous. I knew this one kid who—."

Alexis frowned. "Troy! Please!"

"Sorry," Troy said meekly.

"Of course this could be dangerous," Alexis said, exasperated. "But those guards who caught us trespassing know that we've seen too much. They will be back here any second after they get their orders. And if for some strange reason they don't gun us down, it would be the biggest miracle imaginable."

Creed scowled. He knew she was right.

"We could jump them when they come back," Troy suggested.

"Don't be ridiculous," Alexis snapped. "They'll have guns."

"True."

Alexis adopted a more cajoling tone. "The water won't hurt you, Creed. Just go in feet first. Troy and I will help hold you up. All we have to do is swim to the nearest door or window back into the tower."

Creed folded his arms across his chest. "I'm not going that way."

Alexis looked ready to argue the matter further then changed her mind. She turned to Troy. "Help me throw that chair through the window."

Troy paused deciding whom he was going to follow. "Creed, I think she's right. We probably should go before he comes back."

He helped Alexis fling the chair through the window, while Creed watched. The glass pane shattered cleanly. Troy leaned over the edge, he rubbed his hands together. "This is so insane," he said and leaped out of the window. It was an age before he splashed into the ocean.

Creed stared. "He's got some guts."

Cautiously, he approached the window. The water rocked and rolled far below. Nervous tingles came over him. He did not have to do this. There had to be another way to escape.

Alexis stepped beside him. "You can do it, Creed. Here, take my hand and we'll jump together."

He pulled away. She slapped him. It was so unexpected that Creed could not resist when she pulled him off the edge. A strange sensation of weightlessness washed over him as he seemed to float in the air. Then the wind whooshed against his face as he plunged downwards. Roaring like a starving animal, the water rushed forward to meet him. At the last moment he remembered to shut his eyes. Hitting the water was painful. It smacked his body like a whip, and then swallowed him. He struggled and choked. Something clamped on his arm and dragged him up. He came up gasping and spluttering. Troy was holding his arm. Alexis popped up beside him, treading water. Her beautiful eyes mirrored the water.

After a brief search, they found an access hatch close to water level and a conveniently located ladder. "The first thing I'm going to do when this is over is teach you to swim," Alexis said. Creed caught hold of the rungs, dragging himself up from the water. Thank God that was over. He turned to give Alexis a hand up.

"What are you doing here?"

Three heads spun in the direction of the voice. Standing only two yards away was a tall man in a white coat.

Dr. Taylor Whitefield. Creed recognized him from his picture in the museum brochure. A slender girl walked by his side. They were escorted by four imposing security guards. Weapons were drawn in a matter of seconds. Creed grasped for his gun before remembering that the other guards had already taken it. He felt naked.

He glared at the shiny pistol barrels aimed at his face, deliberating between fighting, running, or surrendering.

Alexis clutched his arm. "Don't fight them," she whispered. And as the situation stood, he was inclined to agree with her.

Creed raised his hands. "Don't shoot."

Whitefield eyed them. "The museum is closed, and you should not be in this area."

Troy grinned nervously. "I told you guys it was getting late."

Alexis looked innocent and confused. "I'm sorry, Sir, we just . . . just got a little lost. We were trying to locate the exit."

Conflicting thoughts crossed Whitefield's face. Troy sneezed. Finally Whitefield turned to one of the guards. "Jones, please escort them off the premises and return them to the island."

With a lingering glance at Alexis, Whitefield turned and walked away. Two security guards followed him and two stayed behind. Troy choked out a sigh of relief. Creed could not believe the man had allowed them to go so easily.

The security guard assigned to guide them sniffed gruffly. "This way."

An unexpected pain crashed into Creed's head. He dropped to his knees. As his vision faded, he made out the grinning face of Trex, gun butt raised. "You aren't getting away this time, kid."

CHAPTER 18

I can't believe you were going to just let them go," Commando scoffed. "Sometimes I wonder which side you're on."

He followed Whitefield through a security door which separated the public museum and research center from the rest of the tower, separating the legal operations from the illegal operations. Whitefield jammed his hands deeper in his pockets as he tried to endure Commando's tirade. The berating had lasted for the past ten minutes and Whitefield was beginning to lose patience.

"How was I supposed to know?" he said. "The last time I saw Skeddner's little girl she could barely walk. When you told me that teenagers had run off with the capsule, I was expecting some hulking athletes. I find it amazing that you let a few little kids get the better of you."

This statement had the desired effect. The blue eyes glowed coldly. Commando had to turn away to prevent himself from tearing Whitefield apart right there in the hallway. He reminded himself why he was doing this. The money. It all came down to the money.

When this whole thing was over, he had claimed the privilege of disposing of Whitefield—oh, he would relish that day. He would take the man apart piece by piece. He had requested a replacement for Whitefield, multiple times, but another man with his degree of expertise in robotics was impossible to discover.

"Alexis and Troy aren't the problem," Commando muttered. "It's the other one. Adam's son . . . Creed."

"Yes, the resemblance is striking."

Commando nodded. "Yeah, but it's only skin deep. Adam was a wimp. The boy takes more after his mother, Oasis." There was a hint of admiration is his voice. "Now she was a brave little thing."

TROY SNIFFED in the tiny room devoid of anything but walls and a door. He sat slouched against a wall, tugging uselessly at the handcuffs biting into his wrists. Beside him, Alexis and Creed shared similar fates. Shifting his weight to a more relaxed position, Creed spoke softly, conscious that there might be listening devices hidden in the room. "Don't tell them anything. Whatever they do, don't tell them anything. Just follow my lead."

Troy and Alexis nodded. They did not have long to wait.

Creed raised his eyes as Trex and Crultt filed inside followed by Commando and Whitefield. Creed couldn't understand it. Whitefield seemed to be working for Commando and yet he had let them go. He hated not knowing who his enemies were. Commando was wearing his customary combat boots, trousers and brown jacket, complete with the Sig P226. His left hand toyed with a keen-edged knife.

Creed felt a bead of sweat crawl down his face. This thing was not human.

Commando bounded forward not bothering with pleasantries or even threats. "Where is it?" he demanded.

There was no need to be more specific. Everybody in the room knew what he was referring to. The answer he got was less than satisfactory. Alexis shut her eyes and Troy shook, but neither spoke. Creed knew Commando would kill them as soon as he knew the location of the data capsule. Again the capsule was their only possible leverage.

"Please, dear," Whitefield said appealing to Alexis. "Commando is not a pleasant person when he is angry. I strongly suggest that you answer his question."

Commando kneeled beside her, bringing his face close to hers. The girl grimaced with revulsion. She had seen that horribly maimed and robotic face hidden behind his synthetic mask.

"Where is it?" The cyborg spat out the words. "You're going to tell me where the capsule is, and you're going to die. That's a fact. You'll just save yourself a little pain if you talk now."

Alexis trembled, wide-eyed with fear. Without a word or warning of any kind, Commando whipped the knife across her cheek. She uttered a sharp cry. A line of red trickled down her skin.

"So you want to be a stubborn little mule, eh? Let's see how brave and self-righteous you are when pain is added to the equation."

He brought the knife back again. Creed could not stand this. He doubled his fists slamming them, manacles and all, into Commando's glaring face. The cyborg was knocked off his feet.

Trex and Crultt rushed forward. Creed caught the butt of a rifle in his mouth with a painful crunch. Using their gun's as clubs, they beat him to the floor.

"Enough," Commando ordered, obtaining his footing and wiping blood from his face. After one final pound to Creed's skull, Trex hauled him upright and handcuffed him to the desk legs. Face swollen from the beating, Creed took grim satisfaction from his brief victory. If Commando could bleed, then at least part of him was flesh. He was not indestructible.

Shoving Trex out of the way, Commando spat bloody saliva from his mouth. "Your parents made the foolish mistake of withholding the capsule. Both are now dead. You feel like joining the club?"

Creed said nothing. He knew his silence was infuriating his captor. Commando grabbed Creed's wrist. "I'm going to start carving you up into strips and make you watch the girl eat them. I think you'll be ready to talk then."

The knife blade flashed. Clinching his teeth, Creed swallowed the scream. The blade severed his finger from his right hand—his trigger finger. Terrible pain screeched through every nerve. Hardly daring to, he looked down at hand. Blood rolled from the stub, dripping off his hand onto the clean marble floor. Alexis gasped. Whitefield seemed almost as surprised as Alexis. "Ah, Commando, I don't think there is any call for such violence."

"Shut up, Whitefield!" Commando hissed, pointing the weapon at him. "Get out of the room if a little blood disturbs your delicate mind. One more word out of you and you'll join him."

He raised the knife again.

Alexis fell to her knees and clutched at Commando's legs. "Stop! You'll kill him. I beg of you, please stop!"

The cyborg looked down at her. "Ah, does Miss Skeddner want to talk now?" He yanked Creed's head up by his hair. "Where is it?"

"Alexis! Don't!" Creed yelled. Commando punched him, smashing the air from his lungs. "Where is it?"

"It's in our motel room on the island," Alexis said quickly.

"What room?" Commando demanded.

Tears flooded her eyes. "204."

The cyborg released Creed, letting his barely conscious body slump to the floor. "Where in the room?"

"I don't know where Creed hid it."

Commando glared down at Creed. "It had better be there."

"Good, very good dear. See that wasn't too hard, now was it?" Whitefield said soothingly. "Commando, return to the island and retrieve the capsule. And this time do not fail." His last sentence possessed a very condescending tone.

Commando gave Whitefield a look of unchecked hatred before turning to Trex. "Stay right here and watch the kids. I don't want them escaping again. I'll be back in an hour."

At the last moment he turned around and locked eyes with Creed. "You and I still have some unfinished business. I'll be looking forward to it on my return." Commando stalked through the electronic sliding doors.

"I hate him," Alexis announced vehemently after the doors shut.

"Alexis, my dear girl, there are some things to bandage the wound in this locker. I apologize for Commando's behavior."

"Oh, be quiet," Alexis snapped with disgust. "You're not sorry. If you were, you would let my father and us go. You're just as much an animal as he is."

Whitefield turned away as Alexis began rummaging in the locker. He spoke sadly—almost to himself, "And now, I have Skeddner's beautiful bargaining chip."

CLOSING THE door behind him, Dr. Taylor Whitefield turned and found himself confronted by his daughter. She was clearly troubled. Had she been listening? Yes. She had definitely heard something. But how much?

He held out his arms to her. "My girl, what are you doing out here? It's nearly midnight. You're supposed to be in bed."

She glanced over his shoulder at the door. "I couldn't sleep. Father, what was happening in there?"

"Oh, that, it was nothing," he responded, attempting to brush aside her question. But Rachel was not appeased. She caught his coat, eyes wide. "I heard her scream. She isn't any older than I."

Whitefield brought her in close. "There's nothing to worry about."

But he knew there was.

CHAPTER 19

"You shouldn't have told him where the capsule is," Creed muttered between clenched teeth. Hydrogen peroxide burned and fizzled in his wound. Alexis dabbed at it with a wad of cotton.

"I don't care," she responded, almost rebelliously. "I wasn't about to let Commando shred you. He would've butchered you. You know that don't you?"

Creed couldn't bring himself to acknowledge her statement.

"Man, I sure hope he doesn't get a second crack at us," Troy said.

When Alexis finished tending the wound, she wrapped it with a clean rag. Something wet dripped on Creed's arm. Tears? He looked up. Lips quivering and eyes glistening, Alexis whimpered. She brushed her eyes on her sleeve.

Creed felt awkward. "Hey, don't cry over me, Lex. I'll be fine."

With his good hand, he traced her dangling blue braid. "We'll both be fine."

For the first time Alexis seemed to lose the fire that had carried her so far. "I'm sorry. This is all my fault." She tried to wipe her eyes but the tears continued to slide down her face. "We should have let the police handle this, like you said. I've only complicated this disaster."

Creed sat up as he heard the distinctive clang of dead bolts being drawn back. Squinting in the pool of light spilling in from outside the corridor, he saw the dark silhouette of Trex.

The young man stomped inside. Creed had a glimpse of six security guards waiting outside the corridor, guns in hand. Apparently, they knew that Creed had the guts to attack Commando and they were prepared for trouble. Trex reached out for Alexis's handcuffs. "Come on, sweetheart. Whitefield wants to speak with you."

The locks clicked open, clattering to the floor. Alexis massaged her bruised wrists. Creed struggled to sit up. "What does he want with her?"

The man's features slipped into a smug grin. "She's gonna find out in a moment."

He caught Alexis's arm, hustling her into the corridor. Creed gritted his teeth. He doubted Whitefield was just going to talk. This might be his only chance.

Creed lashed out with his leg. But Trex was expecting it and dodged. Another guard darted forward from Creed's blind side and slugged him across the face. The blow knocked him to the ground, yet his assault provided enough distraction for Alexis to slip from Trex's grasp.

But before she had taken a step, a guard hit her from behind and she fell next to Creed. She bit her lip. "Creed it's all right, I'll be fine."

With an aching heart, he watched as she was dragged out into the corridor.

The doors thundered shut. The boys stared hopelessly at each other. Troy rolled on his back and restated Creed's question. "What do you think he wants with her?"

He didn't seem to expect an answer, and was not disappointed when he received none. There were no beds in the room so they made themselves as comfortable as the could on the hard floor. After a few minutes, Troy drifted off into a fitful slumber. But Creed was floundering through too much physical and emotional pain to find sleep.

"Oh, God," he whispered, "protect her."

SLEEP WAS the last thing on Commando's mind. He spied Creed's backpack hidden underneath the motel bed. He snatched it up and ripped it open, dumping the contents on the bed. His face contorted under the synthetic mask as a ragged assortment of items fell out, but no data capsule.

Commando spat. That wretched boy. He glared at the small ransacked room. His men were tearing the whole thing apart trying to find the capsule. The scanty chests and night stands were throughly searched. The bed was dismantled. Hyndrix and Crultt began prying up the floorboards.

Commando happened to glance upwards. Something gleamed in the ceiling air vent. Something like a data capsule.

SKEDDNER FELT like he was in hell. Multiple levels of massive factory machinery pounded below him belching steam and foul odors. A pump valve controlled a swift moving waste canal. The roar tortured his eardrums. This was where they built their cyborgs, in the bowels of the tower. The catwalk shook under his feet. Only a railing stood between him and a painful drop.

Whitefield wiped perspiration from his face with a handkerchief. "Not a very pleasant place, is it?"

"Why are we here?"

"Father!" It was a voice that had cried his name a thousand times. A voice that represented his whole world. But it was the last thing Skeddner wanted to hear now.

He spun around. Alexis stood pinioned between Trex and another guard. A chill went through him like an electric shock. The implications were obvious. They would use her to break him. Her cheek bore an ugly cut. Her beautiful face was flushed with dread. Rage boiled in Skeddner's chest. What abuse had she endured at their hands?

In a sudden movement, Alexis pulled away from her guards and rushed to him. She stumbled the last few steps before throwing herself into his arms. The next few moments were a dream. She clung to him, burying her face in his shoulder. He held her so close it hurt. He could feel her tears, her heart, and her fear.

"My darling," he breathed in her ear as he stroked her silky hair. "My darling."

And for a moment time stood still.

But only for a moment. Whitefield cleared his throat. "I see you are greatly attached to your daughter. And I've never seen such courageous devotion from a child. If you would like to avoid a tragic ending to this story, I would advise you to take immediate heed of my proposal."

Skeddner's brain shifted into overdrive. Could he grab Alexis and run? Grab one of the guard's guns?

"Father," Alexis whispered, searching for hope in his gray eyes.

"My dear doctor, I'm waiting."

Skeddner was sick with fear. "Why are you involving her in this? This is not her problem. She is completely innocent in the matter."

Whitefield looked away. Skeddner tried again, pleading now. "She's only a child, Whitefield. Are you so black-hearted that you would bargain with the life of a child?"

"If she is old enough to attempt to rescue her father, she is certainly old enough to accept the consequences." He nodded to Trex who pushed Alexis against the rail and slid out a gun. "Dr. Skeddner, I'm terribly sorry it has come down this. But this is my ultimatum. Build the MCC or watch your daughter die. Make your choice, now."

Trex pressed his gun to her head. She whimpered.

Two wet drops trickled down Skeddner's face. He nearly choked on his words. "I am begging you. Don't do this."

"I'm sorry, Skeddner, but you leave me with no other option. Make the chip, and I will release your daughter. Otherwise, you will force me to annihilate her."

"Okay, we can talk this out, but you need to let her go."

"Shoot her in the knee," Whitefield ordered. From the glint in the man's eye, Skeddner knew this was no idle threat. He could not stand by and watch this man hurt his baby girl. Without thinking he dove for the gun.

Trex spun away and in the process knocked hard into Alexis. She flipped backwards over the rail, barely catching it with one hand. Her fingernails scraped ominously. Her mouth opened in a piercing, terror-filled scream as she lost her grip. A primeval roar rushed from Skeddner's throat as he tried to catch her. But some instinct told him that he was too late. He couldn't reach her. For a second her blue eyes found his. Her desperate plea sliced through his soul.

Then she fell.

Skeddner charged towards the rail, his fingers grasping air. He could only watch her body plummet to the sharp, wicked machines below. She seemed to float rather than fall. He never forgot her scream. Her cry was silenced when she crashed into an enormous power generator. For a brief moment Skeddner had allowed himself to hope that she might have survived. But as she rolled down the machine, raging pistons and exposed gears ripped at her savagely. His hope died. Her body picked up speed, leaving behind a slick trail of blood.

Her skull cracked into a steel support post. Skeddner bit his tongue. Her head snapped back and her limp body, covered in ugly bruises and blood, came to an abrupt stop. The body slid down into the rapid current of the waste canal. The pumps sucked her into their depths. And she was gone.

Skeddner's heart was cut out. His body throbbed and his mind shut down. He fell to his knees, a broken man. He yelled and beat the floor with his fists, tears running down his face.

Yes, he was in hell.

CHAPTER 20

From her hiding place behind a large stack of supply boxes, Rachel gasped. She wanted to scream. She wanted to rush out and save the girl. But her limbs would not obey her. Her mind could not register what her eyes had seen. She fled to her room.

She didn't know how long she lay on her bed crying into the sheets. Her father had become a monster. He had killed a girl.

"Rachel? Where are you?" Her father.

Something in her wanted to hide and never look at his face again. She dismissed it. This was the man who bounced her on his knee. The man who had sung her to sleep.

But now this man had killed a girl.

"Rachel!"

She couldn't bring herself to answer him. Instead she shrank back hoping he wouldn't find her. When she caught a glimpse of his distraught face, her heart broke for him. His eyes were wild with guilt. He pulled her into his arms. Part of her was utterly repulsed, and part of her wanted to never let go of him.

"I love you," he whispered into her ear. "I'll fix everything. I'll. . ."

She wasn't sure she could trust her voice. "Can you fix a dead girl?"

His face went chalky white, and his hands started shaking.

Appalled, she backed away, shaking her head. "I don't know you anymore."

She turned and ran. She didn't know where she was running, only that she had to get away.

WHITEFIELD WAS slumped over his desk with his head in his hands. He couldn't escape the image of Alexis's torn, bleeding body and Rachel's piercing eyes. Rachel knew. Somehow she knew what he had done. The look she had given him would haunt him for eternity.

Commando marched into Whitefield's private office without bothering to knock.

He tossed the capsule triumphantly on the desk. Reluctantly, Whitefield reached out and fingered it. "It's useless to us now. Hulsane does not want *plans*. He wants a fully functional instrument."

"What are you talking about, man!"

"She's dead."

"What?"

"I was trying to convince Skeddner to build it, but he wouldn't and then Alexis fell . . . Whatever leverage we had on Skeddner is gone with her. He will never cooperate now."

"We still have the boys."

"I don't think they will be enough."

Commando rolled his eyes, his robotic camera eye rolling in perfect sync with his real eye. "Forget Skeddner. You build it."

"Don't insult me. My expertise doesn't extend beyond robots and cyborgs. You ask the impossible. I know absolutely nothing of this technology and moreover, building the device was never included in my agreement."

"For your daughter's sake I hope you learn quickly, because I just made a new agreement."

SKEDDNER HAD repented a thousand times. But his failures still stalked him. He had always suspected that Rolls wouldn't bring himself to destroy the research, but he had never investigated the matter. He pounded his head against the wall, considering each painful thump to his skull nothing less than he deserved. Oasis was dead.

Alexis was dead. Both of his precious, precious daughters were dead. Gone because of him, his pride, his fear, and his incompetence.

SMALL RIPPLES played about in the dark water of the canal. The female body drifted into the path of moonlight. It floated by in the gentle current. The body was very still. Deathly still. Blood was spattered on the face and clothes. The eyes were closed and the black hair trailed behind in the water.

A man in a lab coat stood over the body.

CHAPTER 21

Rachel could not sleep. Two days had passed since she had watched Alexis tumble off the catwalk. Time slipped by as she thought about the atrocity her father had committed. She was shaken to the core. She had to do something. A resolve formed in her heart. She tiptoed through the cold halls until she found Trex idling before a locked door. Rachel collected her nerve and walked up to him. She didn't like the way his eyes lingered over her body. "What are you doing here, girlie?"

"Commando has returned and has asked you to meet him in the lobby."

Trex looked at her suspiciously. "In the lobby?"

"Yes."

SOMEONE WAS shaking Creed. He shot up, almost knocking out the girl who was leaning over him. It was the girl he had seen with Whitefield. She held a cautious finger to her lips. "Hurry and wake up your friend," she said in an urgent whisper. She held out his two handguns. "I think these are yours."

Suddenly Creed was fully awake. In the back of his mind, he wondered why this girl wanted to help him, but he was content to ask his questions later. He reached over and shook Troy.

"Huh? What?" Troy muttered emerging reluctantly from sleep. "Dad, is it time for dinner?"

Creed hauled him to his feet. "We're leaving."

The girl was hyperventilating. Her eyes darted back and forth. "We need to hurry. They'll find out I'm here any moment."

Creed pushed the door open, then turned back to the girl. "Where'd they take Lex? I'm not going anywhere without her."

"She's dead," the girl said softly. "I'm so sorry . . . "

Creed's countenance darkened several shades and he caught her by the shoulders, forcing her to look at him. Unbelief shadowed his face. "What are you talking about?"

She quivered under his scrutiny. "My . . . my father killed her," she whispered. A tear tore down her cheek. Bewildered with shock and pain, Creed sank to the floor. He forgot about escaping. He forgot about the capsule. He forgot about breathing. Alexis was dead? At first Creed thought he had misunderstood her, but he had not. His mind rushed back to the airport where he promised not to let anything happen to her.

He had failed. Again.

"Creed," Troy said, "it doesn't matter if that guy got what he wanted from Alexis or not, we're probably next on his hit list."

Creed could not bring his thoughts into focus.

Timidly, the girl touched his arm. "Please come."

"Where's Dr. Skeddner?"

The girl shook her head, "You can't help him."

"Tell me where he is!"

TREX FELT foolish standing in the empty lobby. Five minutes elapsed before it occurred to him that he had been tricked. Duped by a sixteen-year-old girl.

His radio chirped. "Sir, the boys are escaping!"

Trex broke into a sweating run. "Where are they!"

"Level two, sector three, very close to Dr. Skeddner's cell."

Trex hurried for the elevators and collided with an irritated Commando. The collision did not improve Commando's disposition.

With a swift judo move Commando pinned him against the paneled wall. "Watch it, man!" then the blue eyes narrowed. "What's going on?"

Trex swallowed. Commando would find out sooner or later. He might save face if he told the truth. "Commando, sir, the boys are escaping!"

Commando looked ready to put him through the wall. "I told you to watch them! Must I do everything myself?"

WHITEFIELD REMOVED his protective goggles and snapped off his plastic gloves. With a pair of sterilized tweezers he picked up a tiny silicon chip, the outcome of his tedious, painstaking hours of labor. It was the completion of a much larger task that had been decades in the making.

At the beginning, he had nearly despaired. What saved him was the explicit blueprints which Rolls had drawn more than fifteen years ago—explicit to the finest detail. He could not help feeling a kind of awed horror at his handiwork. What he held in his hand terrified him.

But Commando terrified him even more.

THE FIRST thing Alexis noticed when she awoke was that she was not dead. She sent up a silent prayer of thanks. She rubbed her eyes. Someone had washed her and cleaned her wounds. The many stitches in her arms were clearly visible and she knew there must be even more on her legs and back. Her body felt stiff and sore, but nothing like she imagined she should be feeling after hitting those machines. A glass of water and some pills lay next to her on a side table.

She tried to piece together what had happened. She could remember her father's anguished eyes, and then falling. Fear. Blood. Pain. And then everything went white.

How had she gotten here?

Whitefield. Now she remembered seeing him standing over her as she slipped in and out of consciousness. She was surprised to see sorrow and tenderness in his eyes. He had given her pain killers. She wondered if he would come back. Was he an enemy or a friend?

Where was her father? And for that matter, Creed and Troy?

She stood up, found the door, and pushed it open.

CREED LED Troy through the dark corridors. Rachel had said that Skeddner was being held on level 2, sector 3. But she refused to come with them.

An assortment of automatic rifles was stacked in a neat pyramid on a service rack. More evidence that this was not just a museum. Creed snatched up two off the top. He had a feeling he might need them. "Troy, take one."

"I couldn't use this thing if my life depended on it."

"Creed!" He turned, just as a someone threw her arms around his neck. It took a moment to register that it was Alexis. The girl looked like she had been through a war. But she was alive. Disbelieving, he ran his fingers over her checking for injuries.

"You're not dead?" he said at last. It was a stupid thing to say, so he added, "What happened?"

"I fell from a catwalk. I thought I was dead, maybe I was. Dr. Whitefield helped me."

Troy shook his head. "Whitefield helped you? I don't understand this guy! One minute he's trying to kill us, and the next minute he's pretending to be our friend."

Creed pulled her in close. "I'll never lose you again. I swear."

"Hey!" Troy shouted. "I think I just found Dr. Skeddner!"

Alexis broke away. "Where!"

The hall was lined with doors. Troy stood at one waving wildly. Through a small fiberglass window they could see inside the room. When Creed saw Dr. Skeddner, he hardly recognized him. The man was slouched in a chair, head bowed to his chest, wrists chained, stubble shadowing his face.

Alexis came up behind him. "Oh, Father . . . "

The door unlocked from the outside, and Creed pushed it open. Skeddner looked up with distrusting eyes. "It's not possible . . ."

She threw her arms around his neck, pressing her lips to his cheek. Skeddner tried to embrace her, but the handcuffs made his attempts awkward.

"Alexis! You're alive!"

"Yes. I'm all right. Everything's going to be fine."

Creed turned away in disgust. He couldn't stand this. This was the man who had destroyed his mother, and Alexis was kissing him. He felt betrayed by her. He exhaled, quelling the rage mounting in his heart.

"We don't have time for this," he ordered brusquely. He had to stop himself from shoving Alexis away. Drawing a thin pick from his pocket, Creed began working on the cuff lock, which was attached to a long heavy chain bolted to the wall. "Troy, keep an eye down the hall. Let us know if anyone comes."

Dr. Skeddner looked up from his daughter's shoulder. He had picked up on Creed's discomfort. Tears were building in the man's eyes. "I know this is awkward and difficult. I should have told you earlier, but I didn't know the capsule you gave me had the MCC data on it. I didn't realize that was why they killed Oasis. I didn't even know she possessed it. I—,"

Creed raised his hand for silence. "If it's all the same to you, I'd rather not talk about it. Let's just get out. Okay?"

The man nodded slowly. "I don't know how to thank you for protecting my daughter. I heard about what happened at the house."

There was a strained tension building up behind Creed's normally composed face. "It's a good thing someone was there for her. Seems you had another daughter, but you weren't there for her either, were you?"

Skeddner shrank visibly. "Creed, I can explain—,"

"I couldn't save her!" Creed shouted. The pick snapped off in the cuff lock. His face distorted as he tried to keep back tears destined to fall. All the pent up feelings which he had guarded so carefully in his heart were bubbling to the surface like an irate volcano. His voice was breaking and dying. "I couldn't do it. I'd give my life for her a thousand times. But even that wasn't enough to save her."

Alexis placed a comforting hand on his shoulder, "Creed, you did everything you could. It's not your fault."

He shrugged her away. "Yes, it was!"

His head ached with a dull acidic throb. Helplessness drowned out every other thought but one. "I wasn't enough to save her!" he cried, dropping the knife. "I wasn't enough . . . "

Creed could feel his pain seeping out from every pour. With a groan, he slumped to the ground. Curling himself into a ball, he covered his face in his hands.

The older man knelt beside Creed. Tears coursed his careworn face as he reached out to stroke his brown locks. Skeddner's fingers had the effect of a burning torch.

With a startling reflex, Creed knocked aside Skeddner's hand. "Don't touch me! You never cared about your own daughter," he said, spitting out the words.

"My son, I loved your mother more than you can possibly imagine."

"Yeah, so much that you threw her out in the street," Creed snarled, advancing on Dr. Skeddner who stepped back.

"Creed, forgive an old man. I was a negligent father. When her mother died, Oasis was only thirteen just entering the drama of teenage years. Business kept me traveling constantly so that we hardly knew each other. In my absence, I hired a governess, but they hated each other. When I came back, I didn't know my own daughter. I asserted more authority over her than I had nurtured. Oasis had hardened her heart against me. She hated me for leaving her. But I loved her. God knows I loved her."

Creed lunged at Skeddner. The older man tried to dodge aside, but with one reckless move Creed caught him by the collar. Slamming him against the wall, Creed yelled in his face, "Why did you disown my mother!"

"Creed!" Alexis cried, her face wet with tears. "Oh, Creed, please stop!"

She grabbed his arm. He could feel her nails digging into his skin.

"Don't kill him," she whispered. Her words hovered over the room.

Creed halted. What was wrong with him? The anger melted from his body, leaving only the sadness and fear. His strength dissipated with his rage. Bewildered with pain, he released his hold on Skeddner's collar and backed away. "I'm sorry . . . "

"No, the blame is mine. We had a fight, and I was afraid to ask her for forgiveness for the way I'd treated her and then she ran away. If I had, we might all be together now."

Weakness overcame Creed and his legs refused to hold him. He toppled.

Troy suddenly jumped from his post at the window. "Someone's coming!" he reported frantically. "I think they've heard us! We've gotta get out quick!"

Alexis sat frozen in alarm. Creed was crying openly on the floor. Her father was still manacled to the chair. "Alexis get up!" he entreated. "Run!"

She shook Creed, but to no avail. "Creed! Snap out of it!"

Reaching as far as the chains would allow, Skeddner caught Creed by his arm jerking the boy to his feet. Alexis seized Creed's hand, "I'll come back for you, father, I promise."

She dragged the distraught boy to the door. Troy needed no such urging.

"No!" Skeddner shouted, struggling against his chains. "Don't come back, Alexis! Get out of here. Get the police. Dear God, don't let me lose her again."

Troy jumped to the door and flung it open. A man was just coming forward, balancing a tray bearing Dr. Skeddner's dinner. Alexis dove into him, hitting him squarely in the chin. His eyes rolled back as he crashed down. Alexis snapped up the man's gun and guided them into the corridor.

Stumbling forward, Creed was vaguely aware of running, yells, and then gunfire. But it did not matter. His mother was dead. He had not saved her. A bullet rocked past Creed's temple—taking a sliver of flesh with it. He gritted his teeth against the pain. The reality of the wound helped clear the fog from his mind. He had to focus if he was to leave this mess alive. Get Alexis and Troy out alive. The confusion with Dr. Skeddner would have to wait. He shook the thoughts away and concentrated on the present situation. The present, grave situation.

An entire regiment of security guards were chasing them. And they did not seem afraid to use their guns. "Troy, where are the stairs?" Creed asked. "We need to get out into the public lobby. They won't be able to shoot without drawing attention."

From the corner of his eye, he saw the flash of hope which lit Alexis and Troy's faces. "Glad you came back." Troy said, "We gotta get to those elevators."

Creed dashed into a cybernetic equipment and supply room with Alexis and Troy hard on his heels. Through the room and down another corridor, he saw the elevators.

Suddenly two doors slid out of the walls with a hiss of pneumatics, cutting off the hallway and almost crushing Creed between them. It was his lightning quick reflexes that saved him. He threw himself backwards just barely avoiding having his face smashed to a pulp. The doors connected solidly together without displaying even a hairline crack. It was a dead end.

"No!" Alexis cried, her sneakers squeaking as she slid to a stop beside Creed. The floor shook from the pounding of booted feet. Their pursuers were gaining. With frantic fingers, Troy started tapping at the touchscreen which controlled the doors, "I think I can hack this. Just give me a minute."

Creed turned to face the oncoming guards. "You think?"

"I know."

Creed kicked down a giant canister. It crashed, bringing a steel rack of barrels along for the ride. They would provide some cover. But not much.

The corridor went for about forty yards before cutting sharply to the right. This gave him forty yards before he would be able to see the men. Creed dropped into a relaxed fighting stance. He whipped out both pistols, waiting for the guards to round the corner. He knew the loss of his trigger finger would affect his accuracy—but for Creed, a man was a big target.

The first one came head on. A 9mm bullet hit him squarely in the chest. He died with an odd expression of surprise on his face. He crumbled to the ground in a small contorted heap. The body and the echoing report of the gun gave the rest of the guards some warning.

They dove around the corner on their stomachs to produce smaller targets, automatic rifles at the ready. The stillness erupted into a caustic battle. Alexis pulled Troy aside as a shower of bullets rained overhead. Troy continued his job on the floor. Even with the projectiles flying around his head, Creed maintained complete focus. The handguns were blazing in his hands.

The doors slid open.

"I got it. Come on!" Troy shouted as he rushed through, ducking flying lead. Creed backed up, keeping up a steady fire. He and Alexis were two steps from the doors when they closed again with a terrible thump, with Troy on the other side.

Creed felt the cold metal against his back. Their only escape route was gone. "Do you want to surrender?" He did not look at her as he spoke the words. "I will if you want me too."

He saw her surprise out of the corner of his eye. Creed doubted these guards—cutthroats, would even consider sparing their lives. But she deserved that option.

Alexis was saved having to answer. Unexpectedly, the gray doors slid open. She fell over backwards, but was caught before she hit the ground by two strong hands. Two hands, encased in synthetic skin covering a titanium alloy shell, protecting a complex network of optic fibers which in turn, connected to a score of powerful micro motors and feeling sensors.

"Why hello, Alexis," a cold voice hissed in her ear. "What a pleasant surprise."

Alexis struggled uselessly against the crushing cyborg grip. Commando's blue eyes almost twinkled.

CHAPTER 22

When the doors hammered shut behind Troy, cutting him off from his friends, he nearly panicked. The harsh cough of gun fire could be heard through the metal door. Alexis and Creed would die any second—if they were not dead already. He had to open that door.

But as he turned around, he heard the soft rumble of an elevator. He glanced over. Above the door the level numbers were flashing. It was going to stop here, level five. Troy took a hasty glance around him. Where could he hide? He spied the roll-up panel on the wall. It was tall enough for him to squeeze into.

The panel uttered a muted scraping sound as it rose, rolling in on itself, like a small garage door. He leaped inside and pulled down the panel. Not a moment too soon. Booted feet thudded outside the small enclosure. The firing ceased, leaving behind a disturbing silence. Troy swallowed. He knew that the thin panel between them would do little good if he made the slightest sound. He waited in the blackness, cramped and uncomfortable.

He heard the distinctive voice of Commando. "Kid, you have no idea how much you've gotten under my skin."

Troy hoped Commando was not talking to Creed's corpse.

"What was the commotion?" That was Whitefield.

Commando answered, "Just an ill-attempted rescue of Skeddner. Nothing I couldn't handle. And I think we just found a volunteer for our little experiment."

Whitefield sighed. "My girl, your persistence astounds me. Skeddner should be proud to have raised such a courageous young lady."

Commando's voice came again and Troy caught his breath, "Where's your little black friend?"

Troy did not care for the tone in his voice. He waited anxiously for an answer. He was relived when he heard Creed. "I don't know. Find him yourself, robot."

There was a pause. Troy cringed, he expected any minute to hear the blow that shattered Creed's skull. But it never came.

Instead, Commando gave a dry laugh. "You and I are going to have a lot of fun together. Lock the girl up. We'll use the boy."

The sound of boots faded away into silence. The only noise he heard was the soft breathing of the air-conditioning system. Cautiously Troy slid open the panel and stuck his head out. The corridor was deserted.

Until now, Troy had not realized how much he looked up to Alexis and Creed. Especially Creed. He felt weak and helpless without them. They had not expected much from him. Now everything was resting on his shoulders.

He wanted to hole up somewhere and cry.

DEEP IN the belly of the silver tower, a special operating room was set up. Harsh white walls reflected the gleaming scalpels, cruel hypodermic needles and other sharp instruments which lay exposed on the silver tables. There was a sinister looking operating chair accompanied by sophisticated equipment and computer monitors.

Creed had no idea what they were about to do to him, but he doubted it would be a pleasant experience. Doctors fluttered around the room, faces obscured by surgical masks, hands hidden under latex gloves. They began flicking on the bright lights and booting up the computers and other machines. Whitefield was directing them.

Sweat dripped down Creed's face and splattered the pristine floor.

They had dressed him in a pasty green surgical gown. He felt like a rat caught in some ghastly lab experiment.

"I hope they don't kill you with all this fancy equipment," Commando commented as if smelling Creed's fear. "You and I still have a little date together, remember? I'd hate for you to miss it."

"Can't wait," Creed muttered.

Commando leered down at him, "You know you're one lucky kid. One day the historians will look back and remember you as the pioneer, the first person to experience Adam's invention, the invention that changed the course of mankind."

Creed stared at him. His brain whirred in a chaotic mess. Commando's words replayed in his head. Adam?

His father's name was Adam. Adam Rolls?

Was it merely coincidence? Could it be . . . ?

No. Commando had to be lying. There was no way. Impossible. Unthinkable. And yet, somehow, it was entirely possible. It would explain how his mother had the capsule in the first place.

He did not recognize the voice that came from his mouth. "Adam?"

"You don't know your own father, boy? Oasis was a worse mother than I thought."

Stunned, Creed allowed Commando to shove him into a cold, unforgiving chair and slap locks on his wrists and ankles. One thought drummed through Creed's head.

My father did this.

Slipping an operating mask over his face, a doctor pulled a lever on the chair causing it to fold out into a table. Squinting, Creed found himself staring at the bright halogen lamp dangling from the ceiling. The doctors walked around the table, their medical and scientific jargon flying over him. A doctor leaned over him—Dr. Isaac Skeddner.

Creed wanted to strangle him. But all he could do was sputter, "Why didn't you tell me! Why didn't you tell me that my father was responsible for this!"

Skeddner spoke softly, as he pressed small suction pads against Creed's skull. "Son, I'm sorry. It never occurred to me that your mother never told you."

"Well, she didn't."

"She was trying to protect you."

"Like you?"

Skeddner exhaled. "I know I've made some mistakes, but I'm trying to fix them. They'll perform this operation on you with or without my help but you stand a better chance of surviving if I do it. I don't want to lose you, Creed. There's still hope as long as you're alive."

"Skeddner!" Commando hissed. "Don't speak to him."

The Skeddner turned to Commando. "Sklade, you must realize that he might die from complications during or after the operation. It has never been attempted before on a human."

"There are plenty more where he came from. We are writing history. And when you're writing history, you can't allow a few deaths to get in the way. "

Whitefield pulled his mask over his face. "Creed, I truly am sorry."

The last thing Creed felt was a needle biting into his arm. He slipped into unconsciousness.

CHAPTER 23

Alexis uncurled her braid, then wound it back up. She sat on a cramped foldout cot bolted to the wall, the strand of hair coiled tightly around her index finger. She was alone in a small, barren office. Her watch reported that she had been there for nearly twelve hours. Dr. Whitefield had re-dressed her wounds and given her another dose of the powerful pain medication. Drowsiness had overwhelmed her. She had slept for more than ten hours, and felt much better for it. But now she was fully awake and her thoughts were on Creed.

From outside she heard the thump of boots. It grew louder. She hoped they were bringing her some food. She had not eaten. The doors divided. Two guards entered, wheeling Creed on a Gurney. Electrodes were glued to his skull. He looked so terrible that she forgot her hunger pangs.

"What did you do to him?" she demanded. The guards, who were either deaf or pretending not to hear, deposited Creed on the other cot.

"What happened to him?" Alexis asked again, but the guards filed back out of the room and the door slid shut with a clank. She sank to her knees at the boy's bedside. His eyes were closed, his mouth hung slightly open. Alexis could not detect the smallest hint of movement. There was something pained and haunted in his face. The boy was unconscious—or dead.

No.

He could not be dead. She did not allow the thought to linger. She pressed her hand on his chest and felt the faint drumming of his heart.

Good.

She touched his forehead. It seemed to be on fire. She wished she had water or better yet, ice.

"Oh, Creed," she whispered, "What did they do to you?"

His eye lids fluttered open and he moaned softly. "Lex? Am I still dreaming?"

"I only wish that was the case," she smiled. "But I'm relieved that you woke up. You had me worried."

Creed looked dizzy and disoriented. He put his hand weakly to his head and tried to sit up. "I don't feel well."

Alexis pushed him back down. "You don't look well either. You're running a high fever. What happened out there?"

He started to shake his head, but stopped in obvious pain. "I don't know. I just remember being strapped to a table, then they gave me a shot, and everything just fades away . . . " He grimaced. "Lex, I'm so tired and my head hurts."

He sounded so weak and helpless that it pierced her heart. Like a child crying for its mother. So different from the strong, confident, assuring boy she had grown to love.

She stroked his hair. "My poor baby, what did they do to you? Just relax and try to sleep."

Obediently Creed shut his eyes. Alexis stayed by his side until he lapsed into slumber. For the next few hours she lay on her cot and wondered what had happened to him. Her mind was filled with dread.

SKEDDNER COULD see his daughter through the one-way plexiglass window. She was such a trooper. She was battered and bruised, but alive and caring for Creed. He would never have imagined her coping so well. Not that he had ever imagined anything so heinous as this.

Skeddner studied the black undulating lines zigzagging across the computer screen which monitored Creed's brainwave activity. The glowing images of Creed's CT scans were projected onto the far wall.

Commando tapped his fingers against the table. "Well, were you successful or not?"

Skeddner stroked at the three-day-old stubble darkening his chin. "At present he appears stable. According to this readout, everything seems to be functioning properly, so he'll live. But there is still the possibility of damaged cranial neurons or brain tissue. We won't know for certain for another hour or so."

"So was the operation a success or not?"

"I believe so, but there are a multitude of negative side effects apart from immediate death."

Commando leaned over Skeddner's shoulder and hissed, "Since the boy managed to survive, what is preventing us from testing the device now?"

Skeddner could feel the goose bumps rising along the length of his neck as the cyborg's breath struck him. "No, wait until he wakes up, a sudden shock might kill him."

Commando gripped the desk with his robotic hand leaving a deep gouge in the platinum surface. "Skeddner, maybe I haven't made myself clear. I've been waiting an outrageous fifteen years for this and I really don't want to wait any longer."

"Do you want to kill the boy so close to the test's completion? Is that what you want?"

"Fine, doctor, I will wait, but as soon as he wakes I will try the MCC."

CREED OPENED leaden eyes, somewhat surprised to discover that he was still alive. His heart still operated. His lungs still pumped. It was impossible to guess how long he had been asleep.

What had transpired in the surgery room?

He rolled up and off the cot. Lying on her own cot, Alexis whimpered in her sleep, a tear trailing down her cheek. Poor thing. At least she was alive. It could be worse. It could always be worse. He leaned over and brushed her skin with his finger, wiping away the tear.

Creed felt a slight electrical tingle flicker across the back of his head. No, not the back of his head but inside his head. Inside his mind.

Weird.

Before he could completely grasp what had happened, an impulsive, commanding thought entered his mind.

Throw the pillow. Then, as if in a dream, he watched stupidly as he tossed the thin pillow onto the floor. Creed eyed the pillow with confused amazement. Why had he thrown it on the floor? He could not answer his own question. He wasn't given much time to ponder his actions as another tiny electrical signal jolted in his mind. A foreign thought raced through the neurons in his brain.

Stand on the cot.

He had climbed up on the cot. What was going on? His body seemed to be functioning on its own, without any conscious thought. Like a preprogramed machine. Scary. Was it his imagination? It had to be. He was controlling his own limbs, he just couldn't figure out why he was doing these things.

With an effort, he convinced himself that the idea was purely his own, yet he couldn't escape the feeling that there was something bizarre and unnatural about it. He touched the back of his neck. As he ran his fingers up his spinal cord, he winced as he felt a tender scar at the base of his skull where a small patch of hair had been removed.

Another gentle, electric pulse pricked his spine. He stomped over to a sliding door, not positive about what he was going to do. A strange idea sprang in his head. He began pounding on the door and let out a wild shriek.

SKEDDNER WAS ashamed of the excitement coursing through his body. He was in control of the human brain in the next room. Part of him insisted that he was hallucinating. It was still a theory. He and

Adam had not known for sure if the MCC would function in a human being.

Until now.

The CIA had secretly initiated the project decades ago attempting to surreptitiously control the nation's enemies. There were countless military applications for the controlled manipulation of the human mind. Skeddner and Adam had been recruited, but soon realized that the technology they were developing was simply too dangerous.

A revolting smile snaked its way across Commando's face. "How does it work exactly?"

Whitefield drummed his fingers over the keyboard. "A remote links the bio chip to the computer. We have produced a basic set of preprogramed orders, such as fight, stop, run, and jump. Now, if I were to select a particular order, for instance, *walk* . . ."

He entered the command into the computer. Creed, who was standing on the other side of the glass, immediately began walking forward.

Whitefield continued his explanation. "The program suggests specific actions to the brain. A simple command such as *walk* may stimulate different responses depending on the person's interpretation of the command. Since I limited the command to *walk*, the mind decides in which direction. This incredible program allows me to give a general order and let the brain determine how to accomplish the order. But if I were to be more specific, I could instruct the brain to walk in a particular direction. It's actually quite remarkable. Dr. Rolls was a genius."

Commando was impressed. "So, I could say *kill* and he would kill anyone, or I could be specific and say *kill Taylor Whitefield* and he would kill you?"

Whitefield swallowed. "Well . . . yes, I suppose . . . that is the basic, underlying concept."

Leaning over the consul, Commando shoved the engineer away from the computer and proceeded to pound the keyboard.

IT WAS the scream that woke Alexis. She was shocked as Creed slammed his fists against the door. "What are you doing?" She had to shout to be heard above his yells. She stood and moved toward him. He stopped and turned toward her.

Alexis took a step backward. His face was hard and heartless, with an expression she had never seen directed at her. The weakness she had seen the night before had vanished like drifting vapor. He glared coldly, mechanically, with no sign of recognition. Alexis stepped back again. This was someone she did not know.

"Creed?" she asked, praying that she would at any moment wake up from this nightmare. In two strides he was beside her. The formerly assuring brown eyes that had attracted her when they had first met were now cold and steely, reminding her of Commando's eyes. She swallowed. "What are you going to do?" she whispered as her heart began thundering in her chest.

Alexis never saw it coming.

There was a vibrating sting as Creed slapped her face. Her mind went numb. She didn't even think to scream. She only reeled and staggered back. She could not comprehend what had just happened. Creed had lost his mind. Why? Oh, God, why? Looking up she could see him drawing his fist back, preparing to hit her again.

He was smiling.

"YOU'LL KILL her!" Skeddner shouted and rushed Commando. Watching the scene play out on the projector proved too much for him. Skeddner smashed into Commando spinning him away from the console. With a precise movement, Commando wrenched Skeddner's arm back at an awkward angle.

Pain shockwaved from Skeddner's elbow to his wrist. He knew it was broken. Unmasked rage radiated from Commando's hideously deformed face. The cyborg body-slammed Skeddner against the adjoining wall. Right arm dangling uselessly from his side, Skeddner moaned, sliding to his knees. "My girl!" he cried. "Please, please don't hurt my daughter!"

Commando towered over him. "I'll decide who gets hurt and who doesn't."

Skeddner steeled himself for the end. From the corner of his vision, he saw Whitefield fall upon the keyboard, inserting new information into the program. Across the glass, Creed halted his attack mid kick.

Still tapping, Whitefield called over his shoulder, "I still have need of him, Commando! It is impossible for me to run the program alone."

Commando fumed, then spat on Skeddner's upturned, entreating face.

Whitefield turned to an assistant. "Clark, issue a lock down in the tower until further instructions. Cancel all appointments, and tell the museum visitors that we are experiencing electrical difficulties. All visitors must be gone within the hour. And Commando, perhaps you should inform your employer that the initial MCC trial was successful."

Skeddner nursed his arm as best he could and wondered at Whitefield's intervention. Without a hint of doubt, Skeddner knew Whitefield could now run the entire system on his own.

CREED THREW himself headlong onto the small foldout cot and fell asleep almost immediately. Terrified, Alexis shuddered at the opposite side of the room. She did not know why Creed had stopped, but she was relieved and thankful. She crawled into her cot and leaned against the wall as far away from Creed as possible. She was too frightened to sleep, so she sat there with the blankets pulled tightly around her as though they might protect her from the berserk boy.

CHAPTER 24

Whitefield stood in the narrow, secret passage beneath the silver tower. It was difficult to believe that it had finally come down to this. His nimble fingers punched in the ten letter password on the computer keyboard. As the steel door of the hidden vault slid open, a nagging feeling crept up his chest. Was he doing the right thing?

The robot prototype skeleton was standing just inside. Whitefield pulled out the data capsule containing the digital blueprints for the cyborg's design. Whitefield had been accumulating parts for the cyborgs since the beginning. That was part of the agreement. All the pieces were here, just waiting to be assembled. It was only a simple matter of feeding the information from the capsule into the computers.

"Whitefield."

He spun at the sound of his name. Commando darkened the doorway. "Have you finished training the engineers?"

"Yes. You will have no shortage of qualified people to run the system."

"Good. The soldiers are scheduled to arrive in a few hours and Hulsane will arrive tomorrow morning. He expects the construction on the cyborgs to commence immediately."

"I thought as much."

Commando caught Whitefield by the arm. Whitefield shrank back. Commando could be very unpredictable. "Is it possible for me to have the remote link which controls the cyborg connected directly to my brain?"

"It is hypothetically possible. It would require the installation of a transmitter adaptor."

CREED AWOKE suddenly. What a dreadful dream. The images were still playing in his mind. For some strange reason he had been furious at Alexis.

Then he hit her.

Why had he dreamed something so disturbing? It was awful. He shook his head trying to clear away the thoughts, but they refused to leave. He could remember Alexis regarding him with concern, her eyebrows puckering into that thoughtful frown of hers. Then her expression changed to stunned shock. The last and worst mental picture was her face contorted in fear. Terror.

She was afraid of him. Why? The remembrances seemed ingrained on every fiber of his brain. They seemed so authentic. So real. He groaned and put his hand to his brow. The heat radiating from his forehead surprised him. His head was throbbing. He had been so distracted with the dream that he barely noticed where he was. Creed found himself staring at a blank gray wall inches from his face. He rolled over and sat up. Alexis was staring at him, eyes fearful and distraught. She looked exactly as she had in his dream—if it was a dream. Now he was not sure.

She sat huddled on her own cot across the room, hugging her knees close against her chest. She did not make a sound, only continued to stare. An awkward tension rippled between them. Creed could not take it any longer.

"Ok, Lex, tell me what's going on. Why are you looking at me like that?"

When she spoke, she did not answer his question. "How do you feel?"

"My head's on fire; otherwise, I feel fine. What of it?"

She frowned, eyebrows arching. "Are you positive?"

"Just tell me what's wrong."

"A few hours ago, you were acting like a lunatic."

Creed stiffened. "What did I do?"

"You screamed, banged the walls, then . . . then you attacked me."

Confused, Creed stood and took a step toward her. Was she lying? But why would she lie?

"Lex, you know I would never hurt you. I don't know what happened—"

"Stop!" she shouted, and scurried to the farthest corner of the cot. "Don't come any closer. You can talk from your bed."

With a sickening heart, Creed sank back onto the bed. His feelings must have risen to his face, because Alexis added more gently. "I think Whitefield and Commando did something to you last night, drugged you maybe. Don't you remember anything?"

Searching the dark recesses of his memory, Creed stared at the ceiling. "They mentioned MCC several times, but I have no idea what it means."

Alexis ran her fingers nervously over the cot sheets. "Or they might be tricking us, playing a game with our minds."

Her words resonated like a dong in his head. Everything fell into place with stunning, painful clarity.

MCC—mind control chip.

Of course! What a dunce he had been not to realize it before. That would explain everything. This was the secret 'weapon'. This was the evil which was embodied in that small titanium capsule. Having lain dormant for fifteen years, it now matured into a frightening reality.

Mind control.

The severity of the situation almost smothered him. He wanted to crawl into a corner. He wanted to sleep and not wake up. His mind was in Commando's hand. Or Whitefield's. He still wasn't sure where the man stood. How would he know whether he was dreaming or being controlled? Skeddner was right. The thing should have been destroyed.

He took a deep breath. "I think MCC stands for Mind Control Chip."

Alexis wilted. "Oh, God . . . no."

"My father was Adam Rolls."

She looked at him quizzically, not comprehending the significance of the name.

Creed raked his fingers recklessly through his shorn hair. "Adam Rolls, don't you remember? He wrote the information on that data capsule."

Alexis caught her breath. "He was your father? But how . . . I thought . . . "

Sighing wearily, Creed fell back down on the bed and stared listlessly at the ceiling. "Yes. He must have sent the capsule to my mother that would explain everything—well not everything, but enough. Why did she keep so many secrets from me?"

Alexis frowned, "How long have you known that Dr. Rolls was your father?"

"Commando told me just before they knocked me out. Why?"

She almost laughed, "And you believe everything that monster says?"

Creed scowled. "You think I want to believe something that . . . awful? Anyway, Dr. Skeddner confirmed that it's true. I'm scared, Lex. I don't even have control over my own body. How am I supposed to fight back?"

Alexis sidled closer to him and touched his cheek, pulling his face toward her.

"But you have a spirit, Creed. No matter what they do to your brain, they have no power over your spirit."

A MASSIVE freight carrier was docking next to the silver tower. Ramps were lowered from the ship and rectangular boxes were wheeled down, disappearing inside one of the many access ways built into the silver tower.

Commando stood in an enormous, walk-in freezer as the final boxes were wheeled in. The ship was completely unloaded, and not one sailor knew what they had transported across the Pacific.

As it should be.

The boxes were shaped suspiciously like coffins. Around him other boxes were stacked, brushing the ceiling. There were exactly two thousand boxes. The loud whistle pierced the air as the freighter announced its departure. Commando shut the door as the last one was deposited carefully inside. "We must check to make sure none are damaged."

He removed the lid. Inside, lay a man. Eyelids closed as if in sleep, the African-American face was cold.

"Is he dead?" Whitefield questioned softly.

Commando touched the man with his flesh hand. He could feel the slightest pump of pressure. "He lives. The doctors said the hibernation should last for two more days, three at the most. But we need to inject nutrients into the blood stream to keep them healthy. I want them fully functional when we wake them."

Cautiously, the cybernetics engineer reached into the box and touched a necklace which dangled loosely around the man's neck, an army tag. "Lieutenant Trevor Grayson," he read aloud. "How did your associates acquire these soldiers?"

"Let's just say I am a very influential man. I scoured military hospitals. We won't have to train these soldiers how to fight or take orders. Here are your killer minds."

CHAPTER 25

A Sikorsky S-76 Spirit circled twice around the silver tower before touching down on the tower's circular helipad. Two men jumped out of the private helicopter. They were burly with clean-shaven faces, wearing loose-fitting combat clothes.

Hulsane emerged from the helicopter. He was slightly hunched over. A dark cloud of evil clung to him like a cloak. His two black eyes sat close together in his strong angular face. They scrutinized the island only a half-mile away, admiring the white sandy shores, tall palm trees, and rich jungle.

His nose was long, and it flared sharply as he took a long sniff of the clear air. The cool air felt good on his face and shaved head. Yes, he liked this place. Much different from the cold, snowy regions of his own homeland. Much better. He had received word from Sklade that the mind control device had been a stunning success. In his left hand, he carried a long gray cane which he used to steady himself on the steps. The cane had a beautiful ivory handle embellished with small green gem stones. He moved as if he had to force his body to obey his mind, and yet, he could not have been older than forty-five. His body was young, but fragile. Two more men walked closely behind perhaps to catch him if he fell. The five men scanned the empty landing pad as if expecting someone.

"Dimitri, where is Sklade?" When Hulsane spoke there was no doubt or insecurity, only a dominating authority that commanded immediate obedience. The voice did not seem to fit the frail body emitting it. When he spoke his lips barely moved at all which added to the strange affect.

One of the men, Dimitri, answered in a gruff undertone. "Sklade said he would meet us here, sir. Wait, I believe that might be him." He pointed to a lone figure that was making his way toward them. He had blond hair and a pale face. He wore long black gloves. The four guards reached for the handguns hidden under their jackets. This was not Sklade Browning. The blond haired man came closer. Dimitri called out to him, "Who are you?"

"I'm Sklade Browning. Don't you recognize me?"

"It's a trick," Hulsane said. "Kill him."

Dimitri whipped out his gun and fired twice into the man's chest. The bullets bounced off his chest. Unable to conceal his smug smile, the man opened his jacket revealing the chrome alloy chest. "I told you I had been injured and repaired handsomely."

"Impossible . . . " Hulsane muttered. This was indeed a surprise. True, he knew Whitefield had made great progress with the robots—but this! He had never imagined such a thing was feasible. It was something out of a science fiction movie. With an army like this, anything was possible.

"Sklade, you must take me into the laboratory. I will enjoy this visit."

COMMANDO WATCHED impassively as Creed snarled and lunged forward. The boy was yanked back by iron chains which shackled him to the wall. Just out of range Commando stood, arms folded across his chest, silently goading him. Creed wanted to kill him and knew Commando envisioned the same fate for him. He strained forward. The blue eyes were inches from his own.

They were in an expansive room which Whitefield called the Exhibiting Dome. Near the opposing wall, Hulsane sat reclining on a wide couch which had been brought to the room especially for him. Creed disliked him on sight. He was the real boss here. Creed understood that now. Commando and Whitefield were mere pawns which he manipulated to achieve his warped purposes. Hulsane watched Creed with great interest, like a rare animal on display. A powerful supercomputer hummed beside him.

Whitefield continued with his explanation. "And your hibernation drug will render them docile, in a semi-dream state—unlike this boy."

Hulsane nodded his appreciation. Whitefield had rambled for the greater part of an hour describing the intricacies of the complex computer system which linked to the tiny silicon chip attached to Creed's cerebellum.

Although most of the technical terminology and phrases were difficult to grasp, there was one solid fact that Creed couldn't escape. His brain was no longer his own. He felt violated. Nausea churned in his stomach.

Whitefield concluded, "As a final failsafe measure, each chip is also equipped with a tiny explosive which, when activated from the computer, will destroy the brain, killing the cyborg. This unique chip in conjunction with the incredible human mind and my robots, which you have already viewed, will give you a most powerful army unlike any other."

"Yes, this is good," Hulsane chuckled, his lips crinkling into a disturbing smile. "Very good."

"Then I take it that my daughter and I are free to go?"

Hulsane appeared not to hear him. "Well done, Sklade. I believe the time has come. I've waited thirty-five years for this moment ever since as a helpless child, I watched my parents gunned down by those self-righteous, bloodthirsty American soldiers." His eyes darkened with loathing. "Well, I'm not helpless anymore. Sklade, I need anyone and everyone who was directly or indirectly involved to be removed. I'm sorry but that includes you, Dr. Whitefield."

"Excuse me?"

"You've done all I asked, but now you're just a bit too dangerous to be kept alive."

Whitefield paled. With sickening anticipation, Commando leveled his Sig 226P in line with Whitefield's head. Creed strained on his chains. Whitefield was his only possible ally among this crew of cyborgs and murderers. He did not want to see this man killed. Licking his lips with fear, Whitefield groaned.

"I'm afraid I don't understand," he lied, eyeing the weapon carefully. Commando's disfigured face twisted into a thin smile. He was lingering, savoring the moment.

Hulsane chuckled ruthlessly. "Oh, I think you do."

Whitefield blinked, clearly ransacking his brain for any inkling of an idea that might save his life. "But what if there is a malfunction with the cyborgs? What will you do then? Nobody knows my cyborgs the way I do."

Rubbing a green jewel imbedded in his cane handle, Hulsane nodded, his face softening. "Delay a moment, Sklade. I believe his proposition should be considered."

Commando spat, lowering the gun. Hulsane seemed to ignore Commando's reaction, "We won't exterminate Dr.Whitefield yet. Secure him in one of the inner offices and leave a contingent to guard the door."

"As you wish, sir," Commando said stiffly. "Trex, get the boy and lock him up."

Hulsane stood, his action mimicked by his bodyguards. "And I will go see the progress of my cyborgs."

"DISREGARD ALL secrecy and concentrate on speed," Hulsane ordered. The silver tower was not accustomed to mass production of cyborgs. But it was certainly capable. This was the very reason he had authorized its construction more than ten years ago. Mechanics and technicians scurried around the sophisticated equipment.

The emerald studded cane clinked on the hard steel floor as Hulsane walked down long aisles between the assembly lines. Giant pistons pumped and roared around him. A thousand electric motors powered the massive machinery. The coffin-like boxes were ripped open and men were placed on the conveyer belt. Some were missing arms and legs. But that was of no consequence. Only their brains, vital organs, and souls would be used. The human organs would be implanted into robots, transforming them from men to cyborgs.

Staring up from the conveyer belt with sightless eyes was an uncompleted cyborg. Hulsane could see the chest rise and fall in slow, level breaths. Inside the chest, a motorized pump worked the heart and lungs.

Hulsane watched in fiendish delight as a mechanical arm pivoted 180 degrees, clutching a robotic leg in its claw. The silver leg shell was bolted to the cyborg's torso. With repetitive precision another arm reached over equipped with a welding torch. The man's face lit vivid orange as hot sparks crackled from the silver metal like miniature fireworks. Cyborg after cyborg moved systematically along the belts gaining parts as they went.

At the end of the line, the cyborg was pulled to a standing position. Silver plated armor was clamped onto the body covering the network of motors and wires. All traces of the human inside were gone.

A wicked smile creased the man's shallow cheeks as he studied the small United States emblem imprinted on each chest plate. So ironic. This entire operation functioning right under their snotty little noses. All of his predecessors—rest their souls—were only wanting in their strategy. His plan was flawless. What could be better then letting the Americans build their own destruction? One bolt at a time. These hybrids were superior to humans in every way.

He was only improving on God's design.

Hulsane squinted as each cyborg completed the cycle, sliding off the belt into neat rows—row upon row, line upon line. An army. Whitefield had certainly done his research. And Adam Rolls had been blessed with the mind of a genius—a mind destined to control other minds.

The cyborgs would be unstoppable on the battlefield. Hulsane laughed out loud. A battle! There would be no battle, only a silent, fearful death. The cyborgs were sedated in hibernation. But this sleep was monitored and they could be awakened at the touch of a button.

DR. WHITEFIELD STUMBLED as Commando hurried him down the hallway. Commando hauled him up with unnecessary roughness, pinching his shoulder cruelly.

"Get up, you clumsy ox."

He propelled Whitefield into an office room with such ferocity that Whitefield found himself on his hands and knees. Slamming the door shut, Commando locked it carefully and returned the key to his pocket. He turned to the guards. "Stay here and don't let him out."

Although he still longed for the time when he could kill Whitefield, Sklade Browning was satisfied with the day's work. The remaining damper on his day was the fact that Creed was still alive and relatively undamaged. He flexed the mechanical arm fused to his shoulder. Well, that could easily be mended. His phone vibrated. "Yes?"

"Commando," came Hulsane's voice. "I am preparing to launch my army. Come to the exhibiting dome. Immediately."

Creed would have to wait.

"WAKE MY soldiers."

Hulsane's tone oozed with anticipation as he spoke into his earpiece, which kept him in contact with the technicians and engineers behind the glass wall in the main control room. Hulsane stood on the edge of a massive chamber. One thousand completed cyborgs stood rigid before him. All were facing straight ahead in perfect line.

All were built to kill.

They were slightly larger than humans. Their faces resembled skulls. A hard alloy plating covered their bodies, fitting them like a suit of armor. Each carried a deadly, closed bolt submachine gun with a retractable stock—a weapon capable of firing 1000 rounds-per-minute. Additional thirty-round magazines hung on utility belts strapped to their waists.

Upstairs, the head technician punched a series of commands into the supercomputer.

The silver tower stood like a colossal lighthouse in the middle of the sea. Miles of blue waves stretched in every direction. A motor hummed from the apex of the structure. A spring latch flipped open from the wide chrome surface. A long, thick antenna rose from the tallest pinnacle of the tower. The powerful antenna boosted a signal transmitted to an orbiting satellite capable of reaching the farthest corners of the globe.

Hulsane smiled.

CHAPTER 26

The central control hub was built and designed for a sole purpose: operating the ten thousand cyborgs. Hundreds of supercomputers were mounted in racks. Commando scanned the thousand mini-screens which would display what the cyborgs saw once they were activated. He let his imagination run wild.

A large flat screen displayed the major news stations. On CNN an anchorman described the cloudy weather conditions in Los Angeles. If they only knew what was about to happen, the weather would be the least of their worries. In a few hours the world would awake to an unpleasant surprise. And Commando wanted to see it.

Commando wove between the technicians and computers on his way to the exhibiting dome. He had removed the synthetic skin around his face—a living robot skeleton with bits of human flesh, wearing trousers, combat boots and a brown leather jacket.

A few technicians swallowed as Commando stalked past, an uncustomary restlessness in his step. He had checked and rechecked the tower's security systems. Everything was on schedule, but he could not crush the nagging feeling that something was wrong. Maybe it was Creed. Yes, Creed was wrong. But soon he would be dead and it would not matter. Commando would take great pleasure in that.

As the cyborg passed, he glanced out at the thick floor-to-ceiling window. Eight hundred feet below, the ocean tossed and turned. From the east, dark, cumulonimbus clouds came riding on a southwest wind. A storm was brewing. Commando frowned. Hulsane should have chosen a different day to launch the cyborgs.

He voiced his observation to one of the technicians. "If those clouds break, won't that effect the transmitters?"

The man shrugged unconcernedly. "It should be fine. It is strange though. I don't know where they came from; the satellite cameras predicted a clear day."

Commando pushed open the security door to the exhibiting dome and joined Hulsane at the platform. Behind him the head technician pressed a master button.

With eerie unison the dull cyborg eyes lit up to a frigid blue. As one machine and one mind, they came to life. Their chrome faces produced no emotion, but their confusion was obvious by the way they searched their surroundings and stared strangely at their metal limbs. Gripping his emerald tipped cane tighter with excitement, Hulsane stood.

Commando knew what was going on behind those impassive faces. Behind the gears, wires, and electrodes, a human brain pulsated, a human soul existed.

The hibernation drugs had not completely worn off. Hulsane did not want them to. The drugs would help keep the minds in a dream, discouraging any thoughts of their past lives. They would believe anything in a dream.

LIFE RETURNED to Lieutenant Mark Grayson. He could not remember how long he had been unconscious. Even now, he was unsure if he was actually awake. The last thing he remembered was passing out on the battlefield with a bullet in his thigh. His surroundings blinked into focus. He was standing in a sea of machines.

Grayson glanced down at himself. His body was encased with silver armor. In the back of his mind he knew there was something horribly wrong with him. There was no pain in his leg. This had to be a dream. He raised his hand. He could hear an odd, mechanical humming. His body moved with ease. The sun glinted off his armor, sending white flames dancing over him. Somehow he had been inserted into a robot body.

Two men were standing before him on a raised platform. One was disfigured. Half of his body was reconstructed from robotic equivalents. The other leaned heavily on a cane. His thick accent carried to the farthest corners of the chamber. "I know you must be confused. You have been drugged and I, Hulsane, have just awakened you. Let me bring you up to date on the nation's events. America is involved in a civil war and you have a chance to save it. You are her soldiers and you will fight for your country."

Grayson was having difficulty processing this. Had he been fighting in a civil war? He could not remember.

The half-man, half-robot caressed the automatic at his side. "Permission to kill the boy and girl, sir?"

"Granted," Hulsane said. His face was glowing in the blue light. "Yes, we will kill them all. Every last one."

TROY DID not know how long he had been crying. But he did know that tears would not solve his problems. He had to figure out what to do. Except for the occasional guard or technician, the museum seemed abandoned as Troy wandered through the robot exhibits. All visitors had been hustled out under the assumption that there was an electrical fire. But Troy wasn't fooled. The facade was being dropped. The truth was finally rising to the surface.

He couldn't call for help and he couldn't get out. How was he supposed to find Creed and Alexis? Troy ducked away as a security camera swivelled in his direction. It was all over if anybody spotted him. And then an idea popped into his head. He could not believe he had not thought of it sooner.

Okay, he had to figure this out. Focus. Only a few minutes ago, he had passed a door marked security personnel only. Carefully, he backtracked until he found the door. Now, how to get in? To his relief, the question was solved when the door swung open. Troy hid behind the door, almost getting smashed into the wall.

Hyndrix stepped out, his rifle hanging on his shoulder. Holding his breath, Troy waited for the him to move away and then slipped inside just before the door shut. Too late, Troy thought about the possibility of other guards in the room. But he was already committed.

There was another guard at the instrument panels, but fortunately his back was toward Troy. Afraid to even breathe for fear of being heard, Troy scanned the screens quickly. One showed Creed being marched down a corridor by an armed escort.

He felt elated knowing that his idea had actually worked. Okay great, he found Creed, but how was he supposed to free him? The uniformed guard at the desk yawned, stretched in his chair, then pulled off his hat to scratch his head. Troy could not tear his gaze off the man's gun buckled to his side. He gulped.

If Creed were here, the guard would already be knocked out, gagged, and shoved in some locker. But of course, he was not. Troy was on his own.

He looked around for something to hit the guard with. The only thing readily accessible was a chair. Troy wondered if he could lift it and swing it hard enough.

The guard groaned and flopped over when Troy hit him with his improvised club.

Troy locked the door and then slid into the chair. He flipped through the different security cameras. He wiped his sweaty fingers on his pants and reached for the computer keyboard.

"What are you doing?"

Troy almost had a heart attack as he fell out of the chair. He was caught. Slowly, he got to his feet and then blushed when he realized the voice had come from a radio. Troy picked up the guard's radio, the shaky sketches of an idea forming in his head. He had to find the frequency that Creed's captors were using. He hoped Creed would catch on. If he could get Creed out, the rest would be easy.

A thud came from the door. He jumped. Somebody was trying to open it. "Hey, Abdul, are you in there? Unlock the door."

Troy looked down at the guard on the floor. This was bad. Should he try to imitate the guard's voice and answer back? No that would not work.

The banging continued. If Troy did not do something the guy was going to break down the door.

HYNDRIX BANGED harder on the door. "Open up!" He had already tried his key. Abdul must have thrown the bolt. But why? Hyndrix was lifting his phone to call the head of security, when he heard the electronic locks click open. Angry, and slightly leery, he marched in. He could see Abdul's back, where he was hunched painfully in his chair, clutching his stomach and groaning. His hat had slipped down over his face and his forehead nearly touched the desk.

Hyndrix poked his shoulder. "Abdul?"

"I'm sick . . ."

Although Hyndrix was not a sympathetic person by any measure, he could see that the guy was in some serious pain. "Here let me help—Arrrg!"

Abdul spun around, swinging a pipe he had been hiding under his jacket uniform. Of course when Hyndrix realized that it was Troy, not Abdul, in the chair, there was not much he could do about it. The pipe rammed into his stomach. Hyndrix doubled over.

Troy grinned. "I got better."

FOR A full ten minutes, Dr. Whitefield did not even attempt to pick himself off the cold floor. Contemplating his position, he now regretted everything he had done. He should have known that Hulsane would not keep his end of the deal. He was such a blind fool. He moaned aloud.

"Daddy?"

Rachel was standing there. She approached timidly from a dark corner. He held out his arms, desperate for her forgiveness. "I'm so sorry."

"I know."

Eventually, when they let each other go, he discovered that Dr. Skeddner and Alexis were crouched on the other end of the room staring at them with silent accusation. They had been in the room the entire time. Whitefield averted his eyes. He could not face them.

"I hope you're satisfied with yourself, Faulkner," Skeddner said at length. "You've succeeded in unleashing the very nightmare Adam and I wanted to prevent."

"Skeddner, they forced me to do this. I had no choice," Whitefield said, almost pleading. "Commando had bugs everywhere and all the security guards are actually here to keep an eye on me. He was holding my girl hostage."

"You're a despicable man."

"No, Skeddner, I'm desperate, as are you."

"I still hardly believe that you did it. All this double dealing, sneaking, and lies."

"Listen to me, Skeddner. I did it for Rachel. Maybe it was not the best decision, but she was in critical condition, man, dying! My little girl dying right in my arms." His lips trembled as they formed the words. Tears pooled in his green eyes. "What would you have had me do? Sklade offered me a proposition and I had no choice but to accept. You would have done the same thing for Alexis."

"Why didn't you ask me for help?"

"Maybe you don't remember, but we were not on the best of terms. In fact, I had precious few friends. The only man who offered to help me was Sklade Browning."

HIGH ABOVE the cyborg manufacturing room, Creed was marched past a window overlooking the construction. Hundreds of Commandos.

This horror was made possible by his father's mistake.

Creed's hands were cuffed behind his back. He could hear the breathing and footsteps of his six escorts including Trex, two in front, four behind. Creed did not care for the odds. The guards were very cautious and would not come close enough for him to even consider disarming them. Sure he could try, but Trex was probably praying for an excuse to kill him.

What good was he to them anyway? Once they locked him in a cell, the chances of him escaping were slim. Maybe he should try. After all, what did he have to lose? The answer came quickly. Everything.

Suddenly, Trex's radio sputtered. "They're coming! There's an emergency on level three! There are cops down here. We need everyone to get down here right now."

Creed suppressed a grin. He immediately recognized Troy's voice. The guards glanced around uneasily, shifting their guns. A flash of panic blinked over Trex. "Cops? In the tower? How?"

Trex pushed one the guards forward. "All of you go figure out what's going on. I'll take him the rest of the way."

The other guards raced off, leaving Creed alone with Trex and one guard. The odds had just improved. Trex glared at Creed as though reading his mind. "Don't try anything stupid."

His radio barked. "You're a dead man, Trex!"

Trex looked stunned. Then the fire sprinklers suddenly flicked on followed by a pounding alarm causing him to jump. The odds couldn't get much better. Creed flew into action.

He put his elbow in the Trex's face. He kicked, punched, and head-butted like a furious animal until both of his guards lay slumped in the hall.

The alarms and sprinklers shut off.

Awkwardly, he kneeled and patted down the man's pockets until he located the handcuff key. Within seconds, he had freed himself. Troy's voice came through the radio. "Creed! Are you alright?"

Creed grabbed the radio and broke into a sprint. "Troy! That was incredible!"

"Well . . . thanks. But you need to hurry, somebody is coming down the hall."

Creed ran, gun cocked and fully loaded, radio pressed to his ear. "Do you know where they took Lex?"

"They're not far from you. Go left at the next corridor."

With Troy feeding him directions, Creed dodged security guards and navigated the maze of the tower. Troy's voice sputtered from the radio. "Four doors down on your right."

Creed found the door.

"I might be able to unlock the door from here." Troy said, "Hold on a sec."

The lock sprang open. Creed ducked inside to find Alexis, Dr. Skeddner, Rachel, and Whitefield, surprise stamped on their faces.

COMMANDO RESISTED the urge to grind Trex's face into the tiled floor where he lay sprawled in the middle of the corridor. There had been no need to enter the office where Creed was supposed to be detained. The unconscious body of Trex told him everything—namely that Creed was no longer in his custody. He stopped. No . . . the boy was still in his hand. He had Creed's mind.

CHAPTER 27

Taking a firm grip on the locker handle, Creed pulled. With a groan, the door rolled up and he saw two dozen repeating rifles and handguns. Long belts of ammunition lay piled underneath the gun racks.

Whitefield slid an odd looking black cartridge out of a magazine. "As they perfected the nearly indestructible metal for the cyborgs, they also discovered the substance that dissolves it. I thought it might be a good idea to stockpile some."

Slinging a rifle across his shoulder, Creed strapped on extra magazines and passed some to Dr. Skeddner. "Take as many as you can carry."

Everyone armed themselves with guns, including Rachel, Alexis, and Troy.

Any notions of escape were rapidly drifting away. The tower felt like a vice that was slowly tightening, squeezing away Creed's life.

Whitefield looked directly at him. "Time is of the gravest importance. I expect they will launch the cyborgs within the hour, if they haven't begun already. What is your plan?"

Creed had no plan.

They were all looking at him, waiting for him to speak, waiting for the idea that would save them. "What's the best way out?"

"There are helicopters in the hangar bay, level 4-C, and speed boats on the water level. But I fear running will be useless; security has already been alerted to our escape."

"I need you to lead them out."

"Why? I don't—"

"Just do it! Do you have a phone?"

The man drew a phone from his pocket. "Here. It will operate with other selected phones as a radio unit within a two-mile radius, but security personnel monitor all calls. I imagine that they've already severed all communication with the outside world."

"Okay, where is the command center for the robots?"

"On level 14. But it's heavily guarded. There's no chance of getting inside."

"Don't they have an emergency system override?" Troy asked.

Whitefield nodded thoughtfully, "There is an override system you could access on level 16. But there are heavy firewalls, passcodes and access procedures on all the computer bays. Its not as simple as flipping the off switch."

"What are the passcodes?"

"Only Commando and Hulsane know the codes. They never trusted me with that information."

Skeddner offered a suggestion. "When your father designed the original control system he built a backdoor into the program after he realized that the backers of the project had less than scrupulous motives. I think we can still access it."

Creed turned away. "You lead them out. I'm going to stop Commando."

Alexis grabbed his arm. "Creed, you can't go in there. They'll kill you."

"I need to—" a tingle of electricity enveloped his brain. Creed groaned. Not now.

Stay right where you are.

The high-powered radio frequency had just made contact with his MCC, the small silicon chip attached to his cerebellum. The thought was spontaneous. But he knew it was not his own. A foreign agent was tampering in his mind. It was so insistent, so relentless that it was drowning out his sense of reason.

"He's coming . . . " he said shakily. The suggestion was taking over.

Troy frowned. "Who is?"

But Creed did not answer. He stood frozen in a trance. Alexis shook him. Fear poured from her eyes. "Creed, you have to fight it!"

She seemed a mile away and he barely heard her.

You can't fight me.

It was a voice, a presence, penetrating his very mind.

"Run," Creed whispered. "Run!"

They turned and fled. Creed heard the soft hiss of pneumatics, the clink of metal upon metal. Commando stepped out of the adjoining hallway.

He wore no mask, and for the first time Creed saw his horribly maimed face twisted in rage. He wore no shirt, displaying a jagged scar running from his temple across his face and down to his waist where his flesh fused to robotic counterparts. He looked like he had been cut in half and had half a robot surgically attached to him. Behind him, more cyborgs ran up, guns leveled.

And then everyone was running, shooting, and screaming. Creed was swept up in the mad rush.

Stop running.

With an great effort Creed pushed the thought from his mind. A service door appeared on the right.

"On the other side of the docking bay door is a helicopter!" Whitefield shouted at Dr. Skeddner. "Rachel can fly it. Get through that door. I'll hold them off!"

He opened fire at the oncoming cyborgs. Creed was fighting to take a single step. Dr. Skeddner pushed the girls through. Troy tore in after them.

"Creed, get in!" Skeddner yelled.

The only two left in the hall were Skeddner and Whitefield. They stood shoulder to shoulder, shooting up a storm. Whitefield crouched in the hall, "Skeddner, go. I'll hold them off!"

Skeddner dove inside, just as the cyborgs sprayed the hall. Whitefield screamed as a seam of slugs was stitched across his chest. He was dead before he hit the ground.

Troy dragged a crying and screaming Rachel back, as she tried to get to her father. Creed threw all his lean 160 pounds against the steel door, desperately trying to force the hydraulics to close faster. A stream of bullets snaked by leaving smoking holes in the opposite wall. As soon as the door lined up with the door jam, Troy pushed the control panel and the dead bolts slid into place, locking the door securely. They could only pray that it was bulletproof.

Creed sucked in a greedy gulp of air. His breath was coming in gasps. He was not sure if it was the mad dash or the fear, probably a combination of both. Whitefield's death was shocking, even for Creed. Rachel had dissolved into tears. Alexis pulled her into a hug.

"You think it's gonna hold?" Troy panted.

Alexis bit her lip. "A better question would be, how long will it hold. It's going to take a lot more than a door to stop that monster."

Creed directed his attention to the opposing door emblazoned with the words *Docking Hangar*. He tried the handle, but the door refused to open.

A scream from Alexis caused Creed to whirl around. Dr. Skeddner had stumbled awkwardly to his knees. Alexis dropped to his side, panic manifesting in every part of her being. "Father! Talk to me. What's wrong?"

Breathing heavily, his face twisted, Isaac Skeddner could only gasp in reply. Then Creed noticed the growing dark stain on the man's jacket. There was a burning crimson hole in his side. Kneeling, Creed helped Alexis ease the man onto his back. He felt sick. A cursory glance was all he needed. The wound looked mortal.

Alexis cradled her father's head in her arms. "Creed, please save him!"

Her eyes locked with his. The pain, horror, and fear he read in them punctured his soul, but he knew he was helpless to intercede.

The man's face contorted with pain. His once strong voice cracked like a bad connection.

"Get out of here . . . "

"I won't go without you," Alexis answered with pained stubbornness.

"Darling, I'll only slow you down."

Uselessness and failure rose up in Creed's chest. Alexis buried her face in her father's shirt, tears threatening, but she hadn't given up. "Don't say that, Father! You can't leave me! If you go, then . . . I will go also."

Creed was not sure if she was trying to threaten Dr. Skeddner or simply expressing a truth. Dr. Skeddner half rose. "No!" he ordered, then he fell back. The effort had taxed the last reserves of his strength. Alexis, who had bravely held back her tears, began to weep. Creed could do nothing.

The man's voice softened as he saw the agony and distress in his daughter's face. "Oh, darling I am so sorry for everything . . . "

Alexis took her father's hand in hers and lifted it to her lips. Her voice cracked. "It is past, Father. All is forgiven."

Skeddner's eyes drifted past Alexis to settle on Creed. "My son," he gasped, "know that I loved Oasis. I loved your mother. I pray that you will learn from our foolish quarrel. I'm proud to call you my grandson. And don't hate your father, just forgive. He had good intentions. He just made some mistakes."

He looked over at his daughter and trailed his fingers through her long black hair. The door shuddered. "Alexis, go!"

"Not without you . . . "

"Alexis, I'm dying."

Alexis only shook her head, and tried to pull Skeddner to his feet. Her father pushed away her efforts.

"Darling, you've got to live. Creed, get her out of here! Tell me you'll get her out."

"Yes, sir, I will."

With a sigh, the doctor lay back in her arms, as if a heavy load had been lifted from his chest. "I am proud of you both."

Creed held back his tears. A tremendous clatter sounded from the opposite side of the door. Gently but firmly, Creed drew Alexis to her feet, prying her slender fingers from her father's jacket. Tears flowed down her cheeks unchecked. "I'm dying," she said softly. Her words sent a chill through him. He knew she had a habit of speaking in poetry, but this . . .

"Where do we go?" Troy asked, fear almost stifling his voice. As if to accentuate his words, a crash sounded on the opposite side of the door. The cyborgs were hurling themselves against it. It would not be long now.

THE DOOR was shattered by an eruption of flame and smoke. Grenades had been detonated around the doorjamb. It disintegrated in a matter of seconds. The cyborgs charged through the fumes, each one fully armed and ready for action, the unmistakable sound of their metallic feet clanking against the steel floor.

Commando stood out in front, gun extended. His gaze darkened as he performed a quick scan of the room.

"You can't hide from me, boy," he muttered.

Underneath some tool carts and bins, Alexis sobbed silently pressing her face against Creed's shoulder. Creed put a finger to his lips. Skeddner's body was propped between Alexis and Rachel. Creed was unsure if the man was still breathing. Alexis's tears saturated Creed's shirt and chilled his skin. He wanted to comfort her, hold her, tell her everything was going to be all right, but he resorted to just squeezing her hand. He could not afford to stray a single ounce of focus from Commando.

The cyborg's legs were visible. One was made of flesh and bone, but the other was constructed of chrome plates and motors. He had stopped within two feet of their hiding place. If Creed reached out, he could have touched him. Beyond Commando and through the docking bay door, Creed knew he would find the sweeping propellers of a helicopter, as Whitefield had said. The only problem, of course, was getting past Commando.

He considered jumping out and attacking Commando, which might give the others enough time to reach the aircraft. But that would still leave the two other cyborgs, who were watching their commander with unblinking blue eyes, their automatic weapons held carefully at the ready. A grin was forming on Commando's face, something far worse than any grimace or glare.

Come to Commando.

Creed felt the order in his mind. The compulsion was too great and he suddenly found himself standing out in the open. It happened so quickly. Only Alexis had time to even realize what was happening. She tried to grab his arm but he only shrugged her away. One moment he was hiding and the next he was face to face with Commando.

The two cyborg soldiers knocked aside the rolling bins.

Alexis looked at them in a daze. Creed reacted swiftly. He snatched up his gun but the cyborg grabbed his wrist and twisted it from his grasp.

Stop fighting.

Creed felt like he was moving in molasses. His muscles refused to function. He did not want to die like this. But he especially did not want Alexis to die like this. He scowled up at Commando.

"What are you going to do?"

"Take a guess." Commando slid out his semi-automatic pistol. "Any last words?"

As one, the cyborgs leveled their weapons. Creed stared at them, running through his options and preparing a last ditch escape attempt. But if there was no escape, then he was certainly going to take out Commando. If he was going to go, then Commando was going remember it. Then to his surprise, Rachel spoke.

"You can't do this . . . "

"Ah, but I am."

"God will judge you, *robot*."

"I never did like you," Commando said calmly, and fired three rounds through her chest. The force of bullets blasted Rachel across the room. The hot lead ripped the flesh from her—yet there was no blood. Creed watched the unthinkable in muted shock.

Rachel was a chrome FX-6 cyborg, just like Commando.

Alexis and Troy stared, slack-jawed.

Commando's mouth fell agape. He looked ready to explode. Rachel stood at the center of everyone's gaze, the light reflecting off her chrome casing that still had bits of artificial flesh clinging to it. Only her face was flesh and blood. She hurled herself at the still stunned Commando.

CHAPTER 28

Rachel's slight edge of surprise did not last long.

She crashed through a stack of crates and tool racks as Commando knocked her away. She moaned. She had forgotten to switch off the feeling sensors in her body. She wondered if the metal back plates were broken. He would kill her just like he did her father. In all her years of knowing Commando, she had never imagined confronting him. But now she had.

Commando was already up, standing over her. "Daddy's no longer around to piece your miserable body back together."

He yanked Rachel off her feet and flung her as though she were a toy. She slammed into more crates. This time she had the presence of mind to lower her sensors, so the shock was not as bad as before. But she knew that this fight was already over. She had no chance against Commando.

With another great bound he was upon her. The tiny optic fibers carried information back and forth between the human brain and the robotic limbs approaching the speed of light. The hydraulic powered arm flew through the air like an armored bullet train. Rachel reeled, taking the blow to her shoulder.

She was outmatched at every turn.

EVEN THOUGH Creed was shocked by the revelation that Rachel was a cyborg, he took full advantage of her unexpected attack. Spinning on his heel, he broke the cyborg's grip on his arm and used the cyborg as a shield against the automatic fire from the other cyborg.

Bullets ricocheted. Creed wrenched his gun from the cyborg's hand and shot it through the heart, hoping that Whitefield was right about the bullet's ability to penetrate the cyborg's casing.

The bullet burned through the plated armor like acid. Groaning, the cyborg clawed at his sizzling chest, then fell over. Creed spun, shooting the other cyborg who crumbled and clattered to the floor, a smoking ruin.

Troy fired several shots through the docking bay door, and then kicked it open. The private helicopter was like a gift from heaven. No one had to be told to board. As one person, they rushed to the hatch.

Creed flipped the control switch, activating the dome mechanism. As the two massive ceiling slabs parted, a blinding ray of sunlight streamed through. Freedom waited in the sky above. The cold, salty sea air whisked its way inside the silver tower. Outside, far below, the Pacific rolled and rippled like a giant blanket flapping in the breeze.

Alexis crawled to her father and grabbed his shoulder trying to drag his body toward the copter. Creed could only hope he was still alive.

"Creed, help me!"

He came to her aid. Gathering all his strength, he hefted Dr. Skeddner up over his shoulder. With a desperate heave, he shoved Skeddner into the cabin. Alexis jumped in. He yelled after her, "You've got to get the engines started!"

Now for Rachel.

Besides the battling combatants, Commando and Rachel, there were no other cyborgs in the hangar bay. Creed was poised with his finger tensed on the trigger, waiting for an opening without risk of maiming or killing Rachel. Commando seemed to sense his hesitation and fought in tight. The girl was not going to survive those swinging uppercuts long, even if she was half robot.

She had taken a savage beating. Commando was ready to end it. Creed had to take a chance. He fired.

But Commando was ready. The projectile sank into his cybernetic forearm as he blocked it from his flesh and vital organs. Yet the distraction gave Rachel a chance to escape—and she took it. She ran for the helicopter. Creed pulled off another series of rounds at Commando who ducked behind some crates.

A bullet screamed past Creed's face. More cyborg reinforcements. Creed hit the floor, sliding for cover behind a pile of tools carts. Hands shaking, Troy sat in the cockpit hatchway maintaining an unwavering current of fire on the door, keeping the cyborgs at bay. The crossfire was intense, but Creed had no choice.

He raced across the open deck, firing as he went.

One of the cyborgs jumped on the tail propeller and tried to disable it. Troy blew him off. Creed covered Rachel as she tore past him and leaped inside. Even before Creed reached the ramp, the rotators came to life with a tremendous roar, almost knocking him back with a strong blast of air. Leaning from the hatchway, Alexis reached out her hand to him. The helicopter rose off the deck and Creed jumped the rest of the way catching Alexis's outstretched hand. They tumbled inside. In the cockpit, Rachel maneuvered the joystick, sending the aircraft arcing out of the hangar.

Then Alexis was hit.

The hatchway ramp was halfway closed when the bullet torpedoed into her arm, jack-knifing her out of the low-gliding helicopter. Creed heard her scream above the pinging bullets, howling engine and chaos around him.

He would not lose her. He could not lose her.

Without a second's hesitation, he dove after her. He hit the deck landing almost on top of her, their momentum rolling them across the deck. The earsplitting swosh of air told him that the helicopter had escaped the tower. But he and Alexis had not.

Troy, numb with shock, lunged for Rachel in the pilot seat, "Creed and Alexis fell out!" he screamed in her ear. "We've got to turn around!"

She blanched. The helicopter shook as projectiles razed its sides, forcing Troy to grab a ceiling hook to keep from losing his balance. He looked back. The tower was still close enough to make out an infuriated Commando, who for the moment seemed to have forgotten that Creed was only a few yards away. Desperately, Commando targeted the helicopter's fuel tank. His pistol spat angry chunks of lead, but the helicopter was already out of range. A crew of cyborgs began setting up a heavy anti-aircraft gun in the hangar bay, while others were piling into another helicopter. Troy gripped the armrest. No matter how much he wanted to, it would be impossible to go back. Creed and Alexis were certainly dead.

CHAPTER 29

There were three possible exits to the docking bay—the windows, the doors and the elevator shaft. A jump from the windows might kill them, and the cyborgs were pouring through the door. Creed yanked Alexis up, nearly jerking her arm from its socket and made for the remaining exit. The elevator. Commando tore his attention from the fleeing aircraft.

Creed and Alexis collapsed inside the elevator. He slammed the first button his fingers touched. The doors closed on Commando's angry face. The lights above the door blinked on and the elevator plunged down the shaft for level three.

"Lex, how bad is it?"

She was leaning against the wall gripping her shoulder, blinking back tears. "I think it's fine. It's just grazed."

"Here, let me see."

Alexis grimaced as he touched her arm and peeled back the torn, bloody cloth from her lacerated shoulder. She sniffed. "I'm sorry . . . for falling . . . "

He shushed her. "It's not your fault. It could have been any of us."

Tears squeezed from her eyes. "I'm sorry . . . " she said, then crumbled into a sobbing wreck.

Creed shook her. "Lex! Listen to me. I'll get you out of here, but you have to stay strong. Okay?"

She sniffed and nodded. He tore a strip from his shirt and wrapped her shoulder. "You're gonna be alright. The bullet took some flesh but it's not serious. The bone is not shattered. You're a lucky girl."

She managed a pained smile. "I don't feel lucky. What are we going to do?"

"We'll just sit tight. Troy and Rachel will bring help."

For her benefit, he said it with more confidence than he felt. The phone which Rachel had given him shuddered in his pocket. He dug it out. "Hello?"

"Creed? It's Troy! Are you both alright?"

"We're fine."

"We'll turn the copter around—."

"No! Bring the police, the army, the Navy Seals, I don't care— ."

"But—."

"Troy, listen to me! We'll be fine. Just get help!"

Creed shut off the phone as the elevator rumbled to a halt. The numbers above the door told him that they were below water level. The pneumatic powered elevator doors split open. As he and Alexis walked out onto the narrow causeway, they heard a metallic clink. He spun, finger on the trigger. His slug ripped through the cyborg. The second cyborg caught Creed by surprise. He fired but only blasted the cyborg's weapon from its hands. Unfazed the cyborg flung himself at Creed.

Creed had the awful realization that he had just spent his last round. No time to reload.

The cyborg aimed a punch at Creed's jaw, strong enough to put his fist right through his head. The blow flew to where Creed's head should have been, but he wasn't there. The boy dodged swiftly to one side throwing his body into a sideways roll and out of the way of the mechanical fist. All the cyborg pounded was air. Unable to stop its momentum, it flew forward, the acceleration carrying his metal fingers right into the triple pane window. As Creed flipped to his feet, he heard the smallest crack issue from the window. The sound was so faint that it was hardly noticeable in the heat of the battle.

But Creed noticed.

It was like the tiny gust of wind before a hurricane, like the first rain drop announcing a storm, or the smallest pebble which starts an avalanche. He grabbed Alexis's hand and ran. His heart was pounding as he bolted recklessly to the only doorway out of the room.

The cyborg stood still, eyes transfixed on the huge window. Terror had frozen him. At first, there seemed to be no change in the window, then a minuscule drop of water squeezed its way through the small fissure in the thick glass pane.

The electronic sliding doors were their only chance of survival.

More drops were pressing through, each drop growing larger as the crack began to expand. A thin stream of water began trickling down the window and formed a small puddle on the floor at the cyborg's feet. Suddenly the human brain jerked out of its daze. The cyborg sprinted—but it was too late. A terrible cracking sound vibrated across the huge window. Cracks burst outwards from the first fracture, running up and down the window in little slits, like a frozen lake just before the ice breaks.

The doors slid open. Creed and Alexis dashed inside. Creed slammed the button on the control panel that shut the doors. In that last moment, he risked a glance behind. The cyborg was running toward him, but what caught his eye was the huge glass window behind it, holding back billions of gallons of water. The steel doors had almost closed when it happened. The whole glass window shattered.

The sound of cracking glass was accompanied by a roaring rush of water that drowned out all other sounds. Splintered glass exploded like shrapnel. An incredible tidal wave of sea water thundered into the room. White foam frothed and boiled as the monstrous wall of water rushed forward, intent on tearing the tower apart from its foundation.

The cyborg looked pitifully small against the increasing mountain of water rising up behind it. Just as the sliding doors came together, the cyborg and water slammed into them. The entire tower shook from the encounter.

But the doors held.

Creed leaned over to catch his breath. He noticed the water squirting up from the door jam. The door began bulging outwards under the pressure. How long would the tower last under such pressure? Fifteen minutes? Ten?

They took off running again.

THE ROAR of splintering glass, collapsing masonry, and crashing sea water reverberated through the Hulsane's ears. He jumped from his chair, moving faster than he had in twenty years. A female technician screamed. Apprehensive glances shot around the crowded room.

"What in the world . . . ?"

A guard pointed to a security monitor as it showed the swirling flood. "I want the third level completely sealed off!" he called into his headset.

The image of Creed and Alexis racing down the hall flashed across the screen. Behind them, the deluge charged down the hall toward the camera. A second later the camera flicked and went dead. Hulsane rose from his seat like a demon.

"Sklade!" he roared into his phone, "That boy is loose inside the tower!"

"I'll get him," Commando muttered from somewhere in the bowels of the silver tower.

"And, Sklade, I want the boy dead this time. Don't come back without his body."

Hulsane's ever-present bodyguard, Dimitri, shook his head. "Don't worry yourself about him, sir. There is no way a person could survive that."

"You don't know this boy."

TROY SLUMPED in his seat. Every revolution of the helicopter's massive propellers took him farther and farther from the tower. Images of Alexis and Creed torn and blooded in the hangar bay as Commando exacted revenge floated in his mind. Creed said they were fine, but how long could that last?

He tried the phone again, but he could not get any service. They were still too far from the cell towers.

Troy looked back at Dr. Skeddner. The man had not moved in ten minutes. Troy did not check for a pulse, afraid he would not find one.

He stole a glance at Rachel beside him. Shining through her bullet-torn shirt were the chrome plates. With all the danger surrounding him in the last hour, he had almost forgotten about her . . . unveiling. Now as he watched, his stomach lurched with fear. This girl was a cyborg. Could he trust her? Her chrome-plated fingers held the joystick. He tried not to stare, but he could not help it.

Rachel adjusted her radio headset. "Troy, where are we going?"

He barely lifted his head to answer her. "I don't know. Land, I guess."

The radar screen lit up with a red warning blip. Troy groaned, taking his eyes from the GPS consul unit. Behind them, three helicopters roared. "We've got a little problem. Can you out run them?"

Rachel grasped the control yoke. "I'll do my best."

The aircraft leaned forward as she pushed it to the limit. A few random bullets pinged over the helicopter.

Troy licked his dry lips. "At least they don't have any heavy weapons on board."

To his utter chagrin, he realized he had spoken too soon. A powerful blast shook the aircraft. It rocked, then dropped into a dizzying tailspin, smoke issuing from the one of the engines. There was a horrible rattling sound in his ears. Troy felt his stomach in his mouth, but he was too scared to throw up. This was it. The end. He groped for his phone.

A FEW miles away off the Los Angeles shoreline, the clouds had unleashed their payloads. A terrific storm traveled to the silver tower. The water rolled and thrashed like it was possessed, turning and folding over itself in its anger. White foam spewed forth from the turmoil of wild water. The great sea was at odds with everything in creation. It was fighting with the wind and the rain. It was fighting with itself.

Overhead the sky was covered with enormous gray clouds. Thunder crashed across the night. Lightning lashed tongues of strange, fiery-purple energy that cut through the atmosphere. The air was icy cold, so cold it seemed never to have felt the warmth of the sun. Roaring rain hurtled down in the form of hail, splashing into the churning waters far below. The wind bellowed its war cry as the powerful force slammed against the sea causing huge waves to rise over the melee, only to fall down again in a cascade of relentless water. The stormy elements vented their rage on the silver tower.

Creed wondered how much allotted time was left to him. He plowed up the stairs two at a time, with Alexis on his heels. The ominous roar of water could be heard from somewhere below.

The silver tower grew eerie. An inquisitive fish stared inside through the triple-paned plexiglass. Model robots stood frozen in diverse positions, like a gallery of wax statues. The lights were dimmed to conserve power, leaving patches of shadows. The rooms were deserted. Everyone must be on the higher levels—where he needed to be.

Without slowing, Creed rammed a fresh magazine into his gun. His cell-phone shook. He pressed it to his ear. "Troy?"

"Creed, they've caught up with us. They're shoot—," an explosion blew away the rest of his words. Mingled in the eruption was Rachel's scream. The connection crackled off.

"Troy?"

Silence.

Creed scowled and punched redial. "Troy! Come on, Troy, pick up."

Nothing. He almost threw the phone against the wall. He tried a third time with no success. Creed slumped. Despair sucked the life from his soul.

Beside him, Alexis squeezed his arm as she read the grim situation in his eyes. "My father . . . "

"We just have to pray that they made it." Resigned to their plight, Creed began thinking aloud. "Well, what options do we have? Level five, where the speedboats are docked, is flooded. We've got Commando above us and water below."

"DID SOMEONE leave the sink running?" Joe Yates asked looking up from his computer. He heard the plaintive sound of water issuing from outside his office door in the silver tower. The technician stood from his desk and was greeted by 10,000 tons of water which exploded through the door. Boiling foam and water thundered forward ripping through the office walls, sweeping up the objects in the room and adding them to computer equipment, office supplies—and limp bodies already riding the swell.

The scream died on his lips.

CHAPTER 30

K*ill them both. Split up and converge on the targets.*

Commando sent the silent command to his cyborgs. Not even Hulsane knew that he had some under his direct control, and Commando intended to keep it that way. They could come in handy later, in the likely event that Hulsane needed to be eliminated. Commando trusted no one.

The cyborgs darted ahead, their human brains obeying without hesitation. Commando's knee-high combat boots pounded the curving stairs as he bolted down, gun extended. They were closing in. He cocked his good ear. He heard water trickling, sloshing, and draining below. The sealing process had malfunctioned somehow. The tower was still flooding and there was no holding it back.

"I told you we should have gone after that kid," Trex said. "Now they're loose somewhere in the tower. I bet he made the leak."

Commando glared in Trex's direction. "Shut your mouth, before I open a leak in you."

"Sir," the cyborg's silky, indifferent voice rose up to Commando. "We've found them."

CREED COULD feel the numbing coldness of the water even through his watertight boots as he and Alexis splashed down the flooded corridor. He had to get above the water that was drowning everything in its path. And that was barely half the battle. He still had Commando to contend with.

Neon lights illuminated the silver walls and ceiling with an eerie blue glow. Air vents punctuated the length of the ceiling in ten foot intervals. They passed under an air vent that began to drip water. It splashed into the pool which had already accumulated, covering the floor.

Then the next vent started dripping.

And the next.

Before they could react, a mountain of water crashed down. Alexis slipped and fell. Creed grabbed her and hauled her upright. Coughing and sputtering, Alexis tried to wipe her eyes and regain her balance. Creed pulled her clear of the cascade. Somehow the water had found its way to the level above them and was draining. How long would it be before the corridor flooded? The tower would be their tomb.

They ran.

The water level was rising at an alarming rate. It had risen up to their knees. A few minutes later the water had climbed to their chests and showed no signs of abating. Ahead, Creed could just make out a staircase.

Creed dragged Alexis up the flight of stairs. A cyborg appeared at the top of the landing. Creed pulled his gun up and fired. Sizzling and bubbling, the chemical compounds of the bullet burned its way through the cyborg's chrome casing.

As Creed pushed Alexis to the landing, he heard a second cyborg coming up behind him. He turned in time to evade the blow, but not in time to prevent the cyborg from grabbing his wrist. Creed fired quickly, his aim hampered by the crushing grip. The bullet struck the cyborg's leg, sizzling like acid.

His next shot went awry, missing the cyborg by a foot. He did not get another chance. The cyborg kicked Creed and knocked away the gun in the same movement.

A barrage of bullets knocked the robot off balance and pierced his chrome head casing. Alexis had opened fire. Creed stepped back and was shocked to feel nothing solid under his feet.

He had stumbled off the edge of the stairs. He barely had time to snatch some air into his lungs before bracing himself and shutting his eyes. The cyborg, half sank, half tumbled off the flooded stairs, pulling Creed down with it. Alexis's shot had fried the cyborg's optic cables. Its joints were frozen in place, like rigor mortis setting into a corpse. Creed tried, unsuccessfully, to shake off the grip. Finally he opened his eyes. He knew he only had seconds before he ran out of oxygen. He fumbled frantically with the metal hand. He pulled, scratched, kicked, anything to release himself from the robotic hand dragging him to the death he most feared.

ALEXIS DROPPED the gun, which would be no use under water, and jumped into what felt like an indoor swimming pool. She filled her lungs with the precious air then swam to the bottom. It was cold and dark. The salt water stung her eyes. Her groping fingers came in contact with something hard. It was the face of a grinning cyborg. She followed the steel body until she found Creed.

Straightaway she recognized the problem. She had to free Creed. Reaching down, she pulled with all her might. The cyborg gave a jerk and its eyes turned back on. Alexis recoiled. The light from the cyborg's eyes created an eerie, hazy light, illuminating the skull face with a blue tinted halo of light. The head moved a little, trying to see her. But that was all. The rest of the body did not move. Although the eyes had murder in them, all they could do was look.

Gathering her nerve, she touched it. Nothing happened. She continued prying the metal fingers; at least now she could see what she was doing. The metallic head darted forward. The mouth reared open. Just in time, Alexis spun out of the way to avoid being bitten. Her hands were shaking. She stayed as far away from the grinning head as she could while still prying the metal fingers.

Creed's eyes slid shut.

THE WATER clawed at Commando's legs as it rose in steady increments. The relentless flow had found its way inside the tower through numerous entrances. Commando watched the spot where Creed and Alexis had disappeared moments before. They had been under too long. A few more seconds and they would never come up. The surface of the water was still. The murkiness made it impossible to see more than two feet deep. Commando fired, peppering the water with bullets and causing small fountains to splash upward.

Trex began walking back up the stairs. He had no desire to get any wetter. "They must be dead."

Commando holstered his gun. "He's not dead until I see his body." He focused and sent a thought to the silicone chip in Creed's cerebellum.

Surface immediately.

The water remained undisturbed, continuing its unrelenting rise. They must be dead. He sent an order to one of his cyborgs.

Dive. Find the body.

CREED FLOATED through hazy shadows. He felt oddly comfortable. Somewhere in his mind a thought echoed. He should rise to the surface. The surface of what? He did not much care. Iridescent balls of light drifted into his vision. As they came into focus, it occurred to him that they were people—and one was his mother. White robes fluttered around her celestial body. She smiled. He tried to go to her. But she put her hands up. "Not yet, baby. Not until you've finished your task."

PANIC CLAWED Alexis as she struggled for breath. Creed's head lulled and his eyes fell closed. He had stopped fighting for his life.

With a crack, the cyborg's metallic fingers released their hold. Her relief was short lived. Now what? The minute they broke the surface,

Commando would put a dozen bullets in them. This was not fair. Alexis felt her blood pulsing and she was starting to feel dizzy.

Come on, girl, think!

Through the water she saw a narrow passage built into the wall. It was a crawl space between two rooms. Since the passage sloped at an upward angle, she hoped there might be an air pocket at the top.

Alexis got a firm grip on Creed then pushed off the floor as hard as she could and propelled both of them into the opening.

To her relief, her head broke the surface and she gulped for air. Then she started up the metal slope dragging Creed behind her. The slick grade proved difficult. Creed was not breathing. It would have been hopeless, if she had not discovered a thick cord running along the wall. Praying that it was not an electrical wire, she tugged it, pulling herself up. The slope leveled off about six feet above her. She turned Creed over on his back.

"Please," she begged. "Don't leave me."

She clasped her hands together and pounded his chest. She was rewarded with a slight gasp. He was alive. She hit him again, this time with everything she had. He retched up a stream of water which splashed her face. She felt his chest heave as he began to breathe.

"Creed! Talk to me!" she pleaded, shaking him—hitting him.

Suddenly, he opened his eyes. "Lex?"

Exhausted, Alexis collapsed to the floor. Her heart was still hammering in her chest. She knew that this nightmare was far from over.

IT WAS nothing short of a miracle. Troy could still feel his heart pound, one more time, then again. Somehow Rachel had righted the helicopter and pulled them out of the death dive.

The craft careened sharply to the right, jarring everything so violently, that Troy lost his grip on the phone. He could only watch as it flew out the window. It took all of Rachel's piloting skill to keep the craft from crashing into the ocean. Waves jumped like aquatic hands attempting to tear the helicopter from the sky. The Los Angeles shore line rose up before them. The helicopter limped onward, passing over the beach, and entering the heart of the metropolis.

Troy pointed. "Look! There's a police station. Maybe you can land in the parking lot."

It was more of a controlled crash than a proper landing as the helicopter dropped from the sky like a wounded bird. The burning wreck screeched across the graveled parking lot, before slamming into some parked cars. They ripped off their seatbelts. Troy kicked the crumbled hatch door open, grabbed Rachel's cyborg hand, and leaped down to the asphalt. Together they dragged Dr. Skeddner's limp body from the wreckage. Any minute the flames would contact the fuel tanks. . .

The helicopter erupted in a brilliant, orange fireball.

Troy and Rachel were thrown from their feet. A burning heat wave singed Troy's skin. When he regained his footing, police personnel were everywhere. Well, that was one way to get the cops' attention.

They were yelling for them to get on the ground. But Troy had no intention of getting on the ground. "Creed—Whitefield!—hurry!— An army of cyborgs!" His words were jumbled. His mind was jumbled. He tried to start over. "There's a terrorist group at Shell Island with an army of cyborgs!"

Disbelief and ridicule stared back at him.

"What evidence do you have?" someone shouted.

Rachel yanked off her gloves. All sound fell away. Every eye was riveted on the girl's robotic hand. With deft movements she slid up her sleeves, exposing her cybernetic arms. It was a disturbing mixture of man and machine. For a long moment the only sounds were micro motors hissing as Rachel spread her arms for inspection.

"God help us," whispered the officer in charge. "Lieutenant Perry, get Homeland Security on the line."

CHAPTER 31

Creed took stock of his surroundings. He and Alexis were huddled in a narrow crawl space. Naked pipes and wires protruded on either side. He glanced back the way they had come. Down the sloping passage, he could see the giant pool of water. It glowed with a bright blue light. Glints of silver body armor rippled underneath the waves.

Cyborgs. Creed hated cyborgs. Words could not describe how much he hated them. The cyborgs were still searching the bottom of the pool for them. Alexis did not speak until the cyborgs gave up and turned away. "Are you all right?"

Unsteadily, Creed dragged himself into a sitting position. "Yeah, I'll be fine in a sec. Thanks . . . for pulling me out."

Alexis shrugged, "Well, you've saved my life so many times that I've lost count. It was an honor to return the favor."

He pulled out his waterlogged cell-phone and tossed the useless thing away. "Where are we?"

"A ventilation or service shaft I think."

Creed put a finger to his lips. "Shhh . . . You hear that?"

The sound was a dull roar—not water, but machinery. He crawled further up the tunnel on his hands and knees, allowing his ears to guide him. The noise increased with every foot, until he located its source. He was staring down the bars of a grill built into the ceiling of the cybernetic manufacturing room. The powerful whir of machinery deafened his ears.

From his vantage point, he could only see the tops of the technicians' heads as they sat operating the equipment. Roaring and pumping like a living animal, the intricate machinery was assembling cyborgs out of men. A white-suited technician sat at a monitor with his back to him absently draining a cup of coffee. Before him, conveyer belts rolled, transporting hundreds of cyborgs.

Creed jiggled the grill as softly as possible. It was loose. He pulled it up and passed it to Alexis. Grasping the edges of the hole, he leaned down. A quick inspection revealed only two men in the room. Two unsuspecting technicians. Creed landed on the table, amid a stunned audience. He clamped his hand over one man's mouth and knocked him down, spilling the coffee on the man's coat in the process. The other man tried to run but Creed knocked him out with a well placed kick to his temple.

As Alexis dropped from the vent, Creed scanned the control unit for a shut off switch. He soon found it. The pumps, conveyer belts and machinery ground to a stop. They walked down the line of cyborgs which stood like fierce statues in some futuristic museum. Their expressionless, humanoid faces stared at Creed.

Alexis reached out, as though petting a cobra, and touched the cold steel. "They set my nerves on edge."

Creed walked around the cyborgs and studied the computers, the inklings of an idea forming in his mind. "There should be a way to activate the cyborgs."

Alexis followed. "Creed? Why would we want to activate them?"

He fingered a control panel. "I don't think these are programed yet. They might help us."

"Or kill us . . ."

"We're running out of options. We have to take that chance."

Alexis jumped as the cold blue eyes came to life. The cyborg nearest Creed spoke. "Where am I? This isn't the hospital . . . " his voice drifted away as he stared at his metallic hand.

Another cyborg at the end of the line shouted, "What happened to me?"

With this statement the room collapsed into chaos. Screams of disbelief bounced off the gray walls in smooth, identical monotone voices. Completely undone, one cyborg sank to his knees making a sound that Creed took to be crying. An idea formed in Creed's mind. He counted thirty cyborgs. There were others half-built on the assembly line, but he did not think they would be completed in time to be of any use, even if he could figure out how to restart the complicated machinery.

There was a blinding flash of silver and blue, and Creed found himself pinned to the floor with the breath smashed from his lungs. Unlike Commando, this cyborg had no flesh to injure. Creed's fists were useless against a body built entirely of chrome alloy. The cyborg locked his arm around Creed's neck. He could not even swallow under the cold mechanical arm tightening over his throat. The voice in his ear was that silky, disturbing monotone which all the cyborgs shared. "I don't know what's going on, but I want out. Right now."

"What's happening?" another equally monotonic voice questioned from down the line. One of the cyborgs grabbed Alexis.

Creed spoke, careful not to show any fear. "Do not hurt her!" he ordered. She was pinned to a wall, with her arms twisted behind her back, but the cyborgs did not seem to be harming her—at least not much.

The acute edges of the cyborg's bony limbs dug into Creed's back and shoulders as the cyborg pressed his face harder into the marble tiles. He prayed this cyborg's human brain functions were undamaged and it would listen to reason.

"We're on the same side. If you let me up, I can explain."

It was impossible to judge the cyborg's thoughts by its blank expression, but Creed guessed that there was distrust and fear behind it. Creed could not imagine what he would feel if he woke up and found he had been transformed into a robot.

After a tense minute, the cyborg released his choke hold. "Let me have the gun."

Creed tensed, then decided to take the risk. He handed over his weapon. The cyborg looked even more frightening holding a gun. He angled the weapon at Creed's face, motioning for him to stand. "Put your hands behind your head."

Creed laid his palms against the back of his neck. Time goaded Creed. Hulsane would be launching his attack soon. Creed needed this cyborg's—man's help. He still found it difficult to grasp that there was a human being hidden underneath those chrome plates and wires. They were not mindless machines. They were humans—humans, hopefully not yet installed with the MCC.

The cyborg kept the gun on Creed. "Now, who are you? And what is going on?"

The other cyborgs gathered around. The unnerving glow of sixty mechanical eyes, reminiscent of Commando, staring at him did not aid Creed's concentration. But he took a breath and gave it his best shot.

"My name is Creed Trailven. Adam Rolls was my father," he paused, trying to organize his thoughts. The name Rolls appeared to capture the cyborg's attention, Creed had the impression that he knew him. "You were being used for a rogue military experiment. I've just released you. What's your name?"

The cyborg seemed dazed and did not answer for a moment. "Lieutenant Mark Grayson," he said finally. Several other robotic heads swivelled at this. "Grayson! It's me, Jack Coals."

Grayson acknowledged the speaker absently. They must have known each other before they were transformed into cyborgs.

"Well, at least I'm not alone in this bizarre dream," Grayson said.

Relieved that Grayson was calm and coherent,, Creed took the initiative. "Will you let my friend go, and may I lower my arms now?"

Grayson nodded, "Let the girl go." Grayson's name appeared to be respected among the cyborgs. They obeyed without protest, stepping apart to create a path for Alexis. She was at Creed's side in a moment.

"Are you all right?" he asked.

"I'm fine," she said, but her eyes betrayed her. She sidled closer, slipping her hand into his. The circle of cyborgs reformed.

"Creed," Grayson said, lowering the handgun, "Did Taylor Falkner do this?"

Creed nodded, recalling Whitefield's former name. "Yes, but the doctor is dead now. Sklade Browning and a man named Hulsane are in charge. I need your help, Lieutenant, to stop them. They are using a mind control chip and drugs to create an army of cyborgs. He has at least a thousand of you already, but I don't think he plans to stop there."

He was greeted with perfect silence. He could not decide if they believed him or not. "I need a team to create a diversion, while the rest of us break into the emergency control room and override the system."

They stared at him. For some reason Creed had assumed they would automatically jump to his aid. Now, he was not sure. But if he could convince Grayson, the other cyborgs would follow his lead. "Grayson? Are you with me?"

"It's risky. Are you sure there's no way to make outside contact?"

Creed shook his head. "Besides the terrorists, we're the only people on earth who know."

Grayson arrived at a decision. "We don't have much time. If we're going to do this, we need to move right now."

Creed turned to Alexis. "I'd feel better if you stayed here."

She clutched his arm. "I don't want to stay here alone."

Creed fished his mother's ring from his pocket. Slipping the green-studded ring onto her forefinger, he said, "Keep it safe for me. "

Tears began to well in her eyes as she looked at her sister's ring. "I can't," she whispered. "I've already lost my mother, my sister, and now my father. I can't live without you. Whatever happens, I want to be with you."

"Okay," he said, gripping her hand tightly, "then stay close."

CHAPTER 32

Hulsane was disturbed. And he did not like being disturbed. This unexpected flooding was not included in his meticulous plans.

One of the many technicians surrounding him looked up. "Sir, I think we might have another problem on our hands. There seems to be a fleet of military aircraft approaching on the radar scopes."

Hulsane frowned. "Are you saying . . . "

"Yes, sir. They're coming this way. We're receiving a transmission from them right now. I'll switch it to the speakers."

A patch of static crackled. "This is the United States Marines. We demand your immediate unconditional surrender. Disable your robots and evacuate the tower immediately or we will open fire. These terms are not negotiable." More static announced the end of the message.

"Send no reply!" Hulsane shouted, enraged. "This is impossible. How could they trace the signals back so quickly?"

"I don't know, sir, but they should be here within seconds and I expect they'll blow us from the water if action is not taken."

Hulsane knew that everything could be torn from his grasp before the pinnacle of his glory and vengeance. All because of one boy. "By all means captain, retaliate. Give them our best."

If they wanted a fight, then so be it.

His eyes flickered in a lightning flash. "I'll not be conquered now."

THE TEN Apache attack helicopters hung in the air around the tower like giant buzzing insects awaiting the order to engage. They were the initial attack force while reinforcements were mobilizing. James Smith, the team leader, noticed panels sliding open on the silver surface. He knew something was wrong. This was supposed to be an unarmed target. He was shocked to see row after row of mounted antiaircraft guns rear their barrels from the tower. This was not a museum. This was a battle fortress.

"Open fire!" he yelled. But it was already too late.

The last thing he witnessed on this earth was a sky ablaze with a hundred muzzle flashes. Laden with holes and dead soldiers, his flaming helicopter spiraled downward and was swallowed by the sea. The Apaches put up a valiant fight, breaking into evasive maneuvers and scoring multiple hits, but when the fire and smoke cleared, only the tower was standing.

"UNIT RED 3, we heard some disturbance in the cyborg manufacturing room and the cameras are malfunctioning. Go check it out. There might be trouble."

Marvin Crultt clicked his radio, and nodded to his squad. "Roger that. We're on our way."

Something clinked behind him. He never saw what hit him. Grayson exploded out of hiding. Crultt died without a sound. Other cyborgs sprang from their various hiding places. The conflict was brief but deadly. The men stood no chance against the cyborgs. A few were able to get off a burst of machine gun fire only to have the bullets ricochet off the cyborg's plates—killing the shooters instantly.

Two men lay at Grayson's feet. They would not be rising. There was blood on Grayson's mechanical hands. He was still having trouble digesting this. He pried the submachine gun from one of the guard's lifeless hands. He felt more comfortable with a gun in his hand. Around him, his thirty companions had acquired weapons in a similar manner. They were chambering rounds and gathering extra magazines.

He smiled grimly. Sure his body had changed, but his mind had not. This was like any other mission he had conducted. The primary objective was simple. Creed and Alexis broke for the hall.

Grayson started in the opposite direction, firing off orders. "Fifteen of you go with Creed. The rest of you come with me. We are going to raise a storm. "

HE SHOULD never have agreed to work for Commando. Trex could see that now. Unfortunately, all his regrets were too late. There was no way out of this. He knew that somehow the cyborgs had freed themselves and were out for revenge. They had broken through the last lines of defense. Either these demonic cyborgs would kill him, the U.S. special forces would kill him, or Commando would kill him. It was not much of a choice.

He trained his automatic weapon down the hall, hands shaking, as the cyborgs prepared to attack him. He leveled the gun and fired into a silver chest. He was horrified to see the bullets bounce off. The cyborg was still coming. Stumbling back, Trex continued firing and fumbled for his phone. "The robots are going crazy!" He was pleading now. "You've gotta stop them!"

THE CYBERNETIC technicians were frantic. Thirty cyborgs would not respond to their commands. And it was clear that they were coming this way. Every camera showed guards fleeing or being mowed down.

Red warning lights blinked over the computer consuls.

"Sir, despite our efforts at containment, the tower has become unstable. It could collapse at any moment. We should evacuate the facility." Hulsane let out a grunt of anger. A lifetime of plotting, scheming, and anticipating revenge was about to sink beneath the waves. With sudden violence he cracked the emerald studded cane against a computer. He smashed the appliance until the cane snapped in two. Disgusted, he tossed the broken pieces away. "Fine! Fine! Give the orders to move out."

Hulsane watched his men rushing around in a kind of mad scramble. He laughed bitterly to himself. Fools, they were all going to die. The American reinforcements were already circling the tower. There would be no escape. Well, he was not about to give himself up to those bloodthirsty tyrants. He pocketed the data capsule containing the cyborg blueprints. He was not about to let it fall into their hands.

"Where are the capsules with the MCC data?"

"They were left downstairs."

Now regretting that he had destroyed his cane, Hulsane grabbed the railing and started down the stairs.

CHAPTER 33

Creed had memorized the path to the emergency control room. They were almost there. He slid to a stop. Any thought of arriving without a fight was crushed.

Commando was standing there. He was shirtless, silver chest glowing. He was flanked by twenty cyborgs, all of which gripped automatic rifles. "Something told me I would find you here. Trying to be a hero."

Just as Commando leveled his gun the cyborgs which Creed had freed raced up behind him cradling weapons. The leader raised an automatic rifle. "Freeze! Drop the guns!"

Commando froze, slack jawed, gun half pulled. "What . . ."

"I thought I'd pick up some cyborgs of my own," Creed said.

For once, Commando did not know what to do. Neither did his cyborgs. They could only stare. Commando fired at Creed, but one of his cyborgs sprang forward to take the bullet. The hot metal bounced off his chest. Commando had to throw himself down to avoid being hit.

Creed and Alexis dropped for cover as thirty guns discharged at once. The noise was horrific, caustic bedlam. The guns clamped in cyborg hands blasted at everything in sight.

The air shuddered with ricocheting bullets. The bombardment of lead stopped only after they had run out of ammunition. The floor was littered with spent shells and the walls were pockmarked with bullets. But not one cyborg was down. The silver body armor of the cyborgs was impregnable. It smoked and sparked but retained no damage.

When the cyborgs realized their stalemate, they threw themselves at each other. They snapped joints, ripped out cords, and crushed each other with steel fists.

Creed shot a cyborg in the face. The bullet sizzled through its eye. It screamed with pain. With Alexis by his side Creed escaped from the melee of battling cyborgs. He raced down the hall and realized one cyborg was still behind him.

Commando.

Creed dove behind a wall pulling Alexis with him just as Commando fired. Spent shells rattled onto the floor as they were ejected from his pistols. Slugs spluttered and hissed, tearing up the air around Creed. That was close . . . far too close. Creed crouched down breathing heavily, trying to calm his racing heart.

They were on an access ramp. He leaned over the edge and looked down. It was a long way down. If he jumped from here, there would not be enough left of him for Commando to bother with. There had to be another way.

Commando would not wait long before he made a move. Creed risked a glance around the edge of the wall. Even from this distance Creed could see a wicked smile on his skull-like face. The frigid eyes were full of murder and hate. The notorious Sig 266P looked savage in the cyborg's mechanical hand. With the lightning reflexes of fiber optic cables serving as artificial neuronic links fused to his human brain, Commando fired.

Hot lead rushed toward Creed with frightening accuracy, each bullet intended to extinguish his life. Creed yanked his head clear so fast that it hurt. He felt the wind as the bullets zipped by his face.

His heart skipped a beat as he realized how close he had been to death. The wall smoked from the recent barrage of projectiles. Creed scanned the area for any sign of an escape route. He felt the all too familiar electrical tingle. The order came swiftly.

Step forward.

Creed felt the impulsive urge envelop his brain. Everything in him wanted to throw himself from the cover of the wall — directly into Commando's line of fire.

The suggestion was so strong.

It was a brief and violent struggle. His head pulsated as Creed forced mind to yield to spirit. The power of each was so potent Creed thought he would burst from the pressure. The world started to spin. His vision blurred to a red haze.

Then it was over. His head cleared and he was master over his mind once again. He had won.

Creed wiped the sweat from his brow. Then he spun around the corner and fired his gun, aiming for the human part of Commando's chest. The man threw himself back but Creed saw blood spatter the wall. Sklade Browning's blood.

Unfortunately, it was only a flesh wound.

Taking Alexis by the hand, Creed turned and fled for the elevator. He dove inside and slammed the button activating the doors as lead crashed and exploded around him. He slumped against the walls trying to catch his breath.

The elevator ascended, halting at the apex level. The doors opened into complete darkness. Creed felt along the wall until his fingers contacted the light switch.

The control room was eerily empty. The hum of a hundred supercomputers filled the air. He had never seen so much hardware in one place in his life. Floor to ceiling windows encased the circular room giving Creed an uncomfortable sense of openness. He could see the dark water outside. Alexis pressed the control panel closing the doors. Weaving his way through the equipment Creed located the master computer in the center of the room.

He dropped into the swivel armchair and rolled closer to the desk. Outside, crooked streaks of lightning severed the sky. A flat-screen monitor dominated the desk space. A complex matrix of information zipped across the screen. At first glance it was a hopeless mess. At second glance the confusion only intensified. He hunched over, willing himself to concentrate. He jumped when, he heard Troy's voice sputtering from the computer speakers. "Creed? Can you hear me now?"

THE MILITARY chopper was quickly approaching the tower. Inside, Troy admired the expensive army grade laptop which was balanced on his lap. Rachel sat beside him. Troy's fingers flew across the keyboard.

He spoke into his headset. "Ok, Creed. So I'm bypassing the security firewalls so I can remotely access the tower's network. What computer terminal bay are you using?"

"C-45."

"Cool. I'm syncing up our computers right now. Just do exactly as I say and we are going to hack into the control system using your father's backdoor. I just need you to hold off the cyborgs until the computer has time to complete the override process."

COMPLEX LINES of code flickered across the screen as Creed followed Troy's directions. The seconds ticked away.

The long chilling hiss penetrated Creed to his soul. It was half mechanical, half human—all Commando. This time there were no exits. Commando was standing in the only one.

The door panel slid shut behind him before he shot the control pad permanently locking the door. "So we won't be disturbed."

Creed whipped his gun up and pulled the trigger. Nothing happened. The gun was empty and he had no more magazines. He could feel the bile climbing up his to throat.

"Lex, get behind me."

The cyborg laughed. It was one of the most horrible sounds Creed had ever heard in his life. "This game is over," Commando growled.

"It's not over until I'm dead."

"That can be arranged."

Commando charged. Grasping for a weapon, Creed yanked up a chair and swung it like a bat. The cyborg caught the chair with both hands and shoved it back at Creed who was knocked off his feet.

Commando's five chrome plated fingers cinched around Alexis's throat. She gurgled, unable to draw breath. Creed jumped up, slamming his forearm across the cyborg's fleshy elbow. Commando released Alexis, but his elbow took her in the cheek. Creed heard the nauseating crack. He could only hope her jaw was not broken. Her eyes rolled back as she hit the floor. A thin trickle of blood ran down her face like red tears.

She was still. So still. The image of his mother dying in the muddy street flashed across his mind. Alexis appeared so peaceful that it startled him. Her eyes were closed, her black lashes resting gently on her cheeks. If not for the blood dripping down her temple, he might have assumed she was asleep. She could not be dead. She just could not. His mother, and now Alexis.

No.

Commando glanced down at her with unconcern. "Sorry, boy, didn't mean to hit her that hard."

He pointed the gun barrel down at her face, tightening his finger on the trigger.

Creed flung his knife with unerring accuracy. The blade covered the distance in the blink of an eye. Commando dropped the gun and stared at the knife adorning his chest. Fueled with rage, Creed did not even give Commando time to pull the blade free before he launched himself. He pummeled the man with everything he had.

Then Commando recovered. He caught Creed by the hair and slammed his head into the table. Creed's lip split open and red splattered over the computer consul. Throbbing thuds reverberated inside his skull. Commando cracked his face into the desk again.

"A bullet is just too good for you, boy. We're going to finish this business off right."

Creed could nott suppress the scream of pain. He flew towards the desk again with frightening speed. Sparks exploded through his brain. The room started reeling and fading to black. Consciousness was racing away. Just before the world disappeared entirely, he heard Commando's voice grate in his ear. "You might have been my son, but your fool of a mother ditched me for Adam. My only regret is that I wasn't there to laugh in her face as she died."

Creed snapped back, his brain clearing in an instant.

As Commando hurled him down for the final skull-splitting smash, Creed acted purely on instinct. He braced himself against the desk with his arms and used Commando's momentum to catapult them both—himself over the desk—Commando through the double pane window. Chips of shattered glass blasted outwards.

Creed stared at the huge jagged hole in the window. Commando was gone. The cyborg was gone.

Gone.

Barely able to comprehend Commando's demise, Creed staggered to the window. Wind knifed across his face and through his hair. Rain needles pricked him. Outside there was a sloping ledge but that was all. His thoughts immediately switched to Alexis. Turning back he could see that she had not moved. He clenched back tears. Every fiber of his being wanted to rush to her, but he knew he did not have time.

Muffled gunshots exploded in the hall. Cyborg screams of pain and rage vibrated in the air. The only thing separating him from the chaotic battle was a thin paneled door. The cyborgs would break in any second. He could not possibly fight all of them. If Alexis was still alive, the only chance either of them had was to stop the program. He stumbled to the master computer. A complex numeric code flittered across the touchscreen. Wiping blood from his eyes, he tried to focus on the screen. "Troy! What's happening!"

Troy's voice crackled from the speakers. "Umm...yeah, we kind of have a slight problem. There's a password to access the backdoor. I've tried everything I can think of. I can't figure out anyway to get around it."

Creed tried to hold back the panic.

Think!

The soft clink of metal caused Creed to snap his head over his shoulder with dread toward the broken window. A distinctive chrome plated hand gripped the edge of glass, heedless of the sharp edges. Another hand came into view, followed by the horribly disfigured face and cybernetic body of Sklade Browning.

Creed groaned aloud and ground his teeth. He only had seconds. Ignoring every instinct he had, Creed turned his back on Commando. He had no choice. A tiny electric shock zipped through his brain.

Your father couldn't do it. So just give up.

He tried to ignore Commando's impulses but he felt them seeping into his mind. His father had failed here. He could feel the heat burning from the chip. His eyes were blurring. Forcing himself to compose his thoughts, he focused on the computer. What was the stupid password?

Another familiar jolt.

What makes you think you can?

He heard the frightening clank of Commando's chrome foot against the floor. The cyborg was coming.

You don't have half the mind he had.

He clutched his throbbing head in his hands. Troy yelled through the computer speakers. "Creed! You're father designed the program. Think! What would his password be?"

"I don't know!"

It was too much. He was losing it.

"God!" he shouted. "Help me!"

Suddenly an idea hit him. His father had only completely trusted one person. Creed fumbled in his pocket and pulled out his mother's ring. He held it up to the light so he could read the serial code engraved on the inside of the band. Praying that it would work, he keyed it into the computer. Amazingly, it worked. Words popped up on the screen. "Press enter to initiate emergency override shut down procedures."

His finger reached out to hammer the enter key.

Don't you dare!

The screaming thought coursed through his mind, attacking every aspect of his rationality. His mind was on fire.

Then he pressed it. He could not help sighing as the screen glowed with a percentage bar and the words, "Shut down in progress."

It was the warning whisper of pneumatics that saved his life. He threw himself out the chair avoiding the fist of steel-plated fingers by nanoseconds. The chair clattered to its side as Commando's fist whistled past his ear. He rolled to his feet, ready to face his relentless enemy. Blood staining the chrome half of his chest, the cyborg rose to meet him. Creed rotated to position the table between himself and the bleeding cyborg.

The door shuddered as if a tremendous amount of weight was slung against it. Then it gave way. Cyborgs poured through. Creed looked over his shoulder at this new threat. It was a grave mistake. The next thing he saw was Commando's gruesome face an inch from his own. Steel fingers latched on his shirt as Commando lifted him clear of the floor.

Commando flung him through the air, over the table—and out the broken window.

CHAPTER 34

Alexis hurt all over. She blinked as consciousness was restored to her body. Rain spattered her face from the gaping hole in the window pane, probably what had awakened her. She was in the control room. In the center of the room, the override computer continued its shut down procedure.

Then the cyborgs came. She saw Creed's gun lying on the floor. She rolled over and snatched it up. She aimed at the closest cyborg and fired. Nothing happened. Of course, the gun was empty. The cyborg lunged forward catching her arm.

The computer gave a loud beep.

Abruptly, the cyborg loosened his hold and stared at Alexis. Even though his face remained unexpressive, she could sense its confusion. "What's going on?" it questioned in its eerie monotone. "Where is the nurse? I feel funny."

Alexis sighed in relief. Creed had succeeded. The system was terminated.

LIEUTENANT GRAYSON unfolded his cybernetic body from a crouched position, gun raised, water crashing around him. The other cyborgs, who moments before had been trying to kill him, were staring blankly at each other. Grayson sighed aloud. He was accustomed to war, but this had been the worst experience of his life, and he was grateful that it was over. Now he had to get out of the tower before he drowned.

ROTATOR BLADES slicing air, military and rescue helicopters swooped forward over the Pacific Ocean. Troy and Rachel sat huddled together surrounded by a counter terrorist team. Rachel suddenly gasped. "Creed is on top of the tower!"

CREED LANDED sooner than he expected—and it was not in water. The roof sloped outwards from the window and he found himself rolling down inclined panels. Rain slicked every surface as it poured itself out in torrents. The slope leveled off into a small ledge which explained Commando's survival. There were deep gouges in the slope where the cyborg had climbed and scratched his way back to the window.

Creed coasted to a stop. Flicking his drenched hair out of his eyes, he looked up. Commando was standing at the window. He jumped down, half sliding, half walking down the slope. Alexis's face appeared behind him in the broken window.

"Creed, watch out!"

Screwing his face into a crooked smile, Commando threw a flurry of right hooks which Creed managed to duck. He tried to deflect one blow with his arm and got his fingers crushed. Sidestepping, Creed kicked out, catching Commando's human knee. He bounced on his toes and leapt back creating some breathing room between him and the cyborg.

The dome of the tower moaned underneath Creed's feet and shook. The water was destroying its foundation. He dropped into a crouch, trying to maintain his balance. The entire dome rolled like a boat at sea. He did not have to lean over the edge to see the dizzying drop to the water.

Commando meant to kill him. Swinging a powerful right hook, he lunged forward.

Creed dodged. But not fast enough.

The punch slammed into his rib cage smashing the breath from his lungs. He stumbled but stayed on his feet. Racking pain shot up his side. He knew something was broken. The next blow came at his chin. He tried to move. As Commando's fist hurtled for his face, he could make out the tiny screws that bolted his steel fingers together. The fist connected with a massive crack, lifting Creed off his feet. Numbing vibrations zigzagged wildly throughout his entire body. His vision blurred as he hit the dome roof and then refocused.

Commando was standing over him with a gun in his hand. Water mixed with blood streamed down his arm and dripped off the gun muzzle. Commando's lips peeled back into a crooked smile. Creed could see the reinforced steel inside his jaw and mouth as he spoke.

"Tell Oasis and Adam I said hi."

Creed stared up the yawning gun muzzle two feet from his face. He was going to die.

A loud crash of thunder exploded through the heavens, echoing and reechoing in Creed's ears—like the trumpets of judgement day. At first, Creed thought the gun had fired—but it had not. What transpired in the next few seconds was forever burned into his memory.

The world kindled in purple energy as two forks of lighting raked the sky attracted to the tallest point, the half-man, half-robot standing on the top of the thousand foot tower in the middle of the Pacific Ocean.

He was the perfect conductor for electricity. Commando screamed as the fatal energy knifed through his body. Beneath his chrome shell wires and tiny motors sparked then burst into flame. Commando ignited like a torch.

Sklade Browning stood rooted in place, a blazing inferno. Creed rolled to his right desperate to get as far away as possible. He grunted as his injured hand buckled unable to support his weight.

Commando was moving now. Some last dying impulse in the man's legs carried him forward a few steps. The optic camera, which functioned in lieu of his missing eye, glowed as his face was engulfed by the flames. Hydraulic fluid squirted from his body, where it was quickly converted to steam by the intense heat. Small spurts of flame leaped from the man, sailing through the air before falling to the roof and extinguishing on the slick surface. His stumbling legs finally gave way and he collapsed, a writhing, melting mass of man and robot.

CREED GASPED and buried his face in his arms trying to curb the horrendous sight. He could still feel the rolling heat waves, hear the sizzling, crackling flesh, and smell the acidic burning odor. Rain pounded around his head. A dull snap broke from the foundations of the tower. The whole roof began tilting to one side.

The tower was crumbling into itself. The layer of water over the roof acted like a lubricant. Creed was slipping and sliding on his stomach. Gravity pulled at him with unseen fingers. He was accelerating at a dangerous speed and rapidly approaching the edge of building.

Creed's rain soaked fingers groped wildly for a handhold, anything to check his slide. His fingernails grated across the steel alloy which made up the dome. A scraping noise caused him to turn his head. The fried and melded carcass of Sklade Browning, now doused from the rain, glided past him and disappeared over the edge. And there was no way to prevent himself from following. Far below the water roared and churned. In one awful second Creed shot off the dome and into open space.

THE NIGHT sky was alive with helicopters and war crafts as well as search and rescue choppers. Through the cabin window Troy saw people and cyborgs jumping from the shaking tower. Like ants caught in a rain storm, the cyborgs drifted about as the tower began to crumble. He realized that they were sinking and not being helped. Troy shouted above the roar of the helicopter blades, "The cyborgs are human beings. You've got to save them before they sink!"

A cyborg was hauled aboard Troy's copter. Nervously, a soldier clamped cuffs on him as another soldier covered them with his automatic weapon. Somehow the cyborg's monotone voice managed to sound indignant. "I'm a Navy Seal. My name is Lieutenant Mark Grayson. I demand to be released!"

Troy's heart stopped. Hardly daring to believe his ears, he stared dumbly at the cyborg. "Dad?"

Grayson snapped around. "Troy?"

ALEXIS SCREAMED when she saw Creed sail off the tower. A rescue helicopter dropped to the spot where his body had plunged into the icy water.

The floor gave a terrific lurch, like a ship bucking in a torrential storm. Tables, chairs and computers slid across the room as the foundations of the tower crumbled and gave way. Electrical cords snapped, firing up a spray of sparks. The floor cracked, splitting a fissure between her feet. There was no choice but to follow Creed.

She jumped.

The silver tower was in its death throes. Steel skeletal beams bent and snapped. Chips of glass showered across the sea as Alexis plummeted. She broke the surface, thankful to be alive. Wreckage of the tower drifted and bobbed around her. Terrified technicians threw themselves from high windows and slapped the water far below. The silver tower groaned and crashed into the sea sending up a tsunami-sized plume of water. Within minutes, billions of dollars worth of equipment and irreplaceable research had disappeared beneath the Pacific Ocean.

The mammoth tower had fallen.

Alexis treaded water, still searching for Creed. Powerful spotlights shimmered from the helicopters buzzing above her. In the lights she caught sight of him floating limply, face up in the water. She swam for him and held him up.

The grinding whir of a cable wrench hit her ears as the arm swung out over the water. A life line coiled down from the helicopter splashing beside her. Three orange suited rescuers followed. Creed was loaded into a stretcher and hauled up. Within seconds, Alexis found herself being drawn up into the helicopter.

Creed's face was bloodless as the men tried to restore him. They started CPR.

"He was a brave kid," a soldier muttered. "I can't believe he did that."

Alexis dropped to her knees beside Creed. Cradling his head in her arms she whispered, "Don't leave me. Please, don't leave me."

EPILOGUE

Light.

All Creed could see was white light. Where it was coming from, he could not tell. It seemed to be emitting from the ceiling, walls, and floor. It was not a harsh light but the exact opposite—a warm, gentle light. There was no pain. Mentally, he checked his body starting with his head. No one was transmitting any commands into his head. That was good news.

He worked his jaw. The sharp pain was gone. He looked down at the rest of his body. He was lying on a white bed, even more comfortable than the beds in the Skeddner mansion. He felt soothing heat radiating from the bed and basking him in blissful warmth. All the aches were gone from his limbs. He felt like he had been born again. He must have died. Was this heaven?

The room came into focus as Creed's eyes adjusted to the sparkling light. He was not dead and he was not in heaven; he was on a hospital bed.

God must have decided that he still had a purpose.

A huge window offered a stunning view of the sunrise. Exotic urban development sprawled out below him, bathed in an orange glow. He was looking down at the massive skyscrapers. It was like being on top of the world.

Creed gripped the bed's metal side bars to climb to the floor, when he heard an ominous clang. It was a sound he dreaded and had hoped never to hear again—the sound of a cyborg's chrome plated fingers. The feeling of an oasis left him and was replaced with a feeling of fear. He looked up. The room was empty.

He looked down at his hand.

The pointer finger of his right hand was not his own. He gazed with fascinated horror at the chrome plated artificial appendage fused to his hand. Of course, now he remembered. Commando had severed his finger. But its replacement was almost an exact replica of Commando's chrome plated fingers—not exactly what Creed would have chosen.

Deliberately, he curled and uncurled his cyborg finger. An electronic signal raced from his brain—through his nerves—down his arm—where it interlinked with the hair-thin optic cables controlling the micro motors in his finger. The joints were well lubricated and functioned easily, generating a soft hiss, which would be unheard too all but trained ears, like his.

He stroked the bed linens with his silver finger. The fingertip sensors were so sensitive he could feel every fine machine stitch in the fabric. Now he had a small taste of what it was like to be Rachel or Commando. What it was like to be part man and part machine. What it was like to be a cyborg.

The door opened. It was a nurse dressed in a starched white uniform. "Sir, I see you are awake. How do you feel?"

Creed laughed to himself. It was the first time in his life that anyone had ever addressed him as sir. "Honestly, I've never felt better in all my life."

"Yes, the pain medication which you are currently on will leave you in a temporary state of euphoria."

"But Lex . . . is she alive?"

In answer to his question a familiar face appeared behind the nurse's shoulder. The nurse smiled and slipped out the door. For a moment Alexis just stood in the doorway.

Creed grinned. Her face lit up as she smiled back displaying her perfect teeth. Then the spell broke. She rushed forward, throwing her arms around him and almost crushing him in a fierce hug. There was nothing to say.

Creed realized he was crying and did not know why. Like a dream, he watched Rachel and Troy surround him. It was difficult to believe that everyone was alive.

"Hey! Hey! Look who finally decided to join the living!" Troy punched him playfully. "You've been out for three days, man. You'll never guess what happened."

Creed punched him back. "What?"

"My dad is one of the cyborgs, Lieutenant Grayson."

"Your father?" Creed absorbed the news. "Wow."

"We hired an attorney, because there's a ton of legal and political issues to work out, but I think it's gonna work out. I'll have my dad back. Oh, I almost forgot, he wanted me to give you his profuse thanks for your exceptional bravery in the line of duty."

A shy smile brightened Rachel's face as she held out a tentative gloved hand. Creed drew off her glove and kissed her chrome fingers. "Thanks for everything."

She blushed. "Thank you for fixing my father's mistake."

Alexis sat on the edge of the bed and took Creed's hand, her fingers touching his cyborg finger. They both looked down.

"Your poor finger," she murmured, "You were unconscious and they needed to operate, so we told them to go ahead. I hope you don't mind . . . too much."

"It'll take a while to get used to. Did they take that chip out of my brain?"

Alexis shook her head. "No. It was fused to very sensitive nerve endings. They don't want to risk damaging your brain."

Creed recognized his mother's ring which still encircled her finger. "Thanks for keeping it for me. And thanks for reminding me of who I am."

"I only wish I could have done more."

She began sliding the ring off, but Creed stopped her. "No, keep it. I like it better on your finger than mine, anyway."

She smiled and blushed. He liked the way her cheeks dimpled. He grinned back.

Alexis pretended to be aghast. "Creed! I didn't know you were physically capable of smiling."

"The past few days, I haven't had much to smile about, but it's over now."

She took his hand. "Yes, thank God. I know your parents are proud of you. I'm so proud of you."

"I really miss her...my mother was everything to me. You are the only family I have left, and I couldn't ask for a better one. You're like the sister I never had."

She smiled and squeezed his hand. "Creed, now you have two sisters." Alexis slipped her arm around Rachel. "Father officially adopted Rachel today."

Creed blinked. "Dr. Skeddner is alive?"

"Yes, I'm alive. Thanks to you," Dr. Skeddner had stepped into the room unnoticed. There was a bandage over his chest, but Creed thought he had never looked better.

Creed felt tears coming again. "Hey, Grandpa."

Now it was Dr. Skeddner's turn to cry. "Son, when you're ready, we're going home. We are never going to be separated again."

Creed noticed that Alexis no longer had her blue braid. "What happened to your braid?"

Alexis shuddered. "I cut it off. Every time I see blue, I'm reminded of Commando and those horrible cyborgs. I'll despise blue for the rest of my days."

"On that subject, what happened to the cyborgs?"

"Some were destroyed," Troy answered. "A few were saved and taken to secure laboratories. Some had to be carted off to asylums, but a lot escaped. There is a massive manhunt, well, cyborg-hunt, underway right now. Most people can't sleep knowing they're still out there, lurking somewhere. The media is having a field day. There's a hot debate on whether or not the cyborgs are machines or humans. And I'll be at the forefront of the fight. My dad is my dad. It doesn't matter what he looks like on the outside."

Creed looked at Troy with new respect.

Troy caught the look.

"Have any more data capsules been found?" Creed asked.

"I don't know. The entire tower sank below the surface of the water. They're scheduled to dive at the site tomorrow, and I don't know what they'll salvage. Who knows what secrets are lost beneath the waves."

A HUNDRED feet below water level under the wreckage of the silver tower at the bottom of the Pacific, the breathless body of Hulsane settled in its final resting place. His face was frozen in a mask of horror. Locked in an unheard scream, his mouth gaped, allowing the water to swirl freely through his lungs. His eyes bulged. Hulsane had not been prepared to meet his Creator.

Cold sea water ruffled and billowed the gray suit producing the eerie illusion that the corpse breathed. A watertight box the size of a cell-phone lay clutched in the stiffened bony fingers.

The data capsule.

A lone fish proceeded to nibble experimentally at an outstretched leg. It would be joined by others. Soon, all that would remain of the aspirant world-dictator would be bones. But the data capsule had survived.

Some evils will not be destroyed until the end of time.